"EXORCISM FAILS:
1 DEAD, 27 INJURED IN CHURCH BLAZE"

The Monday morning newspapers had a field day.

A man dies on the operating table in Smallville Hospital, his lungs too badly damaged by smoke inhalation for the respirator to cope.

And every reporter drew the salient parallel: a man had died in a blazing wagon 150 years before another died in a burned-out church.

Special emphasis was given to Rev. Grindlay's exorcism. Several survivors quoted his sermon when they were interviewed. Clearly, whatever exorcism the minister had carried out had failed.

Dismally.

If Smallville's residents had been afraid before, now they were terrified.

OTHER BOOKS IN THE SERIES

SMALLVILLE

CURSE

by Alan Grant

Superman created by
Jerry Siegel and Joe Shuster

Hillsborough Community
College LRC

ASPECT®

WARNER BOOKS

An AOL Time Warner Company

WARNER BOOKS EDITION

Copyright © 2004 by DC Comics

Cover design by Don Puckey
Book design by L&G McRee

Warner Books, Inc.
1271 Avenue of the Americas
New York, NY 10020

Visit our Web site at www.twbookmark.com.

Visit DC Comics on-line at keyword DCComics on America Online or at http://www.dccomics.com.

 An AOL Time Warner Company

Printed in the United States of America

First Printing: January 2004

10 9 8 7 6 5 4 3 2 1

For my Father-in-law, Bernard Walker

Prologue

Cyrus Deen hefted the shaft of the pickax in his leathery, callused hands. He raised it high above his head, then, with a slight twist of his body, brought it biting down into the hard-packed Kansas soil. Two, three more times the pick speared into the turf before Cyrus laid it aside and stooped to pick up his spade.

A thin line of sweat beaded his forehead, pooling above his shaggy eyebrows, then trickled down the ridge of his nose. It was only 9 A.M., but already the summer sun burned in a sky as clear as deep blue crystal.

Kansas sky stretches all the way to Heaven. An apt thought for the gravedigger and caretaker of the First Church of Smallville.

His spade flashed in the sunlight as he plunged it deep into the turf the pick had loosened. Working with the ease brought by long years of practice, it took him only minutes to shovel off the top layer of earth.

For almost half a century, Cyrus Deen had been digging graves in Smallville. He'd watched the people of the town build their houses, work their jobs, live their lives. And the one thing he'd learned in all those years was that, no matter how rich or poor they were, no matter how happy or sad, they all ended up in the same place.

A hole in the ground that Cyrus had dug for them.

Death is the Great Leveler, he thought, screwing up his eyes as he tried to remember who the quote came from. His mind wasn't as sharp as it used to be, his memory fading into a seamless rerun of hot summer days and freezing winter nights.

Fifteen minutes later, the new grave was a foot deep and Cyrus's light, checked shirt was drenched in perspiration. Sighing, he leaned his spade against a gravestone and moved into the shade of a huge old lime tree. Sparrows sang in its sunshine-dappled branches.

Cyrus pulled a battered tobacco tin from the breast pocket of his shirt. He snapped a rolling paper from its packet, holding it in the fingers of one hand while he teased out the strong tobacco that would fill it. Deftly, he rolled the cigarette, licked the gummed edge to seal it, then lit it with a match.

Not politically correct to smoke these days, he thought wryly. *But I'll be damned if they stop me.* He darted a glance in the direction of the church. *Beg pardon,* he excused himself.

He leaned back against the tree trunk, exhaling a thin stream of smoke as he surveyed the cemetery. *His* cemetery. The path edges were meticulously trimmed, the grass cut short, the tombstones dazzling white as the sun rose higher in the sky. Fresh flowers adorned the graves.

A lot of people showed scant respect for themselves when they were alive; when they died, at least they had old Cyrus to look after them.

Every headstone in the graveyard told its own story. Over in the corner, an elaborate tomb topped with a life-size stone angel marked the last resting place of Connor

Weighland and his wife, Smallville's first-ever sweet corn millionaires, cut down in their prime by a skidding car. Under their names, the details of their daughter had been chipped into the stone a decade later.

Not far from it was the Langs' grave, certainly the strangest deaths the authorities had ever recorded. For on a fateful day thirteen years ago, a swarm of meteors fell on the town. After a journey through space that had lasted centuries, they arrowed in on Smallville as if Fate herself had written the plot. Laura Lang and her husband died instantly, as one of the white-hot boulders smashed into their car.

A bunch of bloodred carnations stood in the flower holder in front of the grave. The flowers were changed regularly, every Sunday, by the Langs' only child, Lana. Cyrus often saw the girl on her weekly vigil to the cemetery. She'd sit down on the grass beneath which the bodies of her parents lay and talk to them. He'd never listened in, respecting the bond between the living and the dead.

Sometimes, he saw her crying.

The Reverend Grindlay often said that death was the great release, the answer to all life's problems, the peace that came with the cessation of struggle. That might be true for the dead—but Cyrus saw the effect their loved ones' passing had on those who remained.

He knew what death really was: misery for those left behind. Questions left unanswered. Problems unresolved. Pain that never healed. Emotions tortured and shattered like dropped glass.

Cyrus sighed again and used the tips of his forefinger and thumb to pinch out his cigarette. It didn't do to think too much about what he'd chosen for a living, because his thoughts always came up against a solid wall.

I'll die, too. One day. He gave a little shiver. As though somebody had just walked over his grave . . .

He moved back to the grave he was digging and picked up his spade. On Saturday, Mrs. Markell would be buried there; Smallville's oldest resident, she'd succumbed to the weaknesses of age after a full century of life.

The spade drove down into the soil. There was a loud, metallic clang, and pain shot up through both of Cyrus's arms. Drat! He'd hit some obstruction, a boulder most likely. Laying the spade aside, Cyrus knelt in the shallow trench he'd dug and began scooping away earth with his bare hands.

Yes, it was a boulder all right. He unearthed one corner of it, surprised to see that it was squared off, as if it had been deliberately cut. His strong fingers probed alongside and beneath the stone. Strange. It seemed to be more like a slab.

His bushy eyebrows knitted together in puzzlement as he used the blade of his hand to sweep away the loose earth covering the stone. There was something carved into the top of it.

Cyrus bent forward and blew away the covering of dust.

A rough stone cross had been carved in the center of the slab. Around it, running along the perimeter, several smaller crosses had also been carved.

A fallen gravestone, Cyrus thought. *Some poor sucker long dead and almost as long forgotten.*

But there was no name and no date on the horizontal stone. Just those enigmatic carved crosses.

Cyrus took the small trowel from his tool belt, the one he used for weeding between the graves. He loosened the soil around one side of the slab, scraping it away until he exposed the rotten, crumbling wood that lay beneath. The side of a coffin.

A thrill of excitement ran through him. He'd kept a record of every grave he'd dug in the past forty-seven years, adding on the long-lost burials he sometimes turned up. Folks from the nineteenth century, from the early days of Smallville. It gave him a strange sense of purpose; the Reverend Grindlay might look after their immortal souls, but it was Cyrus who tended to their mortal remains.

Gripping the corner of the slab in both hands, Cyrus exerted all his strength as he tried to lift it. It shifted only a fraction of an inch. He'd have to try pushing it aside. Carefully, he wedged his back against the side of the shallow grave, with both feet resting against the side of the slab. He grunted, and straightened his legs, pushing with all his might.

The stone slid a few inches sideways. A terrible smell assailed his nostrils—the stench of ancient decay.

Inexplicably, Cyrus shuddered, feeling suddenly cold despite the blistering sun. He'd spent most of his life working closely with death, but that smell was something he'd never learned to come to terms with.

Steeling himself, Cyrus pushed again. This time the stone slid more easily, moving a good foot or more, exposing the coffin's broken lid.

Cyrus crouched over it, moving slightly to one side so the sun's rays could penetrate the coffin's interior. The bones inside weren't white and gleaming, but dull and dark, as if they had been charred. The skull stared up at him from sightless sockets, its mouth twisted grotesquely. He'd seen that look before. Somebody had died screaming, in agony.

He closed his eyes briefly, and said a silent prayer.

As he straightened to stand up again, he noticed something in the corner of the coffin, behind the skull. A small leather folio case, tied around with a drawstring.

Cyrus reached down, taking care to avoid touching the skull. His fingers closed around the case, and he pulled the package out.

The pouch was desiccated and fragile, and, despite Cyrus's gentle touch, the leather crumbled away in his hand. Inside was a waxed paper bag, its top made fast with sealing wax.

Cyrus's eyebrows lifted in wonder as he slit the wax with his thumbnail. Carefully, he pulled out what looked like a book, or journal. He lifted the corner of the cover and saw spidery handwriting in black ink that might have been written only yesterday.

The Reverend Grindlay had to see this! Local history was a passion of the minister's. For the record, such a find could be like an extra birthday.

Leaving his tools where they lay, Cyrus Deen hurried up the neat gravel path toward the First Church of Smallville.

And an evil from the past stirred in its long, long sleep.

CHAPTER 1

Clark Kent looked around, then stole a surreptitious glance at his reflection in the plate-glass window next to which he stood.

He wasn't too unhappy at what he saw. Not the most handsome guy in school, not by a long shot, but nothing to be ashamed of, either. Thick, black hair that—no matter what he did—always fell back into the same style. An honest, intelligent face. Friendly eyes.

Of course, he could really wow the girls if he showed them what he was capable of. He sometimes wondered how different his life would be if he could demonstrate his powers . . . instead of having to pretend he was average.

There was a babble of voices coming down the school hall toward the exit door where he waited. Clark's heart swelled as he thought of Lana Lang. She and Whitney Fordman had been an item for months. Then Whitney had left Smallville to join the Marines—and good luck to the Marines was the sentiment in the school halls. In Whitney's absence, Clark intended to do everything in his power to crowd out Lana's affections for his rival.

And then they heard the terrible news: Whitney had been killed during military service.

The voices drew closer. Clark threw another glance at his makeshift mirror and hurriedly ran his fingers through his hair. He always felt nervous when Lana was around, perhaps because he knew the love he felt for her wasn't reciprocated. She liked him, as a friend—she'd told him that a hundred times—but that wasn't enough for Clark.

He wanted love.

"What are you preening for, Kent? Got a hot date with a dog?"

Clark's heart sank as he recognized the voice that spoke from behind him. Ed Wall—a good friend of Whitney's. And no friend at all of Clark's.

Steeling himself, Clark turned to face the newcomer. Wall was several inches taller than he, and bulked out from his devotion to sports. His square jaw jutted aggressively as he leaned forward to thrust his face closer to Clark's.

"No, Ed," Clark said as patiently as he could, "I'm waiting for Lana. We're dining together in the intimate confines of the school lunch hall."

"Is that a fact, wise guy?" Wall turned to look at the two lettermen who flanked him—Rob Simpson and Phil Meara, fellow football players who'd also been part of Whitney's little clique. "The nerd thinks he's meeting Lana."

"Whitney wouldn't have liked that," Phil said, with a disingenuous grin. "He wouldn't have liked it at all."

Clark bit back a sharp retort and managed to keep his voice steady. "Lana's an adult," he pointed out, "more than capable of making her own decisions. This has nothing to do with Whitney . . . and nothing to do with you three, either."

Wall scowled. He pushed his face even closer to Clark's. "Whitney asked us to keep an eye on his girl," he said softly, then repeated: "His girl. Get that, Kent? *His* girl."

Before Clark could reply, Wall stabbed a finger at his chest. "Whitney used to get mad when you hassled Lana. But now that he isn't around to look after her, I'm telling you on his behalf—leave Lana alone!"

"I told you, Lana's capable of—" Clark began, but broke off as Wall grabbed him by the wrist. Clark could feel the pressure as the bigger, heavier teenager began to squeeze.

"Let me rephrase my last remark," Wall hissed. "Leave Lana alone—or you are going to be one very sorry nerd."

Clark's eyes narrowed with anger. He only had to flex his wrist, and Ed's grip would be broken. He only had to flick his arm, and even the muscular Ed Wall would find himself spinning through the air.

Suck it in, Clark! he told himself severely. He couldn't afford to lose his temper. Not under any circumstances. Not ever. Because if he did, the secret he and his parents had guarded so well all these years would be out in the open. And his life would be over.

"Are you listening to me, Kent?" Wall said insistently, his grip tightening.

Clark breathed in deeply and felt his anger dissolve. "I hear you, Ed," he replied.

"Good. Keep it that way."

Wall released Clark's wrist and stepped away. His companions were laughing childishly, their sniggers turning to mocking laughter as the trio pushed through the exit doors and left the building.

Clark watched through the glass as Wall and his buddies swaggered over the yard to where a small knot of other teenagers were waiting for them. Clark was surprised to see that his friend, Pete Ross, was among those waiting. He was hanging about on the fringes of the group, but it was obvious that he was part of it.

That doesn't make a lot of sense, Clark thought. *Pete likes these guys just about as much as I do!*

He heard footsteps descending the stairs and looked up to see Lana coming down toward him, accompanied by Chloe Sullivan. The two girls were laughing together, obviously at ease in each other's company. Clark was glad to see it. Since Lana's guardian, her aunt Nell, had left town, Lana had been staying with Chloe and her father.

For reasons that had never been clear to Clark, Lana and Chloe had previously been very wary of each other. But since Lana had moved in with her, they'd become good friends. Chloe had been a tower of strength when Whitney died.

Shoving the memory of Ed's bullying out of his mind, Clark fixed his most dazzling smile and turned to greet Lana.

"Ah! Kent! Just who I need."

The unexpected male voice made Clark start. Out of the corner of his eye, he saw Mr. Melrose, the school's Business Affairs teacher, striding toward him.

Stifling an inner groan, Clark turned to the teacher. "How can I help you, sir?" he asked politely, his gaze darting over the teacher's shoulder to Lana and Chloe. Both girls smiled and gave him a little wave, then moved on.

So much for my lunch with Lana.

Mr. Melrose stroked the neat little goatee that adorned his chin, as if he was trying to remember why he wanted to see Clark. He had a reputation with the pupils for being a little absentminded, but Clark knew him to have a sharp and incisive mind.

"Sir?" Clark prompted.

"Ah yes," Mr. Melrose raised a forefinger in the air. "Lex Luthor," he announced. Seeing Clark's blank look, he went on: "Mr. Luthor is due to give a lecture on business practice to your class next week. I've tried calling him to confirm, but I only get answering machines or secretaries who make excuses for not putting me through."

Lex Luthor ran the Smallville fertilizer plant and was one of Metropolis's richest men. He was several years older than Clark, but the two had become firm friends after Clark saved Lex's life on his very first day in town.

"Is there a reason he's incommunicado?" Mr. Melrose asked.

"I'm not sure," Clark told the older man. "His castle was badly damaged some time ago, and I know he's flown craftsmen over from Europe for the repairs. Lex intended to move into a hotel until everything is completed."

Truth was, Clark hadn't heard from Lex in a couple of weeks. He knew that some of the repairs were major— an entire medieval stained-glass window was only one of the items that had to be replaced—and he'd just assumed Lex was too busy to get in touch.

"I wonder, Kent," the teacher said, "if you'd be good enough to have a word with him. If he's not coming, I'll have to think of a substitute program."

"Yes, Mr. Melrose. Of course."

The teacher strode off down the hall again, leaving Clark looking wildly around him. Lana and Chloe had disappeared, gone on to the lunch hall without him. He ran a hand through his hair again, and hurried after them.

When he reached the door to the hall, he could see the girls sitting at a table with several of their other classmates. There wasn't a space left for Clark.

Oh well. I'm not hungry anyway.

Shoulders drooping, Clark turned on his heel and walked slowly back down the hall.

Sunlight filtered in through stained-glass windows, bathing the interior of the First Church of Smallville in warm, glowing colors. Cyrus Deen had known this building for longer than almost anybody, and its quiet, peaceful atmosphere never failed to impress him.

At the far end of the aisle, Cyrus could see the Reverend Michael Grindlay cutting and shaping flowers for an altar display. The minister had his back to him, but Cyrus didn't call out. Only a minister's voice should ever be raised in church.

Cyrus walked quietly up the aisle's red carpet, glancing down at his feet, afraid that he'd brought soil in on the soles of his work boots. He could imagine Moira Grindlay's shrill voice chastising him—an outcome he always preferred to avoid, if possible.

The minister must have heard his footfall, because he turned while Cyrus was still a few yards away. "What do you think, Cyrus?" He gestured at the large crystal vase standing on the altar, bursting with multihued daisies and chrysanthemums. "Have I done your blooms justice?"

Cyrus considered the floral arrangement for a moment and nodded. "As always, Reverend."

Cyrus didn't only dig graves, and keep the church and cemetery neat and tidy. He had a little plot at the back of the house attached to the church, where he indulged his only hobby—growing flowers. It gave him a lot of pleasure to see the products of his own labor displayed so beautifully, a real tribute to the God he both feared and loved.

Suddenly, Cyrus remembered why he was here. "I've found an old grave," he blurted. "Huge, heavy stone covering it. And look what I found inside!"

He held up the journal in its bag.

"From a grave?" Michael Grindlay's bushy eyebrows arced into a suspicious frown, and he made no move to take the package from Cyrus's hand. "What is it?"

"A journal. A diary of some kind. It's in waxed paper, so it doesn't seem to be too badly damaged."

"A diary—found in our graveyard?" The minister's voice rose a little with excitement, and his hand reached out to take the package from Cyrus. "This is fabulous! Fascinating!" He opened the bag and carefully pulled out the old journal. "I'll take it to my study right now, and—"

"Michael! Mich-ael!"

A shrill, high-pitched voice rang through the church, and the Reverend Grindlay rolled his eyes. "On second thought," he said hastily, "I'll read it later."

Cyrus knew that he'd outstayed his welcome. Moira Grindlay was a good woman, who poured her time and energy into the various Smallville women's groups and supported her husband at every turn. It was unfortunate that her voice didn't match her kindness. Even in a good mood, she sounded as loud—and penetrating—as a foghorn.

Cyrus recognized her impatient tone, and was already shuffling back down the aisle toward the exit when she came through the doorway from the adjoining house.

"Have you finished that piece you told me you'd write for Ladies' Night?" Cyrus heard her demand, followed by her husband's quiet apologies. "And I very much doubt if you've attended to the bells . . ."

Once, and not so long ago, Cyrus would have fixed the electronic bell system himself. But he'd had a couple of dizzy turns, and the doctor advised him to avoid heights. The Reverend Grindlay had been promising to do it for weeks, but had hardly even made a start.

"Michael! What have you done with these daisies . . . ?"

A pity not everyone believes in the sanctity of peace, Cyrus thought.

He pushed open the old oak door. Blinking in the sun's fierce light, he went back outside.

Clark's disappointment lasted only as long as the afternoon break. An apologetic Lana had come up to say she was sorry they'd missed lunch, but why didn't he and Pete join her and Chloe at the Talon after school?

Why not indeed? Clark asked himself happily, as he waited at the school gate for Pete to show after class.

But his sense of pleasant anticipation crumbled when he saw Pete. His friend was tagging along behind Ed Wall and his two cronies, his gaze averted, as if he hoped that Clark wouldn't spot him among the crush of kids.

Ed threw Clark a contemptuous sneer as he breezed past, the others following in his wake like pilot fish around a shark. Pete didn't even look up, attempting to hurry past. But Clark took a step forward, and blocked his friend's path.

"Hey, Pete. Coffee at the Talon? Lana has time off—and she's paying."

Pete lifted his gaze, but his eyes kept sliding away from Clark's, refusing to engage. As if he was ashamed. Or guilty.

"Uh . . . I don't think so, Clark. Not tonight." He hesitated, seeing his friend's disappointed face, before rushing on. "I have a lot to do. Some, uh, some extra homework."

Pete's evasiveness told Clark he wasn't being entirely straight with him, and that puzzled him. He and Pete were best friends. They did everything together, supported each other when they needed it. Heck, they were so close that Pete was the only person in the world—apart from Clark's parents—who knew his secret.

Clark Kent wasn't a human being. He was an alien from outer space who had been carried to Earth by the same meteor swarm that devastated Smallville. He looked like a human, and he thought like a human—but with every passing month, he was discovering new talents and abilities that were anything *but* human. Super-strength. Superspeed. X-ray vision.

Clark had thought that would somehow bring them closer to each other, because in some ways, Pete was an alien, too. The youngest of a large, high-achieving family, Pete was the runt of the litter in every way. Alienated, rather than alien. Still, it gave them a common bond.

But instead, sharing the secret seemed to have had the opposite effect. Pete was always full of excuses for not spending time with him. When they did find themselves in each other's company, there was an awkwardness that hadn't existed before. It was a problem Clark didn't know how to solve.

"Right," Clark said, keeping his voice level so as not to betray his disappointment. "Maybe I'll call you later, okay?"

Before Pete could answer, Ed's voice boomed out: "Hey, Petey! Are you coming with us or hanging around with nerds?"

Pete's face flushed red with embarrassment. He mumbled something incomprehensible to Clark, then hurried away, keeping his head low, not looking back.

Clark stood watching till they disappeared from sight around a corner. Then he set off for Main Street, deep in troubled thought.

Ole Markell's junkyard stood on the eastern fringe of town. Its tottering stacks of wrecked autos and semidismantled farm machinery, all surrounded by a high barbed-wire fence, marked the boundary between Smallville and clear farmland.

The junkyard had been closed since Tuesday, when Ole's mother died. He had so much to do, what with arrangements for the funeral and visiting guests, he'd even taken his guard dogs back to the house with him.

That was just as well for Ed Wall and the half dozen or so others who bent low to the ground as they followed him through a near-invisible rip in the fence wire. Instead of snarling Rottweilers, they met only silence.

Pete brought up the rear, knowing that what he was about to do was wrong . . . but determined to do it anyway. He needed something to make him feel good.

He straightened up and walked quickly over to join the others clustered around Ed in the shade of a stack of rusting cars.

Ed held up a hand for silence, then reached into his pocket to bring forth a bulging polyethylene kitchen bag. Almost in unison, the others moved a step closer to him.

It's like a ritual, Pete thought, even as he himself stepped closer. *Ed's the high priest, dispensing . . . faith to the masses.*

The sun was dropping in the sky, casting long shadows, and the ferocious heat of the day had abated. Even so, Pete felt perspiration bead on his brow. Anticipation, as Wall carefully tipped the contents of the bag into the open palm of his other hand.

Ed tilted his hand, careful not to drop what it held, so that the others could see. Pete stared hard at the seven fat, green berries that lay there. He heard a gasp, and didn't know if it was himself, or all of them.

Ed picked up a berry between forefinger and thumb and held it aloft, silhouetted against the dying sun. Pete could have sworn the berry's green color was swirling around, spiraling up and down. But maybe it was only the sun's light playing tricks on him.

"One each." Ed broke the silence, holding his hand out to the others.

A tingle of anticipation ran through each of them. But

nobody pushed, nobody grabbed. They all took a single berry, Pete included.

"Happy times, dudes." Ed threw back his head, opened his mouth, and popped the berry inside. He swallowed it without chewing, and gave a loud whoop. "Yes, sir!"

The others followed suit, some of them swallowing the berry whole. Pete was one of those who held it in his mouth for a moment, savoring the peculiar taste: like raspberry, with just a zest of refreshing mint. Pete bit into his, and his whole mouth tingled as it filled with the heavy, viscous juice.

"Whoa!" Phil gave a mock-shiver. "Electric teeth, man!"

Everybody laughed.

"I don't believe it," a guy Pete knew only as Donny said. "I feel so strong, I could . . . I could . . ."

"Punch metal?" Ed suggested. He whirled suddenly, his fingers balling into a fist. He punched the door panel of the old Studebaker next to him. Hard. If it hurt, he didn't let it show. But his hand made a deep impression in the aging metal.

"I was going to say—throw a tire." Donny snatched up a worn old retread lying on the ground. Drawing back his arm to its fullest, he half turned like a discus thrower and hurled the heavy tire as hard as he could.

Pete watched in disbelief as it soared high into the air, a hundred yards or more, before arcing down to land out of sight. Wow! He knew from the couple of previous times he'd tried Ed's berries that, somehow, they sharpened your abilities and made you stronger. But that throw couldn't have been bettered by an Olympic athlete.

Ed and Donny and a couple of others began running around, whooping and cheering. Ed lifted a rusting engine block clean off the ground. Phil ripped the rear door off a pickup truck lying on its side. Donny strained and heaved as he tried to lift the front of a wheelless Dodge Charger.

"Somebody give me a hand with this."

Pete grinned to himself. If ever he had any worries, they'd melted in the evening breeze. Stress was suddenly a stranger. Pete grinned again and ran to help lift two tons of automobile.

Two hours later, the strange effects wore off.

People quieted down, became more reflective. One or two complained of a mild headache.

Everybody went home. Except for Pete. He sat on the hood of an old school bus, watching the stars appear in the sky, half-doubled up with stomach cramps. That was the price you paid for the high you got when you went flying on berries.

Pete could live with it. What he found harder to live with was his own life.

He had seven older brothers and sisters, every one of them more intelligent, better-looking, more creative than he. He had a best friend who came from Planet Unknown, who could see through solid walls. The only girl he'd ever wanted—Chloe—was so besotted with Clark, she hardly knew Pete existed. Except as a *friend,* of course.

The planet Venus was shining brightly in the east.

Around it, there was a large dark area where no stars shone.

Like me, Pete thought. *Alone. Isolated.*

He bent over suddenly, retching.

And sick of the whole shebang.

CHAPTER 2

The Reverend Grindlay closed his study door behind him, and let out a long sigh. For a man whose major work was delivering a sermon twice each Sunday, he hardly ever seemed to have a moment to himself. The flowers, arranging the schedules for the various clubs and societies who used the church hall as a meeting place, correspondence with his parishioners and his superiors—all helped themselves to his precious time.

He sat down in the worn leather armchair behind his oversize desk, and allowed his gaze to wander round the room. Floor-to-ceiling bookcases lined two walls, their shelves laden with the minister's collection of Bibles, concordances, and religious commentaries. When he and Moira had first come to Smallville, almost a decade and a half earlier, it was his proud boast that he spent two hours every day studying. His appetite for finding out about his God was insatiable.

But now his daily chores had expanded to fill almost all of his available time, and he often felt like a stranger in his own library. A computer sat on his desk, high technology invading the world of religious tradition.

Eyes closed, he sat back in the chair that over the years had molded itself perfectly to his body. He felt more comfortable in it than anywhere else. For a moment he just sat, breathing lightly, drinking in the scholarly atmosphere he loved so much.

Suddenly, he started. Moira had said dinner would be in an hour—and she hated it when he was late. She could be cranky for days if he let her cooking get cold!

Hurriedly, motivated by the need to avoid his wife's nagging, he slid the package Cyrus Deen had given him onto his blotter. He stared at it for a long moment, savoring his anticipation. Incredible to think this diary—this piece of history—had been buried in his churchyard for . . . who knew how long?

Almost instinctively, the Reverend Grindlay's left hand burrowed into his trouser pocket. His fingers closed around the small object that nestled there, and gingerly, almost guiltily, he took it out. Lying on the palm of his hand was a tiny, green stone cross.

My lucky charm, he thought, then immediately flushed. What does a minister need a lucky charm for? A foolish superstition he could share with nobody else, not even Moira. But it wasn't just any old cross . . .

Thirteen years ago, tragedy had struck Smallville. A swarm of meteors streaked over the town, their journey of billions of miles and hundreds of years destined to end in a small town in the heart of Nowhere, Kansas. Buildings were destroyed, the population was terrified . . . and two good people died.

He hadn't known the Langs long, but had already decided they were decent folks. It broke his and Moira's hearts to see their young daughter, Lana, left struggling to cope with her parents' sudden and untimely deaths. Not long qualified, fired with the desire to comfort his flock, Michael Grindlay took it on himself to visit the home of every one of them. He brought solace to those who needed it, and quiet prayer to those whose faith was shaken. And he did it all with a glad heart.

It was only when he had to face young Lana Lang that he wavered. How to explain to a child that God had stolen away the parents she herself loved more than anything? How to ease the pain that wracked a little girl's broken heart?

The Reverend Grindlay did his best, but in truth it was Lana's aunt, the wild and ambitious Nell, who did his job for him. As he foundered with his words, trying to explain "heaven" and "angels," Nell took the traumatized child in her arms and held her tightly until her sobs subsided and sleep brought her peace.

His failure weighed heavily on his shoulders that night, as Michael walked back to his church from Nell Potter's home. Stars blazed in a velvet black sky. He felt that his God was looking down on him, despising him, judging him an abject failure. Perhaps he wasn't cut out to be a minister, after all.

Deep in thought, he pushed open the cemetery gate, intending to follow the path to the rear door of his house. He hoped Moira hadn't gone to bed. It had been a long day, and he felt drained by the demands of others. He needed someone to talk to, somebody to comfort *him*.

And then he saw it, lying on the path, twinkling in the starlight.

A tiny cross, almost perfect in shape.

He stooped to pick it up, holding it between forefinger and thumb to examine it. It was fashioned from emerald green stone, hard like jade, and surprisingly warm to the touch. Every star in the sky seemed to be reflected in its depths.

He knew immediately what it must be—a fragment from one of the meteors that had exploded in the town streets. But for Michael Grindlay it was more than that, much more. It was a personal message for him. It told him that his God was watching, and was not displeased with what He'd seen. A man can only do his best, and Michael Grindlay hadn't shirked.

For the first time in days, a smile played around the corners of his mouth as he slipped the little cross into his pocket. There was a fresh spring in his step as he walked through the silent graveyard to his house.

That same smile was on his lips now as Michael stroked the cross gently, then returned it to his pocket. Suddenly businesslike, he carefully opened the journal and began to read the spidery, copperplate handwriting.

This is the Journal of Andrew Seddon, sometime schoolteacher in New York City, now determined to seek my fortunes in the Gold Fields of the West Coast, being an account of our trip west in this Year of Our Lord 1856.

We left St. Louis this morning, 53 people aboard 17 wagons, with an assortment of donkeys, dogs, and oxen tethered behind. Before us lie 1500 miles of hard travel and unknown dangers, which we will face happily for the sake of that precious metal which lures us.

We are a motley collection indeed! All but me travel in family groups. There are several from the slums back East, desperate to escape the cities in search of a new life. A fair number seem to come from St. Louis itself, which I found to be a hard town, where a decent man might easily be cheated of his possessions.

And there are Europeans—two German families, and one French, with not a word of English among them. The French family are in the wagon behind me; they bicker and argue with each other constantly, not knowing that I can understand a little of their tongue.

One of the German wagons has a piano strapped to its side boards. At the rear there is an Englishman, middle-aged and of seeming ill health. His complexion is pale and sickly, and he rests under the canvas of the wagon while his stern-looking wife takes the reins.

I confess I am disappointed with our first day's progress. We have come little more than two miles, before stopping to set camp for the night. Though we left shortly after dawn, the heat was already almost unbearable. All children have been ordered to wear hats or kerchiefs on their heads during daylight hours, and I congratulate myself for my foresight in purchasing a wide-brimmed Stetson hat in St. Louis.

Many of us have been forced to wear bandannas over the lower part of our faces because the dust thrown up by our wheels seems to take on a life of its own. It hangs in the air, clogs up the nostrils, seeps into every nook and crevice that affords it entry.

Mr. Huckins, our trail boss, says it will only last until we clear the Great Plains. He did not add— though I know from my geographical studies—that it will be many weeks before we reach that happy day!

I am not overly impressed with Mr. Huckins. While I accept that this rough new land demands rough men to tame it, I would have preferred such a man whose breath did not constantly reek of whiskey. I'll warrant his dirty buckskin jacket and leggings have not seen soap and water since the last wagon train he commanded. A successful one, too, if he is to be believed: 31 wagons and their human cargo delivered intact (apart from minor injuries) to San Francisco.

Yet they say there is gold enough for thousands more.

We had only one injury during the course of today's travel. One of the Farrell family's dogs—Sabre, I believe they called it, a big rangy mutt—has been badly hurt. Some of the children were playing with slingshots as they walked alongside the wagons. One of them, whether by accident or design I do not know, fired a projectile which struck the dog. Startled, the beast turned to seek out its tormentor—and was inadvertently crushed under a wagon wheel.

Poor brute! It is in terrible pain. Had it not been a family pet, Mr. Farrell would have killed it at once. But the children were so upset at the thought, they are trying to nurse it back to health.

It is late now, with a bright moon in a cloudless sky. I can hear the dog's whimpers and occasional howls of pain echoing through the camp. It is not a pleasant sound; indeed, it is most upsetting and not at all conducive to peace of mind.

I need to rest after the day's exertions, but sleep evades me. There is a growing knot in my stomach. Anticipation of what is yet to come? Yes, but it is more than that. I am not usually given to flights of fancy, but the dog's distress—and these endless plains—have unnerved me greatly.

"Michael! Michael, will you answer me?"

The Reverend Grindlay heard the sharp, accusing voice impinging on his consciousness from some vast distance. He blinked his eyes and jerked his head, snapping out of his reverie.

Strange! It was almost as if I was back there with the pioneers . . .

"Michael!" The voice came again, closer now, right outside his study door. "I told you dinner was at eight. What are you doing in there? The food will be growing cold!"

The minister shook his head, making a determined effort to clear his woolly thoughts.

"I hear you, Moira," he called back. "I'll be there in a moment."

His wife's footsteps receded back along the hallway, and the minister sighed.

With a slight sense of surprise, he noticed that his left hand was still in his pocket, gently stroking the little green cross. It felt warm and comforting in his palm, and he let it go almost reluctantly.

He sighed again, and closed the journal. A fascinating insight into the past—a window into the lives of people who lived almost 150 years ago. Fascinating, yes—but not worth incurring Moira's displeasure over.

He'd just have to continue reading it later.

* * *

"Thank you, Jason." Martha Kent smiled as she flipped open the trunk of her car and watched the teenage boy load it with her bags. "It's much appreciated."

"A pleasure, Mrs. Kent," Jason told her, happily accepting the two dollars she gave him. "Drive carefully now."

He turned and began to walk back to the supermarket, while Martha slipped into the driver's seat and started the engine.

She was running a little late that night, a result of the long conversation she'd had with a friend she'd met while doing the weekly shopping. Jonathan and Clark would be home, waiting for dinner. She slipped the car into DRIVE and steered it around the lanes of the brightly lit garage toward the exit gate.

Scant minutes later, Martha left Smallville behind her as she headed for the narrow back roads that led to the Kents' farm.

It was a beautiful, clear night, the stars glittering in the sky. As she turned off the main road, Martha kept the accelerator pressed to the floor. She could see at least a mile up the long, straight road between the fields of head-high corn, and the darkness told her that there were no other vehicles around.

The car barreled up the dusty track, Martha's mind was distracted as she tried to decide if she had enough time left to make a casserole for dinner, or—

Suddenly, her headlights picked out movement at the side of the road ahead. Desperately, Martha stabbed her foot down hard on the brake. There was a slight screech as the brakes began to lock and the tires slipped. Then the antilock braking system cut in, and Martha wrenched at the steering wheel, hauling the car back onto its line.

She caught a glimpse of something large and dark-colored as it ran out from the roadside verge. There was a sickening thump, and the car came to a halt.

Martha sat there for a moment, her heart pounding in her chest. She slipped the lever into NEUTRAL and pulled on the emergency brake, then closed her eyes in awful anticipation as she fumbled for the door latch.

She walked slowly round to the front of the car, terrified at what she was going to find there. If she'd hit somebody . . . !

The glow from the headlights lit up the gently swaying corn by the side of the road, casting an almost surreal light. Hardly able to force her eyes to move, Martha glanced down at the road.

Sprawled there was the bloody, twitching body of a large dog. Martha recognized the animal at once—Rebel, the big old German shepherd owned by the Kents' neighbor, Ezra Brown and his family. It lay on its side, one hind leg lifted slightly in the air, jerking spasmodically.

"Oh no!" Martha breathed.

Tears stung her eyes as she stooped to kneel beside the stricken dog. Its eyes were closed, and it was whimpering softly. She reached out a hand, intending to stroke the dog's ears, to somehow comfort it in its distress.

But Rebel's eyes suddenly opened, and Martha yanked back her hand in surprise. For an interminable moment, the dog's eyes stared into hers: She saw pain there, and puzzlement.

Then Rebel gave a long, low howl. Its body shuddered as a final spasm ran through it. Then it lay still, its sightless gaze still fixed on Martha.

She stood there for a long time, drenched in starshine, as lost and helpless as a little girl, guilty tears running down her cheeks.

CHAPTER 3

The next morning, Clark caught the school bus by the skin of his teeth.

He'd stayed up late, trying to help his father console his distraught mother. Martha was a strong woman, but the knowledge that she'd taken even a dog's life was enough to reduce her to tears.

It had fallen to Clark to go over to the Browns' home and tell the family what had happened. Ezra Brown took the news philosophically; a farmer for thirty years, he'd owned and lost half a dozen pet dogs.

His three children were a different matter. Clark had watched their eyes fill with tears but was helpless to soften the blow for them.

"If Rebel's dead," the smallest girl, barely four years old, said, "does that mean he's not coming back?"

"No, honey. He can't come back."

Clark had walked back home slowly under a perfect starry sky, his mind filled with thoughts of life and death. He looked up at the heavens, all of his own unanswered questions coming back to haunt him. Astronomy was his hobby; he knew full well that the distances between stars amounted to trillions of miles. The time taken to traverse those distances was immense. How could anyone survive long enough to make the journey to Earth?

His real parents must have been aliens, inhabiting a

planet orbiting one of those thousands of stars. Were they still alive? What were they like? Did they know where their son was? Had they deliberately sent him to Earth? And if so, why?

There were as many questions as there were stars in the sky . . .

Now, as Clark swung himself onto the bus, he saw Pete sitting on his own near the front, away from Lana and Chloe, his usual traveling companions. Pete's head was bent low, and he didn't glance up as Clark made to sit down beside him.

"This seat taken?" Clark asked lightly, swaying a little as the bus pulled away.

Pete looked up briefly, and Clark was shocked at what he saw in his friend's face. The whites of his eyes were tinged with green, with shadowy circles beneath, and his dark skin was strangely pallid. He looked like he hadn't enjoyed a wink of sleep.

"Hey, pal," Clark joked, "you're going to have to lay off those wild nights in the Smallville clubs. You look awful!"

Pete grimaced. He was about to say something, but just then Chloe called out from the back of the bus.

"Congratulations, Clark." She grinned broadly. "I never knew you had it in you!"

Clark was glad of the distraction. "I'll catch you later, Pete," he told his friend. "Chloe sounds suspiciously mysterious. I'd better find out exactly what she's talking about."

He made his way to the rear seats, and took his place by the girls.

"Okay," he said with mock severity, "what's the big joke?"

Lana's eyes danced mischievously. "Don't tell me you've forgotten already?"

Inwardly, Clark sighed. He was so infatuated with Lana, even the sound of her voice made the hairs on the back of his neck stand up. "Forgotten what?"

"The e-mail, of course," Chloe announced, holding up a sheet of printed paper. "You sent it last night."

Clark frowned. "I was over at Ezra Brown's last night. My mom was in an accident. With his dog. I had to go explain what happened."

"Is she all right?" Lana was immediately concerned.

"She wasn't hurt, but she's real upset. The dog died."

"So you really didn't send *this?*" Chloe waved the sheet of paper in front of Clark, but snatched it away teasingly when he tried to take it from her.

"What is it?"

"Let me refresh your memory." Chloe stifled a giggle, and began to read from the sheet. "I, Clark Kent, being of sound mind and body, do hereby volunteer my services for participation in the school's Charity Calendar."

Clark looked at the girls blankly. He knew that they were organizing photo shoots for the calendar pictures . . . but he also knew that such things were anathema to him. He would never volunteer for something like that. Not in a month of Sundays.

"So . . . you don't deny you sent it?" Lana asked lightly.

"I . . . I . . ." Clark began, but broke off as his eyes met Lana's, and their gazes held. His heart beat faster.

And, suddenly, he realized who had really sent the e-mail. Ed Wall and his bullying buddies. It was just another way of getting at Clark.

"Most guys ran a mile when we asked if they'd be in the calendar," Lana went on, without waiting for him to reply. "I think you're really brave."

And that was it. He was hooked. One compliment from Lana Lang, and Clark would willingly do just about anything she wanted.

"Thanks, Lana," he said quietly, hoping that his face wasn't as flushed as it felt. "I . . . well, I just want to do my bit for the school."

"You're Mr. July," Chloe told him. "All you'll be wearing is a leather thong and suntan oil."

Clark groaned. *This is the last thing I need.*

But then Lana said, "You're a real star," and blew him a little kiss that made everything worthwhile.

Ed and his friends were leaning against his pickup truck when the bus finally pulled into the schoolyard.

As Clark and the others spilled off the bus, Ed and his gang let out a series of mocking whoops and cheers.

"If it isn't Mr. Beefcake," Ed laughed, pointing at Clark. "Every woman's dream!"

Clark ignored their catcalls, permitting himself a small smile. Far from humiliating him in Lana's eyes, the bullies' action seemed to have brought the two of them closer together. She'd even called him a star.

He was willing to bet that was something she'd never said to Whitney.

It was lunchtime before Clark had a chance to speak to Pete again. He'd been a little unnerved by the way his friend had looked, but hadn't made a point of it because Pete had been so evasive. They'd been best friends for years, though, and Clark was determined to find out what was wrong.

He saw Pete striding across the yard, making his way toward where Ed and Phil and their little clique were sitting on the grass. Clark hurried to head him off.

"Are we still on for tomorrow?" Clark asked.

Pete blinked, but looked blank.

"Saturday?" Clark reminded him. "Are we meeting up as usual after the Farmers' Market?"

Pete's gaze slid away from his. "Uh . . . no," he said, almost shiftily. "Not tomorrow. I've made . . . other plans. I'm going someplace with Ed and the guys."

Clark nodded. He'd heard whispers around school that Ed's gang was intending to party that weekend. No nerds invited.

Pete lowered his head and made to move on, but Clark still barred his way. Pete's behavior was way out of character. If Clark was going to find out what was wrong, he seemed to have no option but to take the bull by the horns.

"What's bugging you, pal?" he asked quietly. "Is it something I've said? Something I've done? Whatever it is, I can't make amends until I know."

Pete had the decency to look embarrassed. "No," he mumbled. "It's nothing you've done."

Clark sighed. It was obvious that was all Pete was going to say on the matter. Reluctantly, Clark stepped aside, and Pete moved off without another word.

Clark watched Ed and Pete high-five each other like long-lost buddies, and sighed again. It hurt to think he was losing his friend, particularly as he had no clue as to why it was happening. But other things troubled him, too.

Pete was the only one who knew Clark's secret. His strange behavior had begun not long after he'd found out the truth about Clark and his extraterrestrial origins. Were the two connected? Clark knew that Pete had a deep-seated inferiority complex concerning his own high-flying brothers and sisters. Could finding out that Clark was an alien—a veritable superboy—have made him feel even worse?

If Pete had decided he and Clark were no longer friends—if he was as tight with Ed Wall's crowd as he seemed to be—for just how long would Clark's secret be safe?

And there was one more problem. Rumor had it Ed's gang experimented with drugs. Would that perhaps explain Pete's behavior?

It was a prospect too awful to contemplate.

"Is this weird, or is this weird?"

Chloe had been surfing the Internet during the afternoon break, and she came up to Clark with a computer printout in her hand.

"Chloe," Clark said, with feigned long-suffering patience, "you discover something weird at least three times a day. What is it this time?"

"You said your mom ran down a dog last night?"

Clark nodded. "Not very pleasant—but I wouldn't class it as weird."

"So . . . how many dogs do you think die in a town the size of Smallville on an average night?"

Clark tried to figure what she was getting at. Chloe was editor of the school newspaper, the *Torch*. A keen journalist, she had a nose for strange and offbeat stories. A lot of unusual things had happened in Smallville since the meteor swarm all those years ago, and Chloe spent much of her time trying to find connections between seemingly disparate events.

But dead dogs? That seemed to be a step too far, even for Chloe.

Impatient at his silence, Chloe didn't wait. "Not very many," she went on, "because Smallville isn't very large. But my dad says Deputy Martin told him the sheriff's people were called out five times last night—five accidents in which a dog died."

"I guess that's unusual, all right," Clark admitted. "But I don't know if it's exactly *X-Files* territory. Like, it couldn't have been the same driver who killed them all."

Chloe shot him a look that said, "So what do you know?" but let the subject drop.

"That was only a by-the-way," she informed him. "I came to tell you it's time to strip and flex those pecs."

She howled with laughter at the look of distress on Clark's face. "I knew you'd never volunteer yourself," she confessed. "Who was it—one of Ed Wall's homeboys?" Clark nodded, and Chloe laughed again. "But I also knew you'd never back out in front of Lana."

"I love it when my friends tell me how predictable I am." Clark shrugged, trying his best to be nonchalant. "Lead me to the torture room."

*   *   *

Clark wasn't exactly a natural at hogging the lime-light. He preferred the quiet life, happy to remain in the background whenever he could. Apart from anything else, his parents had long since instilled in him an extreme caution in everything he did. He could never allow anyone else to uncover the truth about him, because as his father had once said:

"If the authorities find out what you are, you'll end up in a laboratory, or a zoo . . . and your mom and I will go to prison for harboring you."

However, a calendar photo shoot shouldn't be a problem—at least, not from that point of view.

The shoot was taking place over the course of the day in an unused classroom. Lana had tacked a white sheet to the wall for a backdrop and arranged a couple of the Drama Society's spotlights to focus on it. Her camera—a top-of-the-line digital model her aunt Nell had given her before she left town—sat atop a professional tripod.

The girls had draped off a corner to act as a changing room. Clark stripped down to his shorts, folding his clothes across the back of a chair. Lana and Chloe had designed a separate costume and look for each month of the year. As Mr. July, Clark was to wear black, WWWE-style spandex tights, and strike a heroic pose while carrying a pole with a sun symbol on top.

At least Chloe was just teasing about the thong.

He stood there for a long time, staring in disbelief at the spandex, trying hard to overcome his embarrassment and actually pull the tights on.

"What's the holdup?" Chloe called from the other side of the screen. "Not backing out on us, are you?"

"No," Clark said, but his voice caught in his throat. He cleared it, and spoke again. "No. I'll be out in a minute."

Cursing softly to himself for not having pulled out when he had the chance, Clark got into his skimpy costume. The spandex felt like a second skin. Steeling himself, convinced he looked absolutely ludicrous, he pulled the drape aside and stepped out.

Chloe gave a low wolf whistle, and laughed. Lana didn't speak, and Clark glanced up from under his long lashes to see if she was ridiculing him, too. But Lana was staring hard, eyes wide open, as if she was seeing him for the first time ever.

She flushed when she saw him looking and covered her confusion by turning away to fiddle with the camera's light meter.

Clark felt a tingle of excitement course through him. If he'd known this was the effect it would have on Lana, he'd wear spandex every day!

His awkward embarrassment vanished like mist in the morning sun.

"Hey, dig the supermodel!"

Ed, Rob, and Phil were heading for Ed's pickup when they saw Clark come down the school's front steps. He ignored the gibe and would have walked on, but the trio altered direction so they could confront him.

"Bet you feel like a total clown, right, Kent?" Wall jeered.

Normally, Clark would have ignored them and gone about his own business. But he was still glowing from the realization that maybe Lana was starting to see him in a different light.

"As it happens, Ed—no, I don't feel like a clown. I really enjoyed the whole experience." Knowing it would needle the other teenager, he added, "So did Lana, I think."

He paused just long enough to savor Ed's puzzled look, then turned to leave.

As he walked away, he could feel Ed's gaze burning into his back. For an instant, he wondered if he'd done the right thing. Ed and his cronies were already close to being his enemies. Mocking them wasn't going to help matters any.

Then again, he consoled himself, *it made me feel great!*

CHAPTER 4

"I'd like to see Mr. Luthor, please. Lex Luthor."

Clark stood at the reception desk in the marble-floored lobby of the Smallville Hotel. It didn't exactly offer five-star luxury, but it was the best the town had, and it was where Lex had set up home while his castle was being repaired.

"I'm sorry, sir." The receptionist flicked a wayward strand of blond hair from her face. "Mr. Luthor's instructions were very specific. No visitors."

"I'm a friend," Clark said patiently. "Couldn't you just call him and let him know I'm here?"

"I'm sorry, sir. Mr. Luthor requested the telephones be removed from his suite. I can take a written message, if you like."

Clark shook his head. "No, thanks. Guess I'll just have to see him later."

He exited through the plate-glass revolving doors out onto Main Street.

The streetlights shone brightly in the clear night air as he stood for a moment under the hotel's front canopy. He'd already decided what he was going to do. He'd promised he would talk to Lex and confirm his appearance at school the following week, and he would keep his word.

Though the receptionist wouldn't know anything about his visit . . .

The street was relatively quiet, and nobody noticed as Clark turned into the alleyway that ran along the side of the hotel. The only light there came trickling down from the hotel windows above. Craning his neck, Clark could see that there were lights on in the penthouse, on the seventh floor. It was the most expensive suite, and he'd bet his last dollar that was where Lex would be staying.

Six feet above his head, the bottom rungs of the fire escape dangled. Glancing around to ensure he was still unseen, Clark flexed his ankles and jumped in the air. He soared effortlessly upward, and reached out to pull himself onto the balcony.

Soundlessly, he hurried up the fire escape's metal steps, smiling wryly to himself. Ever since he'd saved Lex from drowning when his Porsche crashed into the river, the older man had suspected there was something strange about Clark. He'd tried to catch Clark out several times, even going so far as to hire a detective to investigate his background.

But Jonathan and Martha had meticulously covered every detail of their son's imaginary past, and all of Lex's inquiries had drawn only blanks.

If only he'd seen that jump, every suspicion he'd ever had would be confirmed.

The door from the sixth-floor balcony was locked on the inside. Clark grasped the handle, and had to exert only minimum strength before the lock snapped with a loud crack. He pushed the door open, slipped inside, and closed it again behind him.

He ignored the elevators and walked up the stairs to the top floor.

Seconds later, he was tapping gently on the door to the penthouse suite. No response. He knocked again, harder.

"I'm busy," his friend's voice came from inside. "Go away."

"It's me, Lex. Clark."

He heard a rattle as Lex took off the safety chain, and the door swung open.

Lex looked as cool and sophisticated as he always did. He wore a plain white silk shirt and tight black pants, and looked as if he might be about to step out with a movie star or model. The hairless head, which might look ugly on most twenty-five-year-olds, only made Lex more charismatic.

"Clark," he said affably. "How did you get up here, buddy? They told me my privacy was guaranteed."

"That obviously doesn't apply to friends," Clark replied, avoiding the question. "Aren't you going to invite me in?"

To Clark's surprise, Lex hesitated. "We-ell," he began to say, "it's not really the best time—" Then he thought better of it. "Sure. I'm smack-dab in the middle of something, but there's always time to see a friend."

He waved Clark inside and closed the door behind him.

The large room was decorated in tasteful shades of blue, and the television set in the corner had been unplugged from the wall. The large coffee table, and one of the pair of easy chairs that flanked it, were covered in heaps of books. A half dozen yellow legal pads lay scattered on the bed, covered in handwriting, diagrams, and columns of figures.

Clark squinted, trying to make out some of the book titles. Most seemed to be business studies. The only one he could make out clearly was called *Cassandra's Secret*.

He perched himself on an arm of the chair. "You're obviously making good use of your time, Lex," he remarked, nodding toward the books. "Something special?"

Again Lex hesitated, as if he was reluctant to share what he was reading. "Yes," he said at last, and abruptly changed the subject. "So—how can I help you? Let me guess. The school hasn't heard from me, and they're worried I might not show for the lecture next week."

"You got it."

"And so have they. I'll be there." He grasped the door handle again and began to pull it open.

"What's this, the bum's rush?" Clark demanded. "I haven't seen you for weeks. I thought we might play catch-up. Wait till you hear about my modeling job today—"

"I'd love to, Clark. Some other time, okay?" Lex must have seen the younger man's disappointed look, because he went on more softly, "I really am in the middle of something, Clark. Something important."

"Is it top secret?" Clark asked.

"Far from it. I'm trying to hike the fertilizer plant's profits by a healthy percentage." Lex gestured toward the sprawl of books and pads. "Not an easy task, I assure you. I need time to sort it all out. And much as I like you, you're distracting me."

"Wow. Work," Clark said dryly, as he got to his feet.

Lex's eyes bored into his, and when Lex spoke, his voice was grimly serious. "Self-discipline, pal. It could save the world," he added mysteriously. "Or destroy it."

"I look forward to hearing more, o great philosopher," Clark joked, as he walked past Lex and out through the open door.

Lex didn't reply, merely closed the door.

Clark stood alone in the hall, feeling slightly foolish. He'd intended to tell Lex about Pete and ask for his advice. He knew that, in his wild youth, Lex had been involved with drugs himself. If anybody could help Pete, it would be somebody who'd experienced the same things.

People thought Lex was cruel and ruthless like his father, driven by a lust for money. But Clark knew he had a gentler, more sensitive side.

What was that all about? Clark wondered. He already had one friend acting strangely. Now he seemed to have two.

It must be something in the air.

The Reverend Grindlay tiptoed quietly along the hall to his study, hoping Moira wouldn't hear him. She'd been nagging him earlier about writing the coming Sunday's sermon, but he felt exhausted, with not an original thought in his mind.

He toyed with the idea of having another look at the church's bell system. But he'd been avoiding it for weeks. Another day wouldn't hurt.

Friday was always a busy day for him. He visited the Smallville Hospital in the morning, making his rounds of the long-term-care and terminal wards, giving comfort where it was needed and help where he could.

In the afternoon he spent three hours at the town's old people's home, taking tea with the ladies and playing pinochle with the men. He hadn't missed a Friday in all the time he'd been in Smallville.

Back home, he had valiantly tried to catch up with his correspondence before Moira called him for dinner. He really didn't feel like writing a sermon that night.

He opened his study door and slipped inside, into his own little oasis of peace.

For a moment he just stood there, back to the door, drinking in the smell of old leather and polished wood. He took the tiny meteor fragment from his pocket and stroked it with his finger. Funny how it seemed to absorb his stress and calm him down.

Then he spotted the old journal lying where he'd left it on his desk, and a little thrill ran through him. He'd all but forgotten about it in the bustle of the day.

He sat down in his leather chair, marveled briefly at the beauty of the handwriting, and flicked open the book.

July 17

The prairie spooks me. It seems endless, an ocean of swaying grass and soughing wind that fills the world from horizon to horizon.

And our progress across it is so slow.

The sun has again been blistering hot. Even in the shade of my wagon's canvas, the heat is oppressive, well-nigh unbearable. And there is little shade along our route. Trees are few and far between, generally located along the banks of streams.

I had thought we might see some of the native Red Men, about whom I have read so much in the Eastern newspapers. Huckins says that those around here have been pacified. I did not ask how it was done. Suffice to say, they tend to keep well away from settlers.

Although it slows us mightily, we have stopped twice today when we forded little rivers, to allow the children to frolic in the clear waters. The cattle and oxen, too, appreciate the half hour's respite and the cool water. That which we carry in the barrels lashed to our "prairie schooners," as Mr. Huckins calls the wagons, warms too much and tastes unpleasant.

The Farrells' dog died at last. I felt sorry for the children, but it is a relief to be rid of the poor brute's piteous whines.

July 18

Perhaps it is the heat, acting on the humors of our brains, which caused the unrest which has broken out among some of my fellow travelers.

Last night, well after dark, I heard the German families screaming stridently (though unintelligibly, to me at least) at each other. Whatever the cause of their dispute, it was not settled, because they have not spoken to each other since.

And we seem to have a sneak thief in our midst. Various small items, none of any great value, have gone missing from the wagons. I am guarding my belongings well, though it grieves me to think that, even here, people can be vile to each other.

Or perhaps it was the Farrells' dead dog casting a long shadow of ill luck on us, a theory propounded around our campfire tonight by some of the Irishmen who are traveling together. They swear that in their home village, a dead dog always brings bad luck.

I tend to shy away from such superstitious gossip; and anyway, the Irish are renowned for their tall tales. I rather think they are enjoying a joke at our expense; but, truth to tell, there is little that is amusing in our situation.

The night is cool without being chilly, truly a blessing in this land of extremes. I pray to the Lord we may leave it soon.

July 22

Jack O'Brien is dead. Yes, the Irishman who frightened the others (and unnerved me) with his tales of bad luck himself encountered a fatal ill fortune this afternoon.

In a way, it was Mr. Huckins's fault. The Farrell boy saw him at our meal stop, skulking behind the wagons, suckling a bottle of what we all know to be whiskey. (When questioned, I should add, Huckins claimed the spirits are for medicinal purposes only.)

We set out again without mishap, turning to follow the path of a creek. We traveled for an hour or more, our pace funereally slow.

Away in the distance, I could see a small smudge on the horizon. I took it to be some outpost for which we were heading, though Huckins had never mentioned any such detour.

As we grew closer, I saw it was a homestead, one of those turf huts whose inhabitants call themselves "sodbusters." It is not a life I myself could lead, but I understand that the isolation and lack of human contact are attractive to some.

There was no sign of life, although the family may have been at home. We were not to find out, because Mr. Huckins suddenly and dramatically announced that we had veered off on the wrong trail and would have to retrace our path, but on the other side of the stream.

The streambed was strewn with boulders, bumping and jarring the wagons most severely as we traversed the waters. The banking on the other side was quite steep, and it required several men pushing from the wagons' rear before the horses managed to drag them up.

Perhaps we should have used ropes. Perhaps Huckins had imbibed more than is normal, for he certainly should have warned us of the perils involved. He is the supposed expert here; we are mere innocents abroad.

The French wagon was halfway up the banking. I was straining at the rear, along with Jack O'Brien and three of his stalwart Irish cronies. Suddenly, one of the horses slipped, its shoe ringing on the bare rock. The wagon jolted backward, its rear corner catching O'Brien off guard and dealing him a hefty blow.

He tumbled off the rocks, his body twisting so that he would fall into what looked like a small sandy beach.

It was quicksand.

His arms broke his fall, but not enough to prevent him plunging facefirst a good twelve inches into its surface.

I immediately turned to go to his aid, but one of the others cried, "Don't let go the wagon, or we shall all go over!"

And in truth, he was right. By the time some of the other men had rushed to help us, and the Germans had pulled O'Brien from the bog, the man was dead. Knocked unconscious by the impact and suffocated by the clinging, soupy sand.

What a terrible end! His companions, always so cheerful and full of mischievous laughter, are devastated.

We had no option but to pitch camp while we dug a grave and gave him, at least, a decent burial. No man of the cloth travels with us, so it fell to me to say a few words, Huckins being so inebriated as to be nigh incoherent.

Of course, the tragic event has cast a dark pall over us. We have each retired to our respective wagons. The Irishmen have started drinking. Even the children are subdued.

Huckins says there is little point in trying to go farther today. There are ominously black clouds gathering in the distance, and he fears we are in for a storm. He advises us to remain where we are and sit it out.

I hope his love of whiskey has not clouded his judgment.

The minister paused in his reading. Fingering the green cross, he closed his eyes and murmured a short prayer for the soul of the unfortunate Jack O'Brien.

How many others like him had there been—from Europe, from Africa, from China? The unnumbered dead who had helped build this great country.

There was the sound of a slam at the far end of the hallway. Michael braced himself. Moira knocked loudly on his study door and entered without waiting to be invited.

She glared at the journal lying open before him. "That doesn't look like a sermon to me," she said caustically.

"No, dear," Michael demurred. "However, it is giving me inspiration."

"I'll believe that when I see it written down," Moira sniffed. "Or hear it on Sunday."

Sighing, Michael closed the journal and put it back into its protective bag. Then he reached for his keyboard, called up the word processing program, and began to type.

Lana sat on her bed in her nightclothes, sorting through the contact prints of the photos she'd taken that afternoon.

"Some of these aren't bad," she told Chloe, "even if I say so myself."

Chloe was sitting on the floor on a thick shag rug, riffling through a similar sheaf of photographs.

"Check out Mr. January," she urged her friend. "Who'd ever have guessed geeky Shawn Dellar would look so chic in a fur hat and Cossack boots?"

"And not much else!" Lana laughed.

"Mr. July doesn't look too shabby, either," Chloe went on. "Clark's a strong-looking guy."

Lana didn't reply. She was remembering the strange feeling of shock she'd experienced when she saw Clark half-dressed. She'd known him since they were children; they'd gone swimming together a hundred times. Yet today was the first time she'd ever seen him as . . . a man.

And, she had to admit, she liked what she saw.

"No comment?" Chloe asked slyly.

Lana blushed, and shook her head. She knew that Chloe was strongly attracted to Clark, though Clark didn't reciprocate the feeling. When Aunt Nell left town for her new life, and Mr. Sullivan agreed to act as Lana's guardian, Lana had fretted there would be friction between her and Chloe.

She needn't have worried. Chloe was friendly, highly intelligent, and literally fizzing with enthusiasm and ideas. They got on like a house afire.

"So . . . what's your take on the dead dogs?" Chloe abruptly changed the subject. She had no interest in embarrassing Lana.

Lana shrugged. "It does seem unusual," she agreed, "but without some kind of connecting factor, it's just—well, coincidence, isn't it?"

Chloe nodded brightly. "Meteor rocks?" she prompted. "Connecting factor? This is Smallville. Weirdsville, USA. You can bet your best dress those meteors had something to do with it!"

Lana stretched and gathered up the photographs. "I think I'll go to bed," she said as she stacked them on the dressing table. "Wake me when you can prove your theories." Barely aware that Chloe was watching her, she picked up her pendant from the bedside table and held it up to the light.

The dark green stone turned in the air on the end of its silver chain. Lana reached up her other hand to steady it, then touched it briefly to her lips.

The stone was a fragment of the meteor that had plowed into Main Street, striking the Langs' car, and killing her parents. All she had to remember them by was her childhood memories and this tiny sliver of some alien element.

"I'll never forget you," she whispered, and replaced it on the table before sliding between the sheets.

"You know," Chloe said thoughtfully, "we might not have proof—but I'm certain those stones possess some kind of strange power."

"I assure you, mine doesn't," Lana said sleepily. "Unless you count the power of memory. It helps me remember my parents, that's all."

She closed her eyes and let herself drift away. But her last waking thoughts weren't of her parents.

They were of Clark Kent.

CHAPTER 5

Lex Luthor hadn't slept all night.

Dawn found him seated by a window in his hotel suite, drinking in the rosy glow as the sun's light stole across Smallville. His eyes never left the scene—almost as if it might be the last sunrise he would ever see.

Or, perhaps, the first sunrise he had ever really noticed.

His father, Lionel, was one of the richest men in the world. Before Lex was even ten years old, he had notched up hundreds of thousands of air miles, flying around the planet with his father. But there was never time for sight-seeing.

"I didn't become a billionaire by looking at tourist attractions," Lionel told him. Frequently. All of his trips were focused on one single objective: increasing the size, and profitability, of his business empire. And although Lex was his only son, Lionel often seemed to treat him as if he was one of his commercial enemies.

From an early age, Lex learned to fend for himself. He was often irritated by his father—sometimes angry with him—but never, ever cowed by him. During his teenage years, Lex had run with a fast crowd. He got himself involved in a number of scrapes that maddened his father.

Perhaps that was why Lionel had banished him to the back of beyond.

Smallville was about as quiet a town as you could get, and that's where Lionel had sent his son. Ostensibly, Lex was to run the town's fertilizer plant—according to Lionel, in order to teach him how to run a company.

But to Lex, it often felt like he'd been sent into exile.

He thought he'd figured out what life was all about: dog eat dog. Survival of the fittest, or most ruthless, or luckiest. You're born in a jungle and have to spend your entire life fighting against its other inhabitants. You have to learn how to bankrupt them before they bankrupt you. How to control them through business before they're able to control you. How to destroy them—because, make no mistake, they would do their best to destroy you.

It was a very jaundiced view of humanity, but Lex had never seen any real alternative to his father's philosophy. That's why he'd decided to use this period of confinement in the hotel as a time for growing his business and increasing his profits. He'd ordered every book on business that money could buy, and every autobiography by every billionaire who'd ever written one.

Maybe he could distill the lessons they'd learned into one all-encompassing formula for the creation of wealth.

But his mind kept straying to a single volume that had been delivered with the others, though the title was on no order form that he had checked.

Cassandra's Secret, it was called, the title derived from the tragic Greek prophetess. It purported to be the rediscovery of how to turn men into gods. At first skeptical, wondering what on earth it had to do with business, Lex prepared to scan a few pages and toss it in the trash.

But as he plowed through the densely worded text, he began to reconsider.

The book was based on the work of a Princeton professor, and described how, in ancient times, Mankind lived in a fog of near schizophrenia. Rational thinking was unknown in the world, and all decisions and actions were based on "messages from the gods"—either in the form of dreams and visions, or as auditory hallucinations triggered in times of stress.

According to the author, the archaeological evidence shows that the ancient civilizations began to collapse because of their growing complexity. In order to survive, Mankind had to discover—or invent—a new way of thinking.

The rational mind was born. For the first time ever, human beings could reflect internally. They could make rational decisions based on their own thoughts. The gods who had ruled mankind for millennia were no longer needed.

The visions ceased, and the hallucinated voices fell silent. The old gods withdrew.

Man was on the cusp of becoming a god himself. The Golden Age of Reason flourished in ancient Greece, and for a brief moment in history rational thinking was poised to take over the world.

But unscrupulous men discovered how to use rationality to deceive, manipulate, and plunder their fellows. Greed and laziness crippled man's burgeoning creativity. The evil spread like a virus, contaminating every mind with which it came into contact.

Just like my father, Lex realized. *Always ready to take, never to give. And Dad is far from alone there.*

Now, *Cassandra's Secret* promised to reveal how that godlike state could once again be achieved.

Yeah. Right.

As the sun's rays reached his window, painting the room's interior in shades of golden red, he banished the book from his thoughts and turned again to the uninviting stack of business volumes.

He would switch between the two many times in the nights to come.

By nine o'clock, the sun was high in the sky. In a field on the outskirts of town, Smallville's weekly Farmers' Market was in full swing.

Clark stood behind his parents' stall, serving those who wanted to buy, exchanging banter with those who didn't. He had risen with the dawn and used his incredible strength to load crates of farm produce onto his parents' truck at lightning speed. By the time Martha and Jonathan came downstairs, everything was ready to roll, and their breakfast was on the table, waiting.

"It sure comes in handy sometimes, having an alien son." Jonathan smiled—although market day was probably the one day of the week when Clark felt least like an alien.

"Good morning, Mr. Deen," Clark said, as old Cyrus stood peering at the boxes of fruit and vegetables. "Looks like we've got another great day."

"Hmmph," Cyrus snorted. He peered suspiciously up at the sky through craggy brows, squinting his eyes against the bright sun. "Nice enough now, maybe, but there's a storm brewing. A real humdinger, too."

Clark looked surprised. The sky was a deep blue bowl,

marked only by a few, fluffy clouds at high altitude. "You're kidding, right?"

The old man picked up a bag of apples. "You mark my words," he said ominously, "before the afternoon is out, we'll be up to our ankles in rain."

He handed over some dollar bills, took his fruit, and moved off.

Thoughtfully, Clark watched him go.

"Did you hear that, Dad?" he asked, as Jonathan and Martha returned from the coffee booth with three king-size cups. "Mr. Deen says we're in for bad weather."

His father gazed up at the few distant clouds and nodded. "Could be he's right. It's been hot enough, and if there's moist air coming in from the west . . ." Jonathan Kent had farmed Kansas soil all his life and knew well the sudden and surprising extremes the weather could take. "Cyrus has been here a while longer than me. If anybody knows, it's him."

The Reverend Grindlay slipped the gear lever into first, let out the clutch, and the old VW Beetle rattled away from the church.

He'd bought the car at the end of his first week in Smallville. He liked it so much, he'd had it ever since. It was in surprisingly good condition, considering its age, thanks to the mechanics at the local garage.

"That reminds me," he said to Moira. "The car's due for servicing. I'll take it in next week."

In the passenger seat beside him, his wife looked up from the shopping list she was compiling. "Right after you fix the wiring?" she asked, softening her words with a smile.

"You know, Moira, I can't remember the last time we took a vacation."

"I can. We went to Metropolis. You didn't like it." She smiled again. "For that matter, neither did I. We came home again."

The old car drove past the town limits sign. Michael could see the market ahead, and he indicated to turn left into the parking lot. But as he spun the wheel, the front of the car suddenly lurched. There was a loud crack, and the front fender slammed into the ground.

Michael and Moira lunged forward, caught by their sea belts before they could injure themselves.

"Are you all right, Moira?"

"Just a little shaken." Moira rolled down her window, and looked out. The front wheel had snapped and come completely off the axle.

"I think you may have waited too long for that car servicing."

Halfway through the morning, Clark saw Pete walking around the field with his father. Pete glanced in his direction, but when Clark waved a greeting, his friend looked quickly away again.

Pretending he hasn't seen me. It's getting to be a habit.

Clark didn't know whether to feel upset or angry, and finally settled for a mixture of both. He and Pete had been through a lot together. Clark had sat in vigil by his friend's hospital bedside when Pete was comatose. They'd faced trouble, and danger, together—and come through, still friends.

Pete's discovery of the truth about Clark's origins

should have cemented the bond between them. Instead, they seemed to be growing farther and farther apart.

"Hey, Clark."

His heart skipped a beat as Lana's voice broke in on his grim thoughts. She and Chloe were arm in arm, shopping together for the Sullivans' weekly groceries.

"Why are you scowling on such a beautiful day?"

"Deep in thought," Clark replied lightly. "You know— mysteries of the universe."

"We're going to take in a movie tonight," Chloe told him, "followed by a pizza. Are you up for it?"

Before Clark could answer, he caught sight of Pete again. He was standing near the market's entrance, deep in conversation with Ed Wall. Ed jerked his head toward his four-by-four, and the two clambered into the vehicle. Clark remembered the rumors he'd heard at school about the "party" Ed and his cronies were hosting that weekend.

On a sudden impulse, Clark turned away from the girls.

"I'll see you later," he told them hurriedly. Seeing their blank looks, he added, "Emergency. Have to rush."

He walked swiftly across to join his parents, who were talking to the Reverend Grindlay. As he approached, he heard the minister saying, ". . . couldn't believe it. I've been driving for twenty-five years, and I've never seen anything like it. The front wheel just literally snapped in two. Lucky we were slowing for the parking lot when it happened, or Moira and I could have been killed."

"Excuse me," Clark interrupted. He said a hurried "Good morning" to the minister, then—more urgently— to his parents: "I've just remembered I told Pete I'd go along with him this afternoon," he said apologetically. "Is it all right if I leave early?"

"No problem," Jonathan told him.

Clark didn't wait to hear any more. He spun quickly on his heel and headed for the exit.

He could see the rear of Ed's truck disappearing up the road. The location of the party had been kept a secret, because the only people invited were Ed and Phil's little clique. If Clark wanted to know what his friend was up to, there was only one way to find out.

Glancing around to ensure he wasn't observed, Clark sneaked off the roadway and into a field. Surrounded by gently swaying cornstalks that towered over him by a foot or more, with the sun's rays filtering through the green vegetation, it felt like being in an alien world.

He took a deep breath and started to run.

"What's up, Petey?" Ed yelled over the blare of music from the car's stereo system. "Not in the mood to party?"

Pete was crammed into the backseat with three other teenagers, with Phil up front and Ed at the wheel.

"You bet," he replied, but there wasn't a lot of conviction in his voice. Apart from anything else, he hated being called "Petey." It reminded him of his mom and dad when he was just a kid.

He couldn't deny that he liked the feelings the strange green berries induced in him, but he was very conscious of the deleterious effect it was having on his friendships. He'd felt like a total jerk, ignoring Clark the way he did back at the market. But what other choice did he have? He couldn't tell him what the gang was up to, because he knew Clark wouldn't approve.

It was okay for Clark. He had all these superpowers. He needn't fear anybody, or anything.

"Well, gird up your loins, my friend," Ed laughed. "Berries, boom box, and babes . . . this is going to be a doozy!"

Ed slammed his foot down on the gas, and the pickup's wheels sent up a cloud of dust as it roared along the road.

The pickup was traveling at nearly sixty miles an hour, but, incredibly, Clark was able to keep up with it.

His legs pumped like pistons as he flashed through the rows of almost ripe corn. Approaching a junction, he allowed himself to slow momentarily. His superkeen hearing came into play as he scanned the roads to the side for the sound of traffic. When he heard none, he flexed his leg muscles and leapt.

He soared through the air, eight feet above the ground, his spectacular jump carrying him clear across the roadway and into the cornfield on the other side.

It was a total mystery what Pete and his new friends were up to, but Clark's suspicion that they were using drugs was growing stronger. Chloe had written a well-researched piece on cannabis use for the school newspaper about a year back, and as Clark ran he mentally ticked off the "signs of drug use" she had listed.

Pete was being secretive. He'd found a new set of friends. His attention span seemed to have shortened to the point where he'd lost interest in his schoolwork. He had dark circles under his eyes and seemed tired all the time.

All circumstantial evidence, with a dozen other potential explanations.

One way or another, Clark was going to find out the truth.

Pete looked out of the window as Ed raced the truck along the narrow, straight track, leaving a row of wildly waving cornstalks on either side. He didn't recognize the road they were on, although perhaps that wasn't surprising since most of the roads around Smallville had little to distinguish them from each other.

"Where are we headed?" he demanded, but Ed merely laughed.

The truck swung off the roadway onto a barely visible dirt trail that cut straight as an arrow through the cornfields. They bombed along it, leaving a plume of dust in their wake.

Three or four miles farther on, the landscape changed slightly. The ground dipped along the banks of a small river. The low terrain was wetter, almost boggy in places, with thickets of willow trees scattered among the vegetation of the riverbank.

Just ahead, a gate had once barred the way. Long exposure to the elements had turned its metal to flaking rust, and its retaining chain had long since snapped and broken.

Ed guided the truck expertly around the obstruction and slowed to a halt by a clump of willows.

"Welcome to Wall's World," Ed announced. "Everybody out."

Pete and the others disembarked from the car and stood looking around them.

"Al fresco, right?" one of the other teenagers asked.

"No Als at all," Ed replied. He pulled his large, still-blaring ghetto blaster from the front of the car and set off toward the trees. "Follow me, dudes. And don't forget the six-packs."

A couple of the others hoisted the beer from the bed of the truck. Pete frowned to himself as he shuffled along behind them. Ahead, hidden in the sprawling group of willows, he could make out a scattering of old corrugated metal huts. A blind man could have guessed they were ex-army.

Their windows were virtually glassless, apart from the odd shard still projecting from the frames. The low buildings' paint had blistered and flaked in the relentless Kansas sunshine, exposing large areas of rust.

"What the heck is this place?" someone wanted to know.

"History lesson," Ed said, as he led the way through the thick undergrowth toward the largest of the huts. "Back in the 1950s, it looked like there might be nuclear war between us and the Russkies. The government built and stocked a series of atomic shelters in isolated locations, so if the bombs went boom, at least the local officials would survive. This"—he gestured to the main building—"is an atomic bomb shelter."

He broke off at the sounds of approaching engines. A bright red pickup truck was racing down the track toward them, followed by an old Chevy Impala. Ed raised a hand above his head and waved to the newcomers.

"Right on time," he grinned.

The door to the long, low shed was hanging half off its

hinges. Pete watched Ed give it a vicious boot, and it swung open with a screech of tortured metal.

Inside, it was cool and dark and musty. Pete squinted, adjusting his vision to the deep shadows. A thick layer of dust and debris lay everywhere. The charred remains of a table and a few chairs lay heaped together in a corner under a gaping hole in the metal roof.

Phil snapped on the flashlight he carried in one hand, its beam illuminating the shed's interior.

"Looks almost like the bombs did land," he muttered. "Not much of a venue for a party, Ed."

"O ye of little faith," Ed intoned, before breaking into a wild laugh. "This is just the chill-out room. The Party proper is downstairs."

Phil swung his flashlight, and for the first time Pete noticed an area of deeper shadow halfway along one wall. As they moved closer, he could see that it was a trapdoor in the floor. The wooden door had rotted and collapsed years ago, exposing the set of steps that led downward. The stairs themselves were metal, and seemed to be in a reasonable state of preservation.

Ed's footsteps echoed hollowly as he led the way down. Pete followed directly behind him, feeling more than a little trepidatious. Just what the heck would they find down there?

There was a high-pitched squeaking, and a dozen bats fluttered around them. One of the girls shrieked, and the bats flew off to find another roost.

A second flashlight came on, and Pete was surprised at what their light revealed. A small natural cavern by the riverside had been artificially enlarged until it formed an irregular chamber about twenty yards long and fifteen wide. Several small tunnels ran off the sides of the main chamber. One of them was partially collapsed, half-filled with earth and rock that had fallen from the ceiling. A trickle of water splashed from it, pooling in a small reservoir in the center of the cavern.

"Oh, gross!" Phil shone his flashlight into the mouth of one of the side chambers, lighting up a large untidy stack of tin cans. Their labels were faded, most of them peeled away and rotting on the earthen floor. Some of the cans had ruptured, splitting open to reveal their contents: food.

"Can't you just imagine it?" Ed asked, laughing. "The great and the good of Smallville, squatting down here in the dark, living on canned food and river water." Pete knew Ed reveled in being the center of attraction. The linchpin at the hub of the clique. The Man. And since Ed was the only one who knew where the magic berries grew, his popularity was assured.

"Man, it would almost be worth having a war to see that!"

Ed snapped an order to the others. "Get the candles lit, and the storm lanterns. And somebody open a beer for me, okay?"

Clark heard the raucous music before he saw the two trucks and the Impala parked in the dappled shade of the towering willows.

He'd lived in the Smallville area all his life, yet he'd never been aware of this place's existence.

Pausing behind the wide trunk of a tree, he brushed the dust from his clothes with his hands, pondering what his next step should be. Dark clouds were beginning to scud across the sky. A wind was whipping up, rustling the leaves of the willows. The storm Cyrus Deen had predicted was getting closer.

Cautiously, Clark crept up to the door from which the music was coming and peered inside. Nothing.

He didn't need the aid of his peculiar X-ray vision to see the trapdoor set in the floor and the muffled light that flickered from it. He moved silently closer and began to descend the metal steps.

Halfway down, he froze. There was a cavern below ground level, brightly illuminated by candles and storm lanterns. A boom box was blasting out heavy rock music, a screaming lead guitar echoing from the cavern walls.

About a dozen teenagers of both sexes were clustered around Ed, like disciples hanging on their master's every word. And Pete was among them. Hidden from any possible view by the turn in the stairs, Clark could see the teenagers' expectant faces as they silently stretched out their hands toward their leader.

Like some medieval priest dispensing religious favors, Ed dropped one fat, green berry into each upturned palm.

Not pot then, Clark thought. *But what?*

All attention was focused on Ed and his berries. Taking advantage of the distraction, Clark slipped quietly down the rest of the staircase and darted into the shadows of one of the side tunnels. He had no idea what his next step would be.

For the moment, he would content himself as observer.

"All together now," Ed commanded.

As one, the teenagers lifted their hands to their mouths and gulped down the juicy green fruits.

Outside, the scudding clouds had coalesced into one solid, black mass. There was a single bright flash of lightning, followed almost immediately by a massive peal of thunder.

The first fat raindrops splashed down, running down the willow leaves, bouncing off the hard, parched soil. Too dry for far too long, it repelled the water like a raincoat.

Within minutes, a curtain of driving rain had enveloped the whole area.

Trickles of water meandered together, forming into larger rivulets that themselves became miniature streams.

Ominously, the water level in the river started to rise.

CHAPTER 6

Pete felt elation coursing through his veins like a tangible object.

All of his fears and worries and insecurities faded away, dropping from his mind like icicles melting in the sun. Only the good feelings remained. He felt absolutely amazing.

The candles' light seemed to be flickering in time to the heavy bass from the boom box, alternately lighting up the cavern's interior then plunging it into shadow. The sound of the music reverberated off the walls, building to a solid crescendo of driving noise.

Sound and colors melted into one.

Pete moved away from the little knot of people still clustered around Ed. He began to dance, his body moving in time to the beat.

A girl in a white tank top and denim jeans slid up beside him, matching her sinuous movements to his. Pete glanced at her face. Beams of green light seemed to play around her eyes, flickering in time to the rhythm of the music.

Unbidden, a huge grin stole across Pete's face. His eyes must look like that, too. Cool!

Almost all of the teenagers were dancing by then, lost in a fog of pounding bass and rimshot drumming.

I wonder if this is how the cavemen danced, Pete

thought, and his grin turned into a laugh that seemed to roll and rumble around the entire world.

Clark's heart was heavy as he crouched in the shadows, gaze riveted to his dancing, swirling friend. It wasn't that he didn't like to see Pete happy—they'd been best buddies for years, and Clark was well aware of the insecurities that sometimes plagued his friend. He *wanted* Pete to be happy.

But not like this. Not collapsed to the floor in the grip of hysterical laughter, with a dozen others dancing around him as if he weren't even there.

"Shirley's *my* girl, you creep!"

Clark started as Phil's strident voice cut over the throbbing music. He swiveled his head to see Phil angrily confront one of the other boys, engaged in an old-fashioned jive routine with a pretty girl in red.

Shirley Grainger. Clark knew her slightly from school.

The smile on the other teenager's face turned into an ugly snarl. Clark recognized him as David Lomen, another sophomore, although he didn't share any of Clark's classes.

"We're only dancing, moron," Lomen snapped back. He was smaller than Phil, but broader and stockier. His hand swept up to stab a finger accusingly into Phil's chest. "Get a life, why don't you?"

Around them, the others continued to dance, oblivious to the mood of menace that had Phil and David in its grip. Even Shirley didn't seem to notice, spinning and swaying sexily in a world of her own.

Clark frowned as Phil knocked David's hand aside and grabbed the smaller teenager by his shirtfront.

"You wanna dance?" Phil sneered. "Then do it over there."

Clark watched, astonished, as Phil literally lifted Dave off his feet and hurled him through the air toward the mouth of the side tunnel where Clark was hidden.

Quickly, he shuffled backward, away from the entrance, as Dave's body thudded into the wall beside it. He shook his head to clear it, lurched to his feet, and charged bodily at Phil.

Where did he get strength like that?

The two grappled with each other, and other dancers yelled in protest as they tried to avoid the struggling bodies.

Clark sighed, moving back deeper into the tunnel. The way Phil had thrown Dave like that—it couldn't have been natural. Perhaps the drug—whatever it was—enhanced the taker's strength, in addition to whatever else it did.

Keeping his eyes on the fight, determined not to be discovered, Clark groped behind him to make sure the way was clear. His hand brushed a pile of damp earth and encountered something rough.

He turned. Part of the tunnel wall had collapsed over the years, making it near impossible to back up any farther. Away from the light of the main cavern, it was dark and gloomy, but even without using his super-vision, Clark could see that he'd unwittingly unearthed a small sack.

Puzzled, he drew it toward him. The rotting material disintegrated, exposing a waxed paper pouch inside. It contained something round and hard, about the size of a fist.

He stuffed it into the waistband of his pants and turned back to the fight.

Outside, the rain fell in sheets. Water poured off the parched fields, too dry to absorb it, and ran directly to the river. Driven by the rising wind, the swollen waters lapped ever higher against the banking.

A rusted metal grille, its mesh choked with the river-borne debris of years, groaned under the weight of water pressing against it. Choppy waves crumbled away the soil at its sides. Suddenly, the river surged under a squall of wind.

For the first time in many long years, water poured through the grille.

Pete swayed and shuffled, feeling that the music and his own senses had formed some kind of union. He *was* the music.

He was jerked out of his reverie as two struggling bodies crashed against him, almost knocking him over. Impatiently, he shoved them aside—and felt an immediate thrill at the strength that surged effortlessly through him.

Ed was right. *This* was living.

Who needed school? Who needed a family that made him feel six inches high? Who needed friends from outer space?

Pete peered at the two teenagers, who had pulled themselves apart and were now rolling lithely back to their feet. Unable to fathom why they should be fighting, and not really caring anyway, Pete closed his eyes and let himself drift away.

More solidly built than Phil, Dave had the extra advantage of having studied martial arts at night class. He'd only gone for the one semester, but it had been enough for him to pick up a smattering of karate and judo.

As Phil lunged at him, Dave took a half step to the side and grasped his opponent's arm. Using Phil's own momentum against him, Dave flicked his wrist to send the other teenager careening through the air.

The music reached a crescendo as Phil crashed into the cavern wall with a sickening thud and lay still.

Sudden silence descended. The CD in the stereo system had ended. The dancers froze in midmotion, Pete's eyes snapping open as he returned from his dreamworld. Several faces turned toward where Phil lay unmoving.

Ed gave a laugh, and moved closer to his fallen friend. "Hey, c'mon, man," he said airily, "quit fooling around."

Suddenly, Pete's joy vanished, and he felt terrified. The bright, flickering candle flames seemed to dull, casting a gloomier, more oppressive light. There seemed to be a dull roaring sound, growing by the minute, but nobody else appeared to have noticed.

Pete gave an involuntary start as he thought he saw a huge, leering skull grinning down from the cavern ceiling. He blinked, and when he looked again it was merely the light cast by a guttering candle.

"Uuh." There was a groan, and Phil opened his eyes. "Did anybody get the number of that train?"

Ed hooted with laughter and reached a hand to pull his friend to his feet. "Welcome back, man. We thought you'd gone off on some private trip."

Phil rubbed the back of his head. "So," he demanded,

as if he'd forgotten all about the fight with Dave, "what happened to the music?"

Before anyone could reply, the roaring Pete had heard grew much louder. One of the girls pointed to where the channel had been cut to allow river water to enter. The trickle of water that ran down it had swollen considerably, spewing out into the pool in the chamber floor.

The chamber wall behind was bulging, as the deluge of water sweeping down from the river sought to find a way through to a lower level.

Almost instantly, it did.

The wall crumbled and fell away, and a tidal wave of filthy, muddy water swept into the room.

Even hidden by the twist in the passage, Clark knew at once something horrible had happened.

He scrambled back down the tunnel, his feet splashing in water that was ankle deep and rising fast. He reached the entrance and gasped in shock at the sight that greeted him.

Torrents of water were pouring in through several breaches in the wall. One of the storm lanterns and several of the candles had already been washed away, pitching the chamber into an eerie half-light. Teenagers screamed as they waded waist deep, slipping and sliding as they fought to make it to the safety of the stairs.

Ed got there first, hauling himself free of the water and onto the metal. He reached back behind him to grip Dave's hand and pull him to safety. But two of the others, in sheer blind panic, grabbed on to the rusted handrail and tried to pull themselves up.

There was a shriek of metal under unbearable pressure, and the whole staircase pulled free of the wall.

Clark watched, horrified, as it hung in midair for a moment, before toppling over on top of the thrashing melee in the water.

Somebody's going to drown!

The thought galvanized Clark into action. He waded into the treacherous, swirling waters. Screaming, Phil's girlfriend Shirley was floundering where she'd fallen, ignored by the other teenagers as they fought to find their own way out.

Clark grasped her from behind, yanking her to her feet. Shirley lashed out reflexively, her fist smacking into Clark's head with surprising force. It looked like he might be right about the berries' effects.

"Stop struggling," he hissed, "and I'll get you out of here."

The second storm lantern vanished under the flood, leaving only a few candles on high shelves to give out an entirely inadequate light. Clark tightened his grip, pulling Shirley behind him as he waded quickly toward the fallen stairs.

The teenagers were thrashing around in near darkness, but Clark's super-vision gave him as clear a view as daylight. Despite their panic, Ed and Dave were trying to raise Phil high enough over their heads for him to reach the flooring at the top, where the stairs had been. But even their enhanced strength wasn't enough.

"Let me handle this," Clark said thickly, hoping that the water's roar and the cries of fear would be enough to prevent his voice being recognized.

He thrust the terrified Shirley into Ed's arms and flexed his legs, ready to leap upward.

Strong hands closed round one arm, and he found Dave trying to use him to stay upright. Somebody else was clutching at his legs, not so much trying to pull him down as drag themselves up.

Roughly, Clark shook off the clutching hands. His legs powered him straight up into the air, soaring easily the fifteen or so feet to the platform. It shook as he landed, and he guessed that it wouldn't hold for much longer.

Below, the water level was rising inexorably, and the chamber was filled with screams and cries for help.

Clark used his superspeed to run outside.

Heavy rain was still falling, one of those intense Kansas summer storms that seems to presage the end of the world. Casting around, he grasped a piece of corrugated metal protruding from the side of the building. He tugged hard, exerting his superstrength to rip the metal all the way along the side. It came free with a horrendous noise, ripping off struts and beams from the wooden frame underneath, until he had a length of metal about twenty feet long and three feet wide.

It ought to do.

Dragging the long strip behind him, he ran back into the shed.

"Look out below," he called gruffly. "Coming down."

He lowered the strip carefully into the gaping hole where the top of the stairs had been.

Seconds later, Ed struggled up, using the attached struts as hand- and footholds, pulling Shirley along behind him. Ed wiped water from his face with the back of his hand and peered through the gloom.

"Who—?" he began, but a voice from below interrupted him.

"Phil's hurt his arm." Clark recognized Pete's voice. "Pull him up. And hurry—the water's still rising."

As Ed turned back to assist his friend, Clark shot outside. He circled round to a missing window and stood in the pouring rain, watching to ensure that they needed no further help.

One by one, the teenagers emerged from the basement chamber.

In slicker and boots, Cyrus Deen lowered his head against the wind and driving rain and struggled through the cemetery.

He'd been in his small home, just a couple of streets away, sipping a glass of lemon tea as he watched the storm from his living-room window. He liked a good storm, but this one was disappointing. There'd been some thunder and lightning to start with, but it had soon been overwhelmed by the downpour.

A sudden thought occurred to him, and he set down his glass and hurried to the cupboard to fetch his rainwear.

Mrs. Markell's grave was almost dug—but he'd forgotten to put a tarpaulin over it. If it filled with water, the burial on Monday couldn't go ahead.

Must be old age catching up with me, he chided himself as he left the house and headed for the churchyard. *A dog shouldn't be out in this.*

He stopped off at his hut to pick up a tarp, then headed to the grave. Already, a good six or so inches of water had pooled in the bottom. The wind lashed him mercilessly, making him curse aloud as he struggled to weigh down one end of the tarp at the side of the grave. At least the minister wouldn't have heard . . . !

The wind dropped suddenly, and he took advantage to pile earth on the tarpaulin edge. But as he picked up the other side, the wind gusted again. It caught the tarpaulin, filling it like a sail. Cyrus clung on to prevent it blowing away, and it whipped him off his feet.

He fell heavily. His head struck a glancing blow against the adjacent tombstone. Sparks flashed before Cyrus's eyes. Groaning, he tried to roll around and hoist himself to his feet. But his galoshes slid on the treacherous muddy soil. His arms flailed as he tried to regain his balance, without success.

He plunged headfirst into the open grave, one arm buckling beneath him and snapping as it took the whole weight of his tumbling body. Cyrus screamed, and lost consciousness.

Still the rain fell, running in tiny tributaries that joined on the slopes of the steep pile of earth that stood at the graveside, running down into the grave and filling Cyrus's nose and mouth.

Clark watched as the subdued teenagers filed out of the building and headed silently back to their vehicles. Everybody seemed to have escaped without injury, and the near tragedy seemed to have brought them down off their wild trip.

Pete was last out. He hung around for a moment, giving the others time to be swallowed by the rain and trees, then called out, "Clark?" Clark stood where he was, not moving a muscle. "Clark, I know you're there," Pete's voice came again.

Clark stepped out to face his friend. "You followed me," Pete accused him angrily. "That's the only way you could have known where we were."

"I was worried about you," Clark explained. "Anyway, it looks like it was a good thing I did. Not everyone might have gotten out, otherwise."

If he'd expected gratitude—or guilt, or shame—from Pete, he was disappointed. His friend glared at him maliciously.

"You weren't asked here," he snapped. "You weren't wanted."

"Pete, we're friends—" Clark began.

But Pete broke in savagely, "Wrong. We were. My friends trust me. You obviously don't." He spun on his heel and stalked off, muttering over his shoulder: "So beat it and get yourself a life. Spaceboy."

Spaceboy. The word echoed over and over in Clark's mind.

He stood there for a long time, heedless of the rain that drenched him, soaking him to the skin.

CHAPTER 7

The storm passed within hours, leaving the air clean and refreshed and zinging with negative ions.

By the time darkness fell, the clouds had disappeared.

In the old barn at the back of the Kent farm, Jonathan had converted the loft into a place where Clark could have the privacy a teenager needed, and where he could practice his favorite hobby, astronomy.

He was in there now, his expensive semiprofessional telescope directed at the constellation of Boötes, for no other reason than he had to point it someplace.

Clark spent hours there every week, scanning the skies, combing the cosmos for the answers to the questions that resonated at the very core of his being: *Who am I? Where do I come from? How did I come to be on Earth, where I have superstrength, and super-vision, and superspeed?*

Dispiritedly, he snapped on the lens's safety cover. His heart just wasn't in it tonight. Pete's scornful insult kept coming back to haunt him, like a malevolent ghost. Spaceboy. That's who Clark Kent was. Spaceboy the alien, origins unknown. Present a mess. Future uncertain.

He didn't fit. Didn't do berries. Uncool. Geek. Nerd. Spaceboy.

Clark made a determined effort to shake off the cloud

of depression that threatened to settle on him. He glanced around the loft's interior, lit by a lamp. The bookshelves groaned under the weight of dozens of books on astronomy. He noticed the pouch he'd found in the tunnel at the old nuclear bunker. He'd put it on a shelf in the den when he arrived home, in dire need of a shower and a change of clothes.

He picked it up and slit the seal with his thumbnail. Carefully, he reached in to draw out the contents.

There was a folded sheaf of yellowed newspaper clippings, still bone-dry after who knew how many years underground.

Clark looked at the date next to the headline: July, 1850. He gave a low whistle, and turned his attention to the leather bag, which, by the feel of it, contained something spherical and hard. The knot in the leather drawstring was almost solid, but Clark patiently untangled it rather than using his strength to rip it open.

He pulled open the top, revealing a small crystal ball inside, of the type a fortune-teller might use.

Clark turned it in his hand, holding it up to the light, marveling at the crystal's translucence and apparent lack of flaws.

He slipped it back into its pouch before looking again at the newspaper cuttings. There were several dozen of them, some very fragile indeed. He feared that just breathing on them might cause them to crumble into dust. They were all from European newspapers of the time, some in French and German, though the majority were in English.

GIFTED SEER SPONSORED BY ENGLISH LORD, he read on the front page of the *London Daily Digest* of

1851, above artist's renditions of both men. The accompanying text, in the tiny print typical of the era, told how one Victor Marchmont Gray had been so successful in foretelling various events, an English aristocrat had become his patron. A blurb promised the full story of the discovery of a long-lost treasure could be found inside. Meanwhile, Mr. Marchmont Gray would be conducting a Grand Tour of Capital Cities, where he would demonstrate his peculiar talent for the crowned heads of Europe.

Amazing, Clark thought. *In a couple of minutes, I've learned more about somebody who lived a century and a half ago than I know about myself. I came in a spaceship. I was adopted by good people. End of story.*

Irritated with himself for sliding back into doom and gloom, Clark glanced at his watch. Almost time to meet Lana and Chloe. He didn't particularly feel like seeing a movie, but if Lana had suggested sitting in a field in the rain for two hours, he'd have been happy to comply.

As long as she was with him.

He put the clippings back in their envelope and replaced them, along with the ball in the pouch. He returned it to the shelf and hurried down the ladder.

CHAPTER 8

"What are you doing, Michael?"

Moira Grindlay's piercing voice sliced through his headache like a razor. Guiltily, he put down the cut-glass brandy decanter he'd been examining.

"You still haven't finished your sermon."

Michael sighed. "No, dear," he said, long-sufferingly. "To be honest, the wheel's coming off the car this morning really shook me up. I haven't felt quite right all day."

"Nonsense. We're both fine. Why shouldn't you feel right?"

The minister lowered his gaze and sighed again, this time to himself. With her cropped dark hair and elfin face, Moira was a pretty woman—especially when she smiled. Which didn't seem to be that often anymore. She seemed to wear a permanent severe look, matronly almost.

As if she were slowly forgetting how to laugh.

He came to a decision. Deliberately, he picked up the decanter again. Defiantly, he poured a stiff measure of brandy into a glass. He wasn't a drinking man—anything but, in fact. Even at social events, he rarely touched alcohol. But the accident this morning had bothered him, although nobody was hurt, and the only pain involved was to his insurance company's bank balance.

He could feel Moira's disapproving stare, but he didn't

meet her eyes. "I'm going to my study," he told her, picking up the brandy glass. "I'll see you later."

He went directly to his study, breathing a low sigh of relief as the door clicked shut behind him. He raised the brandy glass to his nose and inhaled deeply. The pungent odor made him shudder.

Sitting down at his desk, he reached for Andrew Seddon's journal and gave another shudder. Was it this diary—as he feared—that had really unsettled him? Wagon wheel breaks. Car wheel breaks. It seemed such a strange coincidence.

Ruefully, he shook his head. *Is this what decades of faith bring?* he wondered. *Fear of coincidence? The Lord knows all, the Lord wills all,* he reminded himself.

That, and a sip of brandy, made him feel better. Fingering the little green cross, he opened the journal to where he'd left off.

And the first words he read sent a chill racing up his spine.

July 23

I have not written for many days now.

So much ill fortune, in such a small band of people, is disheartening. Indeed, some of the Irishmen are muttering that it is Divine Retribution. Although for what, I have no idea.

We had such a storm the other night, the like of which I swear the world has never seen. Lightning turned the midnight into day. Thunder shook the very ground on which our wagons stood. And the rain!

I have seen blizzards in New York, and once a mighty hailstorm. But never have I seen such a storm as this. The very skies, it might seem, turned to liquid.

Not one of us managed a wink of sleep. I could only huddle under my canvas, cold and wet and miserable, wondering if I had indeed done the right thing in joining this expedition. Not that I had much choice in the matter, all things considered.

Yes, I did punish my pupil, William McBain— for his impudence—with a beating. Yes, when his father confronted me to complain, I lost my temper and struck him as well. It was foolish, and unforgivable, and I have regretted it ever since. It was the end of my career as an educator.

Better by far, I reasoned, to travel to where I was unknown, where I might make a clean break and a fresh start, with the opportunity—unlikely as it might be—of finding gold enough to render all thought of work superfluous.

Ah, gold! Do my companions dream of it also, motivating them to continue on this most Hellish of journeys? I sometimes wonder how the original pioneers, with far fewer resources than we, managed to find their way across this vast continent.

Yet here I am, trapped with my companions on these accursed, endless plains. The weather is foul, Huckins is drunk, and the French are squabbling again. Have we embarked on this great adventure only to fail so soon after our departure? After all, we already have one dead man. The Irishmen wanted to hold a wake for their kinsman, but we buried him at once, for surely his body would have spoiled in the incessant heat.

Enough of such morbidity, I bid myself. If I am to enjoy a new life, I must approach it with enthusiasm and optimism.

Though it is hard to feel that way at this very moment. The sun is high in the sky, but we haven't moved an inch today. Huckins and a few of the others have gone in search of a trio of horses that somehow broke loose during the night.

The canvas from one of the German families' wagons disappeared completely in the storm, though the event seems to have healed the rift with their countrymen. All sat down together in the shade of a wagon, working to stitch up a spare canvas they had wisely brought with them.

The mysterious Englishman has been forced to introduce himself. His wagon was blown bodily over one night by a squall of wind. Fortunately, he and his wife came to no harm, and their horses were uninjured by the twisted harness.

Victor Marchmont Gray, he is called, lately of London and Europe. He gave no clue as to his occupation, although his superior demeanor and quiet but confident voice suggest he may be one of the minor aristocracy. Fallen on hard times, perhaps, else why would he be heading for California in search of gold? Be that as it may, he had not the skills to right his wagon single-handedly.

Nor, for that matter, had I.

Of the sneak thief, there has been no further sign. A small blessing, but a blessing nevertheless.

Thus it is that I bring my journal up to date, in the hope—vain, perhaps, but very real to me—that one day, perhaps I can publish the story of our travels as a book.

*   *   *

The Reverend Grindlay found himself clutching the tiny green cross so hard his fingers hurt. He pushed the book away from him and closed his eyes. His headache seemed to be returning. The brandy hadn't helped, for now his stomach felt queasy, and there was a sour taste in his mouth.

He needed fresh air.

He tiptoed along the hallway and exited via the back door. He loved Moira with all his heart—but the last thing he needed just then was to hear her complaining voice.

The cemetery was . . . quiet as the grave, the deep silence broken only by the faint rustle of leaves and the occasional drip of rain from the trees. Slowly, he followed the gravel pathway that wound around the graveyard past the sea of headstones. In just a few words, each one told the story of a life.

Stone angels pointed sightlessly to Heaven. Cherubs graced the final resting place of long-gone, long-forgotten citizens of Smallville. And the occasional carved skull and crossbones provided a grim reminder of what death was all about.

A hundred yards away, the streetlights gave off a cheery glow. Michael breathed deeply sucking in the clean night air, starting to feel like himself again.

From the corner of his eye, he saw a tarpaulin twitching lethargically in the slight breeze. He walked toward it, careful to keep his feet on the gravel paths that Cyrus Deen kept in such pristine condition.

What would I do without him? Michael wondered. *The man is simply a treasure.*

The tarp was snagged on a headstone, blown there during the storm, no doubt. The minister grasped its corner, and gave it a violent shake to rid it of the rainwater puddled in its center.

It was only as he pulled the tarp toward him that the yawning grave beyond was exposed. Grindlay hesitated. The tarp was large and heavy, and he doubted his ability to replace it in the dark. Perhaps he should call Cyrus . . .

By then, his eyes had adjusted to the dim light. For the first time, he was able to see into the partly dug grave.

He recoiled in shock and disbelief.

At the bottom of the grave, half-floating in a pool of muddy water, lay the lifeless body of Cyrus Deen.

Pete slouched along Main Street, hands stuffed in the pockets of his black windbreaker, head down to avoid the bright neon lights. His eyes usually stung for a few hours after eating Ed's berries, and that night was no exception.

But that wasn't the only reason he felt so bad. His cruel gibe at Clark—his *friend*—spiraled round in his head until he felt it was driving him insane.

On Saturday nights, he usually met Clark and Chloe at the Talon. Lana was manager and part-owner of the coffee shop, but stole as much time as she could with them. Pete hadn't been there for a couple of weeks. Since Phil had first told him about Ed's magic fruit, and Ed himself invited Pete along to one of their after-school sessions.

Perhaps it was time for him to make amends.

The incident at the nuclear shelter had really spooked him. He'd never been so afraid in all his life. Any of them—or even all of them—might have died in that flooded bunker. Clark had only been there because he wanted to help his friend. Because he cared.

And how did I react? Pete asked himself miserably. *Like a total jerk!*

He crossed the street and made for the Talon's beckoning lights. Pete had always liked the cafe, warm and cozy, and the scene of many happy evenings with his friends. It would be good to see the three of them again.

He glanced up as he approached the plate-glass window. Through it, he could see Clark sitting at a table with Chloe and Lana. All three were laughing loudly at some joke—not the guarded laughter of strangers, but the easy, open laughter only friends could share.

Pete felt a stab of nausea run through him. Suddenly, he felt as if *he* was the alien. The one who didn't fit. The one who didn't belong.

They didn't need *him.*

Nobody needed him.

Sick to the pit of his stomach, Pete spun away from the window and shuffled off into the night.

"Okay," Clark was saying, "I can't deny I'm a science fiction fan. Our stomachs are strong enough—and our brains weak enough—to enjoy anything that features a rocket and ray guns. But *Plan X from Outer Space* was beyond even my capacity for enjoyment."

The girls laughed again, then Chloe did a double take. "What is it?"

"I just saw Pete." Clark and Lana looked dubiously at her. "I'm telling you," Chloe insisted. "He was standing right in front of the window, watching us."

"So where did he go?"

Chloe shrugged. "I don't know. Maybe I should go see."

She made to rise, but Clark put a hand on her arm.

"I saw Pete earlier," he told her. "The mood he was in, the last person in the world he wants to see right now is me. I think we should let him be."

Chloe shot him a puzzled look but sat back down at the table.

Clark had been debating with himself whether or not to tell the girls about that afternoon. Smallville wasn't a large place, and it was inevitable gossip about Ed's shindig would be all over the school on Monday. Thankfully, only Pete had seen him; none of the other partygoers had even the slightest idea that he was there.

Not even Shirley Grainger, who might have died without his presence.

So he told Lana and Chloe about the party, allowing them to infer that it was Pete who had reported it to him. The girls listened wide-eyed to the tale, gasping at the thought of being trapped underground in a dark, flooded chamber.

"Refills?" The voice of Yvonne, the middle-aged waitress, interrupted Clark's story. She stood by their table, coffeepot in hand.

"Please," Clark said politely, leaning back to allow Yvonne to top up his drink. He hoped she wasn't intending to stay, because Yvonne had the reputation of being one of the town's most ardent gossips. Sometimes it seemed like the Talon was the town's information hub, where all the news—true or false—was embellished and passed on to the customers.

"Leonard Marco was in earlier," Yvonne began, and

Clark braced himself for the inevitable, interminable story that would follow.

But just then the telephone behind the counter rang. Yvonne reluctantly excused herself and went to answer the call.

Clark finished recounting the events of the afternoon, careful to leave out all mention of his own involvement. And of drugs. That thought was constantly there, hovering in the back of his mind, a problem he was delaying tackling because he didn't have a clue where to start.

He'd just finished when Yvonne came back around the counter, her face white with shock. She walked slowly up to their table.

"That was Vera Little on the phone. Her husband's a deputy sheriff." She lowered her voice conspiratorially, as if she was afraid of being overheard—though the three friends were the cafe's only customers. "She says Fred was called out tonight—to the church. They've found Cyrus Deen facedown in a grave. Stone-cold dead."

CHAPTER 9

Clark hadn't been inside the First Church of Smallville before. His parents weren't churchgoers, although Martha always considered Clark's mysterious arrival to be the answer to all of her prayers.

He walked up the wide main path to the front entrance, feeling uncomfortable in his suit and tie under the hot morning sun. His mother had made a fuss about how good he looked, and how she didn't see him dressed up often enough, but what she really wanted to know was: Why are you going to church? However, she'd had the good sense not to ask, for which Clark was thankful.

Most of the people going to the service were known to him, and he exchanged nods and smiles and handshakes with a few of them. He could see the curiosity in their eyes, but made no attempt to explain himself. Pete's dad was there, with several of Pete's older brothers and sisters and their families.

"My family can fill that church on its own," Pete used to joke. That seemed a long time ago.

He was surprised to see Shirley Grainger, dressed demurely but as pretty as ever. He caught her own look of surprise as she noticed him, and gave him a little wave.

Clark entered, and found himself a pew at the rear, under one of the Victorian stained-glass windows. He liked the church's dignified silence, liked the way the morning sunlight streamed through the colored glass and the way the soaring voices of the choir rang around the high rafters.

The Reverend Grindlay was considered to be an excellent minister. He had a firm grasp of Scripture, gave honest and good advice when asked, and was always there when anyone in Smallville needed him.

The first hymn ended. As the congregation reseated itself, amid much coughing and throat-clearing, their minister surveyed them from his pulpit with a somber face. Several times, he appeared to be on the verge of speaking, but he halted each time.

Composing himself, Clark thought.

"Many of you will have heard," the minister began at last, "that yesterday afternoon, Cyrus Deen sadly passed away. Like most of you, I knew Cyrus for many years. He was a gem of a man, a diamond, a credit to the God he so assiduously served." He paused, and blinked away a threatening tear. "I also counted Cyrus as a personal friend. His passing will leave a deep, empty space in many lives in our community."

He closed his eyes and raised his hands in the air. "Let us pray."

Dutifully, Clark closed his eyes and listened to the heartfelt plea for Cyrus Deen's immortal soul.

When the others mumbled "Amen" he opened his eyes.

There was a different expression on the Reverend Grindlay's face. He was about to preach his sermon, and he obviously felt on firmer ground.

"A few days ago, Cyrus brought me something he'd discovered in the graveyard, right here outside this church. It was the journal of a teacher, a man who had forsaken the world of education to embark on a quest to find gold. What he found instead were hard times."

Glancing around, Clark saw that every eye in the church was zeroed in on the minister. He was a good public speaker, his voice rising and falling at precisely the right times to create the mood and atmosphere he wanted.

"Fierce heat. Torrential downpours. Violent storms. Freezing nights." The minister looked up, and his eyes twinkled as he went on: "Much like Smallville today, in fact."

A low hum of polite laughter rippled round the church.

"Seriously, though, life back then—a mere 150 years ago—was hard in ways we can barely credit. Imagine your daily routine without electricity. Or how about drawing all your water from a stream, and boiling it before you can drink? All of your worldly goods piled inside a rickety wagon, with a fifteen-hundred-mile journey ahead. Could any of us today endure such hardship?"

The Reverend Grindlay paused to emphasize the rhetorical question. Then he went on and answered it himself. "To be honest, I like to think we could. I like to think that if you scratch the surface of Smallville folk, you'll find the spirit of the pioneers underneath. We are hardy people. We endure. We must learn to live with our grief, to accept the pain that the Lord decrees must accompany the joys of our lives."

Clark would have been impressed—and relieved—if the minister had left his subject there. But another ten minutes on the same theme was to follow. Clark found his attention wandering. He remembered the pouch he'd found. The newspaper pages were dated around the same time as the schoolteacher's journal. Idly, he wondered if there might be a connection.

A final hymn, and the service was over.

As Clark filed out of the church, a number of the congregation had gathered around the minister outside, shaking his hand and congratulating him on his uplifting words.

Clark stood quietly by, waiting his chance.

"Hi, Clark," a voice said brightly by his side.

Shirley stood there, smiling.

"Hey, Shirley. I didn't know you were religious."

"Ditto."

"I'm not." Clark gestured toward the minister, deep in conversation with two elderly ladies. "I'm . . . I have some business with the reverend. And you?"

Shirley looked a little sheepish. "I'm here because . . . well, I don't know if you've heard yet, but Ed's party yesterday almost turned into a disaster." She bit her lip, as if debating whether to say more. "I was terrified. Panicked. I could have died."

"Wow," Clark said, hoping that he sounded like he was hearing this for the first time. "What happened?"

Shirley shrugged. "That part's not important. What matters is—it made me *think*. I could have died," she repeated.

The incident—and rescue—had clearly made a deep impression on her.

"I lay awake last night, trying to make sense of it all," she continued. "We weren't doing anything wrong—not very wrong, anyway. And yet . . ."

"I'm not surprised it's made you question things." Clark jerked his head toward the church. "Did you find any answers in there?"

"Not really. But it was comforting." Shirley smiled, and Clark noted again just how pretty she was. "It's made me come to a few decisions, too," she said firmly. "Life's too precious to waste. We can never know when we'll die, so the only sensible thing to do is make the most of life while we can."

She halted, and took a deep gulp of air before rushing on. "I wondered if you'd like to date me sometime."

Clark's jaw dropped in sheer surprise. Never in a thousand years would he have guessed that's what she was going to say.

"Bu . . . but aren't you and Phil Meara an item?" he stammered, not knowing how else to react.

"Phil's a jerk," Shirley said flatly, brooking no contradiction. As if Clark would disagree. "I learned that yesterday, if I didn't know it already. And I've always kind of liked you, and I thought, well, if I don't ask, I'll never know if you might have liked me, too."

Clark was still flummoxed, at a loss for words. Vaguely, he was aware of the last of the churchgoers leaving through the gate, and the Reverend Grindlay going back into the church.

"Um, can I take a rain check on that, Shirley? Urgent business. I'll see you at school."

He loped past her, hoping that he wasn't being too rude, and hurried to catch up with the minister.

"Reverend Grindlay. Do you have a moment, sir?"

The minister considered the tall, dark-haired teenager for a moment. "Clark Kent, isn't it? Glad to see you're taking an interest in your immortal soul, Clark. Too few of your age bother."

Clark flushed. "I'm afraid I'm here under false pretenses," he admitted. "I . . . I need to talk to you."

"Then you've come to the right place, son."

Less than a mile away, Pete Ross lay in bed.

His mother had wakened him three times, but he flatly refused to get up. He lay with his head under the sheets, feeling a general, all-over malaise—nothing he could specifically name.

He'd wakened during the night in a cold sweat, dreaming he was back in the nuclear bunker. In darkness. Afraid. Going to drown in that terrifying flood. It had been a good half hour before he fell back into an uneasy doze.

"Peter!" His mother's voice came from outside his bedroom door. "Your father will be home from church soon. He'll be furious if you're still in bed."

"I hear you."

But he buried his face in the pillow. What did he have to get up for?

"Well?"

The Reverend Grindlay broke the awkward silence that had fallen since he'd shown Clark into his study, and they both sat down.

"I can't help you if I don't know what the problem is."

Clark nodded. Best to just come straight out with it. "I think someone I know may be taking drugs."

"Do you know what drugs, exactly?" the minister

asked, his voice clipped and suddenly businesslike. "Soft drugs—or worse?"

"That's part of the problem," Clark confessed. "I don't know what it is they're taking . . ."

He broke off, immediately realizing his mistake.

As had the minister. "They?" he echoed. "I thought you said a friend."

Clark groaned audibly. "There may be more than one. But from what I could tell, it wasn't pot or heroin, or anything like that. They were more like fruit than pills. You know—berries of some kind."

"Many natural substances alter consciousness," the minister told him. "Cacti like peyote and mescal. Jimsonweed. Brazilian vines. Fungi like Amanita muscaria, psilocybin, and a dozen others." He frowned, trawling through his memory. "Berries, though? I can't say I ever recall reading about anything like that."

"I only saw them from a distance."

Abruptly, the minister changed the subject. "Have you spoken with your friend's parents?"

Clark shook his head. "I can't. They wouldn't understand." He shuddered to think how Pete's high-achieving family would take the news that their 'baby' was doing drugs. "I think it would only make the situation worse."

"Teachers, perhaps? That is," the reverend added quickly, "if the friend in question is of school age."

"It wouldn't help. Believe me."

Clark could just imagine the furor he'd cause if he told the principal. Pete, Ed, and Phil, and all the others, could end up being expelled. They might get police records, even be locked away. He couldn't do that to them. What they were doing was wrong, but nobody had been really hurt.

"What I really want to know is, what can I do?" Clark said, impassioned. "To change his mind, I mean. To talk him out of it."

Michael pursed his lips. "It's possible peer pressure got him into this. I doubt if the words of one friend, no matter how persuasive, will get him out."

"So I'm completely helpless?" Clark asked in frustrated desperation.

"Not at all." The minister fixed Clark with his eyes, and the teenager found himself unable to look away. "You can be there for him. When he needs you, be there."

CHAPTER 10

Smallville was a grim place that Monday. Even the sun seemed to have deserted it, leaving a leaden-hued sky that somehow matched the mood of the townsfolk.

It had been years since two funerals took place on the same day.

At school, classes had been doubled up, so that the teachers could attend the services and pay their last respects to Cyrus Deen and Mrs. Markell.

Chloe and Clark shared a double study period and decided to spend it together in the small office of the *Torch,* the school newspaper which Chloe edited. She was also chief reporter and principal photographer—although Lana was showing an aptitude, too.

In fact, Chloe did almost everything but make the coffee, a task she left to Clark. And Pete, when he dropped in. Which wasn't often at all, recently.

At the moment she was bent over her keyboard, trying halfheartedly to expand a minor story into something that could fill the front page. Not a lot had been happening lately: The five dead dogs story was no more than a footnote, a curiosity, and Cyrus Deen's untimely end, while tragic, wasn't exactly grist for the school paper's mill.

Of course, she knew what the perfect lead would be: SCHOOL DRUG RING EXPOSED! She'd be guaranteed that everyone would read that issue, it might even get into the local papers as a stringer. But that was just fanciful thinking.

"It's no use," she announced at last, pushing her chair away from her desk and spinning her seat around so she faced Clark. "We go to press tomorrow, and we're going to have a blank front page!"

"How about a piece on the wrestling show?" Clark suggested. A traveling WWWE-style wrestling group had hired the high school gymnasium for Friday night, intending to put on a number of exhibition bouts.

"Sure," Chloe replied sarcastically. "All-American fun for the whole family. Iron Man Vasquez against Merlyn the Mauler. Big Lizard versus The Fist. Or will anyone manage to last three minutes with Kid Psycho, and claim a thousand bucks?" She snorted derisively. "Great stuff, Clark. Visual, too. Only thing is, we don't know the results. They don't start fighting till Friday night."

Clark grinned. "Cheer up. The worst hasn't happened yet," he reminded her, "not since you took over the paper. I'm sure you'll think of something." He gave a little whoop. "In fact, I just thought of something myself. I was at church yesterday—"

Chloe raised her eyebrows, but Clark ignored her questioning look and hurried on, "The Reverend Grindlay said that he had a journal, dug up in the churchyard. It's 150 years old. There has to be a story in that."

"Hmm." Chloe was noncommittal. "I was rather hoping for something with a bit more . . . mystery. You know?"

"I've got just the thing," Clark said excitedly, recalling the package he'd found on Saturday afternoon. "A crystal ball, and newspaper clippings about a fortune-teller."

It didn't sound like much of a newspaper story to Chloe, but her interest was piqued. She was a sucker for the unexplained, the paranormal, the supernatural. And if she could mix in a conspiracy theory or two, well, that was icing on the cake.

"Where did you get them?"

"From a friend." Chloe's keen senses detected the note of evasion in his voice, but she let it go for the moment. "Would you like to see them?"

"Yes."

"They're in my den. You'll need to come over after school."

Chloe gave a low whistle. "An invite to Clark Kent's den? I thought it was only Princess Lana Lang who got to visit the Forbidden Zone." She saw Clark flush and smiled as she shook her head. "Hey, I'm only teasing. I'd be delighted to visit the barn. And in the meantime, I think I'll call the Reverend Grindlay, see if he's willing to give me an interview. And if you're looking for something to do—" Chloe swiveled her chair so she was facing her computer screen. "I'd love a coffee."

Lex Luthor stood underneath the massive chestnut tree in one corner of the cemetery, watching the large knot of people clustered round Cyrus Deen's grave. Despite the dullness of the day, Lex wore designer shades and a dark mourning suit that might have come off the runways of Milan.

He knew neither of the deceased. But he wasn't there to pay his respects.

Cassandra's Secret, and the reference material it had inspired him to research, had caused him to rethink his attitude. Despite determined efforts to submerge himself in the factory's finances, his attention kept straying to the new things he was learning.

One book he'd found turned a belief system that was twenty-three hundred years in the making upside down.

According to the author, until around three thousand years ago, Mankind lived in a more or less hypnotized state, with little awareness of the individual self. Like ants, or termites, with big brains and opposable thumbs. All decisions, from the personal to the societal, were based on auditory hallucinations presented as dreams and apparitions.

Hence the wonders of ancient Sumeria and Babylon. Hence the pyramids of Egypt, and the temple of Stonehenge. The monuments of the Incas, and the Olmecs, and a hundred other cultures. Gargantuan structures built by what were, effectively, hivelike minds.

But the increasing complexity of social life, compounded by massive refugee displacements, brought a plethora of conflicting deities together. Ten thousand gods and goddesses, each with his or her own voice, all speaking together, produced intolerable stress.

Something had to give.

The something was man's mind—or, at least, his mode of thinking. The brain's software adapted, rearranged itself, and modern consciousness was born. For the first time ever, men and women were truly free, able to make their own rational decisions.

The Golden Age of Greece flourished.

Had it continued, that astonishing burst of human creativity, we'd have been on the Moon at least a thousand years earlier. By now we'd be immortal, making our homes out there someplace, in the stars.

Instead, we got the Dark Ages. We got war after war after war, until we said the last war was the worst ever. Then we went back to war again.

As the minister's faint words drifted in the lifeless air, Lex walked quietly out of the graveyard and headed back to his hotel.

"Heard you were out with Lana Saturday night."

Flanked by his cohorts Phil and Rob, Ed had physically barred Clark's path to the lunch hall.

"Congratulations," Clark replied breezily. "Your ears are working perfectly."

It was the wrong thing to say. Ed leaned into him, crowding him back against the wall. With Phil and Rob glowering at him from either side, Clark was well and truly trapped.

Unless, of course, he used his superpowers.

And, of course, he couldn't do that.

"I don't like a wiseass, Kent." He nodded to each side. "Come to think of it, Phil and Rob don't, either. So I'll tell you what we're going to do." Ed's jaw tightened as he thrust his snarling face into Clark's.

This is getting to be a habit, Clark thought unhappily.

"If you don't leave Lana alone, we're going to beat you to a pulp. Last warning. *Capisce?*"

Despite his superficial calm, anger was seething in Clark's breast. How dare these creeps tell him whom he could or couldn't see? He was sorry that Whitney was dead . . . but life didn't stop for everybody else. They had to move on. All of them.

Just then, Clark caught sight of Shirley Grainger, walking by with a girlfriend. A wicked impulse leapt to his mind, and it was all he could do to keep a straight face.

"I understand, all right," Clark said innocently, "but you've got it all wrong, Ed. You shouldn't be worried about me going out with Lana." He gestured in Phil's direction. "Phil should be worried about me going out with Shirley!"

Ed's brows knitted together as he tried to figure it out. Clark didn't wait to offer further explanation, but took advantage of his bombshell to shove past them and jog off after Shirley.

He could feel Phil's eyes watching him, burning into his back with thunderous rage.

"Remember what you asked me yesterday?"

For a moment, Clark thought Shirley was going to blank him, pretend she'd never said anything about them going out. Some sort of revenge for him rushing off so rudely.

"Have you decided?"

"Yes. How does Wednesday night sound? Do you like bowling?"

"Love it!"

"I'll call you."

Clark was surprised to realize just how good he felt. He didn't often ask girls out. In fact, he couldn't remember the last time. Mostly he spent his free time pining for Lana.

Maybe this would give him the boost he needed.

"So this is the famous Kent Cave."

Chloe looked around the barn's interior, impressed with what she saw. She walked up to Clark's telescope and sighted along its barrel. She frowned, then walked over to the big work hatch Clark used as a window.

She squinted in the fading light, peering into the middle distance through a faint, gathering mist.

"That wouldn't happen to be Lana's aunt Nell's house down there, would it?" she asked finally.

She smiled to herself as Clark flushed with embarrassment. "Lana doesn't live there anymore," he said, superfluously. "And besides, I'm going out with Shirley Grainger."

Chloe was astounded. Clark Kent—date a girl who wasn't Lana Lang? But her astonishment was followed by a pang of regret. Why couldn't he have asked *her* for a date? She'd have jumped at the chance . . . though Clark was so wrapped up in Lana, he'd never paid her any attention, except as a friend.

"Congratulations," she managed to say at last. "You're a real dark horse, Clark. How in the world did you hook up with Shirley?"

"Believe it or not, she asked me."

Chloe cursed inwardly. So that was the secret!

She snapped her thoughts back to why she was there, watching as Clark took a package off a shelf and opened it with extreme care. He held out the crystal ball to her, and she took it in both hands.

"It's a crystal ball, right?" he asked.

Chloe nodded. "As used by fortune-tellers and prophets for a long, long time. South American tribes used them. Native American shamans often used something similar, gazing for extended periods into a bowl of water, where the future was supposedly revealed. Same thing for the ancient Celts," Chloe went on, warming to her subject. "In fact, I'd be surprised to hear of any ancient race which *didn't* treat a flawless crystal as something very special."

She thought for a moment. "There's speculation even Neolithic tribes used them. Then, of course, there's Dr. John Dee, perhaps the most famous scryer—"

"Come again?"

"Crystal gazer," she explained. "Anyhow, you get the picture."

"Where do you pick all this stuff up, Chloe?"

"Here and there," she told him vaguely. "The more flawless the crystal, the greater its power. Although the real power is in the diviner, of course."

"This guy seemed to have it. This Victor Marchmont Gray."

Clark had taken the clippings out of their covering while she spoke. He handed the top one to Chloe, and she read the account of Mr. Gray's rise to eminence as a teller of fortunes. His discovery of long-buried treasure, restoring a hapless family of aristocrats to their former prominence.

"And the others?" she asked.

"More of the same," Clark replied. "Some foreign." He pointed to a few clippings he'd laid aside. "I haven't separated these out yet. They're so dry, it wouldn't take much to destroy them."

"Can I take them home for the night?"

"Uh . . . I'd rather you didn't." Chloe had guessed that's what he'd say. "I know you'd be careful, but I'd hate anything to happen to them."

"No prob. Mind if I take notes?"

CHAPTER 11

August 1

Madness, all is madness!

If I did not know better, I would swear some infernal power had set out to torture us with such travails that we shall never reach California.

We made almost four miles today, and were fortunate to do so.

For there is a crisis with the Germans. As far as I can fathom, the daughter of one family (the Krantzes? Kantzes?) was caught by her husband sharing a foolish moment of stolen passion with the eldest son of the other family.

The two men came to severe blows and were separated only when Huckins and several others waded into them with wooden staves. Blood—German blood—was shed before the set-to was ended. It is tempting to hope that things will settle down now, and we can proceed apace.

But I have severe doubts.

We saw some Red Men yesterday. They were not the noble savages depicted in the Eastern magazines. They seemed to be approaching us, but Huckins cried out loudly, and waved his arms.

They gave us a wide berth as they continued on their own journey.

One of the horses was discovered to have been eating some poisonous weed. Its noisy and frequent bowel movements have been our constant companion for most of the day. Together with the continuing heat, it is all too much for me.

Had I a gun, I would shoot the wretched beast myself.

August 3

Scripture tells us that the darkest hour comes shortly before the dawn.

Seldom have I prayed so fervently for that to be the case.

For surely our expedition—started with such high hopes only weeks ago—has been cursed.

We made fair distance yesterday, for Huckins finally took it upon himself to shoot the suffering equine. Its owners will miss it, but I am sure they are as glad as am I that we shall have some fresh horsemeat tonight. Dried beef has much to commend it as a life preserver, but little to boast of in culinary tastefulness.

What a blessed relief it is, not to have that infernal squealing at every step of the way!

But now, may the Lord preserve us, we have murder to contend with!

It seems that the cuckolded German waited until he had been left alone (which was not for some considerable time, as he had worked himself into a towering frenzy of rage). Then, taking a knife from his wagon's supplies, he waited for the chance to work his evil.

When his rival in love left camp to fetch water, he must have followed. We heard his dreadful screams, but by the time we had discovered his whereabouts, it was too late. The foul deed was done, and the perpetrator fled into the prairie.

Huckins and the others brought his mutilated body back for burial.

Of his assailant, there has been no further sign.

Several of the menfolk have taken to carrying their guns, or large blades, in case the killer returns to seek more victims. I do not think that he will, for his grievance was specifically directed. And now the object of his grievance was dead, surely he would have no reason for revenge on us.

But just to be safe, rather than sorry, I have taken to carrying a knife.

I am too dispirited to write more, and I am not alone in that. Seldom in all my years have I seen a more unhappy and less enthusiastic collection of people.

The Reverend Grindlay recognized the double rap on his office door at once. Moira.

He flipped the journal closed as his wife pushed open the door and entered, ushering a young woman before her.

"Michael, this is Chloe Sullivan," Moira introduced them. "She's a sophomore at Smallville High. She'd like to interview you for the school newspaper."

"I realize this isn't the best time," Chloe apologized, "but our press day is tomorrow, and we don't have a lead story, and I thought—"

The minister silenced her with a gesture. "Sit down,

my dear." He indicated a chair upholstered in dark green leather.

He turned to his wife, who was hovering in the background. "Thank you, Moira," he said pointedly.

Moira looked disappointed as she let herself back out of the study.

Chloe didn't beat about the bush. She spent the first ten minutes finding out about the minister's background and achievements, his likes and dislikes . . . anything at all to warm up her subject.

But what she really wanted to know—the meat of her interview—was about the journal. Michael was happy to show it to her, describing the passages he'd already read while she took notes in shorthand.

"—also an Englishman on the wagon train," the minister told her, "a Victor Marchmont Gray. There were at least three European families, two from Germany and—"

"Hold it." Chloe raised a hand. "Back up, please. This Victor Gray you mentioned . . . ?"

It was the same name as the man described in Clark's newspaper clippings. She'd hoped there would be a connection between the two. Now it seemed that there was—and Chloe was beginning to feel increasingly intrigued. She had a news reporter's nose: If there was a story to be found, she would dig away until she found it.

"Michael!"

Moira Grindlay's voice interrupted them, muffled almost to normal volume by the sturdy wooden door. "What am I supposed to do with all these flowers?"

"For the hospital," the minister said to Chloe. "The flowers, that is."

He heaved a sigh as he got to his feet and turned the journal around to face her. "I'll have to leave you for a little while. Feel free to read all you want, but please—"

"Be careful." Chloe nodded emphatically. "Don't worry, sir. I will be."

Chloe skimmed swiftly through the yellowing pages, pausing every few moments to take notes—especially concerning the bad things that had happened. And there was a surprisingly long list of them.

She almost flicked straight past the entry for August the 6. It was only a fleeting glimpse of the name Victor Gray that made her stop and fully read the journal page.

We have found the cause of all our woes, the dreadful center around which these terrible events have revolved.

Or, at least, most of us think we have found it.

Or should I say—*him*? Victor Marchmont Gray.

It was one of the Frenchwomen who recognized him when she saw him returning from the latrines after dawn. She has no English, of course, and had great difficulty making Huckins understand her. I was flattered that they called on my expertise with languages to aid them, and I received many thanks for my work of translation.

It appears this Gray is a seer, a teller of fortunes and dabbler in the forbidden arts of the occult. Not exactly, I would hazard, in keeping with our biblical exhortations. And if this hysterical woman was to be believed, he was actually in league with demons. And no minor demonry, either, but senior members of that odious order, no less, mayhap even Satan (Lord preserve us!) himself.

I find it vexing that such an aristocratic demeanor can conceal such a foul, demonic heart. But there are, I am aware, numerous precedents. Any ungodly person is a fair target for the unwanted attentions of the lower orders of Creation. The Good Book bids us always to be vigilant.

Huckins has called a public meeting for six this evening, taking care that Gray and his wife know nothing of it. We have been promised we will all have the opportunity to air our views.

Meantime, I am praying for guidance in deciding what must be done.

So . . . they figure there was a supernatural cause!
This is getting better and better. Impatiently, Chloe turned the page and began to read the entry Andrew Seddon had made the following morning.

The demon-lover has fled!

Somehow, he found out about our plans and, under cover of darkness, managed to make good his escape. If proof were needed of his guilt, then this single action provides it. It is plain as the nose on my face, he is guilty! And, far from being alone in that awful judgment, the verdict is unanimous.

Had he stayed, Gray would have received a fair trial, for that is what we all agreed upon at the meeting last night. There were many who called for summary justice, and Huckins, I think, leaned that way himself. The Irishmen, of course, cried loud and long for a lynching. Good sense prevailed—but there will be no trial now.

Huckins maintains he is tracker enough to flush out the inexperienced Englishman, and many of the other men are sufficiently angry to accompany him. They have armed themselves, and I fear for our tormentor's safety should they catch him.

Gray's wife has thrown herself on our mercy. She weeps incessantly, all the while protesting her poor husband's innocence.

Chloe's eyes flew down the spidery writing, a work of art in its own right, seeking out the next entry of interest.

—found him some miles from here, hiding in some kind of subterranean chamber close by a stream. Unsurprising, really, that a demon should seek out the darkness beneath the earth for shelter. It is their natural place.

Gray refused to go quietly with them, and had to be taken by force, putting up such a struggle as might have troubled even pugilists—

Chloe remembered the pouch Clark had found. Obviously, it had been lost by Victor Gray during his struggle with his pursuers. Chloe could picture him, alone, afraid, cowering in the darkness as an armed mob bayed for his blood. And although they seized him and dragged him screaming back into the sunlight, they had evidently missed the objects he had taken with him. A crystal ball, and a pack of clippings about his talents.

Chloe's mind was racing. She knew instinctively that this was going to make an amazing story for the *Torch*, one of the best she'd ever run. But she needed to know how it all ended. She turned the page, and halted in her tracks.

The journal came to an abrupt end after the very next entry. Chloe began to read, her eyes widening in horror as she progressed down the page. She transcribed the words as fast as she could, her hand a blur.

Then she heard the Reverend Grindlay's footsteps coming back down the hall.

No use. She'd just have to memorize the rest.

When the minister entered, she was closing her notebook and getting to her feet.

"You're finished?" he asked, a little surprised.

"Yes, thanks. I think I have everything I need." She paused at the door. "Tell me—have you finished reading the diary yet?"

"I'm afraid not. So much has been happening this past week, I just haven't had the time."

Boy, are you in for a shock! Chloe thought. Aloud, she said: "I'd better be going. The copy's due at the printer tomorrow morning."

"May I have a copy when it's done?"

"Of course. Good night. And thanks again. You've been a big help."

Chloe left the church and hurried home as fast as she could, the incredible story already taking shape in her mind.

Chloe double-clicked with her mouse, and almost instantly the monitor filled with words.

CURSE, she read, followed by three icon boxes marked Definition, Examples, and Believers. She clicked on the first of these and waited while the computer screen rearranged itself.

It was midnight, and she was sitting in her room at home, hunched over her computer. Lana had already been asleep when Chloe arrived back from her visit to the Reverend Grindlay, and her father was dozing in front of the television. Tiptoeing upstairs, Chloe had gone directly to her computer and started working.

Curse: word or words calling down punishment, destruction and injury upon someone (often a cause of misfortune or ruin).

The Examples icon brought her a choice of thousands, thanks to the incredible power of the Internet. Chloe selected a few at random and speed-read through them, noting down everything she might be able profitably to use.

She learned how many of Australia's aboriginal tribes believed implicitly in the efficacy of curses. A shaman need only point the "killing bone" at a victim for his target to waste away and die, often within days.

She learned how indigenous peoples the world over—Native Americans, Amazonian Indians, Asian and African tribes—all believed in the power of a good curse.

Changed days, she thought. *A curse is something you yelp when you drop the car hood on your fingers. But if half the world believes in curses, why should Smallville be any different?*

Bracing herself, she called up her word processing program.

The research was over. It was time to start work.

CHAPTER 12

For once, Clark had finished his chores early. When the school bus came, he was waiting for it at the foot of the drive instead of having to chase it halfway to school.

He was prepared to give Pete another chance. But when he went to sit down in the vacant seat beside his friend, Pete groaned dramatically and turned to stare out of the window.

Why do I bother?

Clark kept on walking up the aisle. Lana and Chloe were seated together as always, but Chloe was fast asleep. Her head lolled against the bus window, and every time they turned a corner, Lana had to prop her friend up so she didn't fall.

"She was up all night, working," Lana explained, as Clark glanced askance at his sleeping friend. "Seems we're going to have a newspaper this week, after all."

Clark lowered himself into the seat behind the girls.

He was glad to see that Lana still wasn't wearing her pendant, the one fashioned from the green stone of the meteor that killed her parents. He didn't know what it was about the meteoric stone, but every time he'd been exposed to it, he'd had terrible reactions: violent sickness, weak and aching muscles, and an inability to think straight.

It made life difficult when merely being with the girl he loved reduced him to Jell-O.

"They sent the wrestling tickets," Lana told him. "I bought four, in case Pete wanted to come with us."

She glanced at Pete, half a dozen rows in front of her, but his attention was still on anything outside the bus. Lana frowned. "He barely said good morning to us. He's like a bear with a sore head. Do you know what's wrong with him, Clark?"

Clark did, but it wasn't something he wanted to share. Not even with his closest friends. He shook his head, and said simply, "I only wish I did, Lana."

"I just hope he comes out of it soon." Lana sighed and changed the subject. "I thought we might meet up at the Talon tomorrow night. I finish early, and there were some generous tips last week. My treat."

Clark's heart sank. "I'm sorry. I can't make it tomorrow," he apologized. "I . . . I . . ."

He found himself wondering why he'd ever agreed to Shirley Grainger's request. Because he found her pretty? Because he hoped it might make Lana jealous? Or were his motives darker—to spite Phil Meara and the goon squad?

He'd half expected Chloe to have already told Lana about his date with Shirley. But obviously, Chloe found the school newspaper more important than the details of his lovelife.

"I'm going bowling with Shirley Grainger."

Lana's eyes widened.

Jealousy? Clark wondered. Hoped. *Or just plain surprise?*

Whichever, she recovered herself well. "Cool. I'm

sure you'll enjoy yourselves. Shirley's a nice girl. And very pretty," she added, half under her breath.

Clark could hardly disagree.

The rest of the journey was spent in uncomfortable silence.

As the bus pulled into the schoolyard, Lana shook Chloe's shoulder. Her friend jerked awake and rubbed away the tiredness in her eyes.

"Where are we?" she asked, peering out through the window. "Oh no! I meant to get off at the printer's. I'll have to walk now."

"You finished the issue, then?" Clark asked as they made their way to the front exit.

Chloe grinned and held up her satchel. "All in here," she said proudly.

"Any chance of a sneak preview?"

"Any chance of a hundred-dollar bribe?" Chloe countered. "You'll see it tomorrow."

She stepped down off the bus, and hurried back out the school gates. "Make excuses for me," she yelled over her shoulder, and Clark gave a thumbs-up to her retreating back.

Lana was already heading up the stairs to the school's main entrance, and he hurried to catch her up.

Ed and his gang were fooling around at the foot of the stairs. Phil glared daggers as Clark passed, but didn't say a word.

Mid-morning, Lana was called out of Mrs. Andersen's English class.

When she came back, she was pale and it was obvious to Clark she'd been crying.

"What's wrong?" he whispered in concern as she took her seat.

Lana blinked back a tear. "That was Mr. Gault. It's Czar. He's sick."

Czar. Clark knew the horse well, having rescued it from near-certain death when it was sucked into a bog. Lana never knew, of course, because he'd had to use his superpowers.

While Lana was staying with her aunt Nell, Czar had been stabled at the Gault farm some miles away.

"I'm sorry," was all Clark could say. He longed to take her in his arms, draw her close, and comfort her.

Instead, he had another hour of Mrs. Andersen to sit through before Lex's lecture.

Chloe was half-dozing at her desk, but she was alert enough to overhear Lana's whispered words.

A horse then, she thought, *a horse now. Just like in the journal. Wow. Is this issue going to kick!*

Clark guessed that Lex's suit had set him back at least a thousand bucks.

But in Lex's case, it wasn't the clothes that made the man. Rather, it was the exact opposite. Lex Luthor had style, the way most people have two arms and two legs. Naturally.

It wasn't something he ever had to work at. Lex could dress in a paint-spattered coverall and still draw every eye in the room.

They were best friends, but Clark sometimes hated him for it.

Lex gave him a surreptitious wink, and Clark smiled in return. That was another thing about Lex. He had charm, too.

Nobody could hate him for long.

Lex stood behind the desk, and briefly surveyed the thirty or so sophomores who'd turned up to hear his words of wisdom. Some of them were watching him curiously, while others chattered to their neighbors, and still others doodled or read.

No point keeping them—or myself—waiting.

He lifted a document off the desk in front of him and raised it in the air. "You've come here today expecting a lecture on Business Practice. You may be disappointed, or intrigued, to learn that we are ignoring the agenda." He ripped the document in two and tossed it casually into the wastebasket. "Instead, I'm going to foment revolution."

Lex hadn't planned what he was going to say, relying instead on his ability to improvise, trusting he'd be guided by his instincts. He was surprised himself when his inspiration came directly from *Cassandra's Secret*.

"First off," he began, "let me ask you all a question. What is the essence of business?"

He looked expectantly around the class.

"Profit," someone called out.

Lex shook his head. "Wrong. Profit may be the motivation for business, but it's certainly not the essence— the single core value on which everything else is built. Anyone else?"

Nobody took him up on his offer.

"Honesty," he informed them. "Honesty is the essence of business. Without it, no business could ever exist. Because if the business was dishonest, nobody would ever deal with it."

"Are you saying there are no dishonest businessmen?" the same voice that had suggested profit called out.

"Far from it," Lex disagreed. "A high percentage of businessmen are, to put it not too finely, crooks. But that doesn't cancel out my assertion. Even if a company CEO is the biggest liar this side of Pinocchio, the business he leads must be honest, or it won't be long before it's history."

So far, so good. But let's see what they make of this.

"Now, can anyone tell me the essence of religion?"

"Belief?" Chloe ventured.

"Faith," Lex emphasized. "That is, believing in something without any rational proof of it. Let's assume I have a vision. I conclude that it's a message from God, for whatever reason telling me to go slay the tribe in the next valley. My soldiers polish their swords and sharpen their spears. But then somebody else—say, Clark Kent there has a vision. He thinks it's from God, too—only, in Clark's vision God says beat the swords into plowshares and make peace with those pests in the next valley."

He stroked his chin thoughtfully, letting his words sink in before he spoke again.

"So . . . whom does the tribe believe? Me, or Clark? How do they know which—if either—is the authentic messenger of God?"

A sea of faces stared blankly back at him. Nobody made any suggestions.

"Let's complicate it further. Let's say a dozen tribes-men have visions—or, for that matter, all of them do. How do they decide which is the correct decision?"

"They don't," Chloe said clearly. "Unless the god concerned is willing to show himself to all, none of them have anything but their own personal vision to fall back on. Any one of them could be telling the truth—or lying."

"And that's my point," Lex concurred. "Why should any man believe in another man's god?"

He shrugged. "But enough of that. Let's get off religion. Anybody hazard a guess as to the essence of politics?"

A dozen voices spoke at once. "Government."

Lex looked dubiously round the room. "Well, superficially that might be so," he admitted. "But what's the one single thing without which there could be no politics—at least, not as we know it?"

He watched realization dawn on Chloe's face. A slow smile lit up her eyes.

"Deceit," she said confidently. "If politicians stopped lying, the whole edifice of government would collapse like a house of cards."

"You've hit the nail squarely on the head." Lex was pleased that at least one of them was keeping up with him. With a little thought, it wouldn't be long before the others were putting two and two together and coming to some very surprising answers.

"We can apply that question to almost anything. What is the essence of law, for instance? Ostensibly, it should be justice. But I'd bet there's not a soul in this room who really believes that."

"It's deceit again, isn't it?" Chloe asked rhetorically.

"If you can deceive, you can manipulate. And lawyers are infamous for using emotion to sway juries, especially when their factual evidence doesn't cut the mustard."

"A harder one: What is the essence of the Internal Revenue Service?"

The class clearly didn't think it was that hard. "Collecting taxes." "Acting as ordered by the government." "Responsibility for sharing the national wealth."

"These are all superficial functions, people," Lex pointed out. "The essence of tax collecting is coercion. In effect, they tell you: Give us what we demand, or we will make you suffer. Fines. Garnishments. Prison."

"Aren't you being a little unfair?" Shirley Grainger asked. "I mean, taxes are used for the good of all of us."

"It might work that way in theory," Lex said wryly, "but ask yourself this: Who *decides* what's for the good of all of us?"

"The government, of course."

"And what did we just conclude about politicians . . . ?"

He let his voice trail away, smiling to himself as he watched them make the connections.

"So a bunch of liars use the threat of force to steal my money—and I'm supposed to believe them when they say it's for my own good?"

Most of the class burst out laughing, and Lex waited for the noise to subside before he went on.

"Ask anyone in the world what they want out of life, and they'll give you the same answer: happiness. We *all* want to be happy. Yet, look at the mess our planet is in. War. Famine and mass starvation. Torture. Terror."

Suddenly, he slammed his fist down on the desk, and his voice rose a notch. "*None* of us wants these things!

They're the exact *opposite* of our very deepest desires. But with every year that passes, the situation seems to get worse. The hands of the Atomic Clock jerk on toward midnight . . . and nobody ever does anything to stop it."

His words hung in the air.

Lex himself shook his head, as if despairing.

When he spoke again, his voice was calm and measured. "Soon, you teenagers will be going out into the world to make your marks. You'll all start out with good intentions. You may even achieve some good things along the way. But in the end, you'll succumb to the system. The system of deceit and manipulation, of coercion and official theft. And you'll think it's normal. You'll go to the mall on Saturday, and you'll never even notice the grim, unhappy faces that advertise grim, unhappy lives in a grim, unhappy world.

"And nobody else will notice yours."

He shook his head again, trying to convey some of the infinite sadness he felt. "The single most important piece of advice I can give you is this: Think for yourself. When you stand alone in the cold, impersonal light of the cosmos, there will be no gods to help you. No presidents, or kings. No astrologers or gurus. The only person you can rely on is yourself. To that end, question everything you're told—by your parents, your teachers, your government."

He gave an impish grin. "And me, of course."

Several pupils started to applaud, but Lex held up a hand to still them.

"One last thing. In evolutionary terms, the human race is a cat's whisker away from destroying itself and its environment. Time is running short. You are the generation who must clean up the Augean mess that others have made. It's up to you to save the world. Don't let us down, okay?"

The applause was loud and long, but Lex didn't stick around for questions. He'd Xeroxed a sheet of suggested reading material and slipped out of the class while it was being passed around.

"When you stand alone in the cold, impersonal light of the cosmos . . ."

The phrase resonated in Clark's head. Wasn't it a perfect description of his own plight? And how did Lex go on?

"The only person you can rely on is yourself."

"How's Czar?"

As usual, Chloe was hunched in front of her computer. Lex's list lay beside it, and she'd already ordered several of the titles he recommended, via the Internet. But Chloe put it aside when Lana entered the room. She'd gone straight from school out to the stable where she kept Czar.

"Dr. Ancrum says he isn't doing well. Evidently he ate some kind of toxic weed. But he was really pleased to see me, he made such a fuss."

Chloe could see she was close to tears. Lana had owned the big chestnut horse since she was a little girl, and a strong bond had developed between them. She got up from her chair and put an arm around Lana's shoulder.

"Come on. Sit down and tell me all about it." Chloe

hated seeing her so upset, but felt helpless. What did she know about horses?

"But it's not just Czar," Lana said miserably. She dabbed at her eyes with her sleeve. "Clark told me he's going out with Shirley Grainger."

Chloe frowned. "That bothers you?" she asked, puzzled. Lana had always made it clear that she looked on Clark as no more than a friend.

"It seems to," Lana replied, looking as if she didn't understand herself. "I know I loved Whitney, and Clark's always been just a good friend, but . . ."

Her words fell away, and she sighed heavily. "I just don't know what's wrong with me lately. Since . . . since Whitney died, my emotions have been all over the place." She eased Chloe's arm away, and stood up. "I'm going to have an early night."

Chloe sat thinking for a few minutes, then gave up. Women? Who could understand them?

Not even other women, it seemed.

CHAPTER 13

The Reverend Grindlay cracked the top off one of his breakfast eggs and sighed. In a way, they seemed to symbolize his marriage.

Once, not long after they'd met, he'd told Moira that his favorite childhood meal was soft-boiled hens' eggs with cinnamon toast. She never forgot. The day after they married, she presented them to him for breakfast.

And the day after. And the day after that, and . . . Well, he'd been eating soft-boiled eggs for fifteen years.

Religiously, Michael thought to himself, and couldn't help smiling.

What had started as a gesture of love had turned into something tedious. Ossified. A ritual that would never change.

And so it was with much of the rest of their marriage. The early excitement was gone, but the clichés remained, trapping both of them in what could only be a downward spiral.

The minister sighed again and reached for his toast.

Moira came into the room, waving a newspaper in her hand.

"Have you seen this?" she demanded, her voice alive with noisy outrage.

"No, I haven't," her husband snapped crossly, "mainly because you just showed it to me."

"Then feast your eyes," Moira said, with a note of triumph, as she cast it down on the table.

On top of his toast, Michael noted.

"Yes, feast your eyes," Moira repeated. "And weep."

The Reverend wasn't used to this melodrama. He picked up the newspaper, recognizing it as the *Torch,* the school newspaper that girl Chloe had interviewed him for. This should make interesting reading.

He stared at the front page in speechless horror.

"Check this, guys!"

Ed Wall held up a copy of the *Torch,* showing off the front page to Phil and Rob and Pete.

"I don't believe it, man," Phil hooted. "That's really going to set the seal on this one-horse town."

"It certainly explains why I can't get a girlfriend." Rob grinned.

The others laughed. But not Pete. Incredible as it seemed, what he'd just read might actually make a whole lot of sense.

Lana gaped at the center spread, hardly able to believe what she was reading. So this was why Chloe had stayed up all night!

The whole idea was ridiculous! Absurd! Chloe must be high on something!

Then again, there was that strange business with the horse. And now Czar was sick.

Lana was reluctant to jump to conclusions. But . . . *could* there be something in it, after all?

She just wished Chloe had talked to her about it first.

*   *   *

Principal Reynolds picked up a copy of the *Torch* from the desk in the school hall and made his way to his office.

He always enjoyed the walk from the front door, his steps echoing in the near empty halls. It reminded him of his own days as a pupil. Gave him a sense of continuity. Purpose, even.

He slid his electronic security pass into the door lock, pursing his lips at the knowledge that such precautions were necessary. The big cities might be hotbeds of madness, but there was no guarantee their violent behavior wouldn't spread. Smallville had its share of hotheads and troublemakers, and the thought of a weapon in the hands of one of them made his blood run cold.

Tossing his coat onto its hook with practiced ease, the principal snapped open the newspaper. The banner headline made him groan.

Chloe Sullivan is a highly intelligent girl. She has a brilliant future, he thought. *It's just a pity that future isn't here already . . . to get her out of my hair!*

Clark shook his head, not knowing what to feel. Amused? Horrified?

He blinked and looked down at the newspaper again, just to make sure his sight had been functioning properly the first time. There, in banner headlines set in forty-point type, he read:

THE CURSE OF SMALLVILLE?

Full Story Inside!

Apart from the paper's title, there was nothing else at

all on the front page. His heart sinking to someplace around his knees, Clark opened it, and began to read.

Chloe had ditched almost everything they'd worked on together. Social news, classroom gossip, and academic results were ousted completely. The entire issue was given over to "the curse."

Page 2 boasted a photograph of the Reverend Grindlay, with an abbreviated biography beneath. The rest of the page was taken up with a summarized version of Andrew Seddon's journal, though not dwelling on the pioneer's travails in any detail.

And with no mention of any curse.

The third page was a pencil portrait of Victor Marchmont Gray—Chloe must have drawn it herself, from memory, Clark figured. She'd only seen the newspaper for a half hour. Her talents never failed to amaze him.

Accompanying the sketch was the story of the seer's rise to fortune and prominence, using quotes from many of Clark's newspaper clippings.

He had to hand it to Chloe. She really was a one-woman show.

The Reverend Grindlay pressed the little green cross hard into the palm of his hand, stroking it with his index finger.

"It's scandalous," Moira complained. "An absolute disgrace! She seemed such a nice girl, too. That she should come into my house, disturb my husband, then—"

"Moira, please," he said as calmly as he could, recognizing the stress that underlay his words, "I am trying to

read. When I have finished, you may make as much fuss
and noise as you like. But for the moment, please—"

He looked into her eyes and said fiercely, "Stop shout-
ing in my ear!"

Moira looked hurt, and he knew he should have taken
the time to apologize and smooth things over. But he
avidly wished to read on, horrified yet at the same time
fascinated by what the girl had written.

Page 4 was headed, simply, The Curse.

Underneath was an entry from Seddon's journal—one
that Michael hadn't yet read. He ran his eyes down it
with a growing sense of panic.

August 7

I do not know who first cried "Witch!"

I do, however, know that many took it up, chanting the word until it filled the air and no longer
seemed to have meaning. It was more like the sibi-
lant wheezing of some mighty traction engine than
the speech of human beings. The French and some
of the Germans joined in. Though it shames me
somewhat to admit it, priding myself on being a rational man, my own voice could also be heard in
the hubbub.

Some of the older children began throwing rocks
at the prisoner, and he suffered several gashes and
bruises before a bellowing Huckins sent the mis-
creants scurrying for safety. From the protests of
some of the others, they'd have preferred to see
Victor Marchmont Gray stoned to death.

We bound him with stout ropes and shut him in
his wagon. Several voices cried for us just to move

on, and leave him there, to meet his fate at the hands of violent Nature.

Wolves might get him, or some of the savage Red Indians who are rumored to abound, but who—if our experience is typical—are pathetic wretches rather than mighty warriors.

Huckins said no, possibly because he had sobered up. He maintained we would drag Gray all the way to California, where he would stand trial before man and God for the evils he had brought on us through his meddling with the Infernal.

This decision was not well accepted by many of the others, including myself. At our present rate of progress, all the gold in California would be discovered before we reached our destination.

Nobody knows who started the fire.

There are many who might have done it, though it would not be fair to voice any suspicions I might have. Suffice to say, it was an Irishman, Jack O'Brien (May God rest his soul), who had died first.

The canvas on Gray's wagon went up in seconds. Flames leapt ten feet in the air, dropping flaming gobbets into the interior, setting light to Gray's clothes and chattels.

Moved by Gray's desperate screams, some of the men ran forward, intent on dragging the demon-lover out of his own personal Hell. But the kerosene lamp chose that moment to explode, showering burning oil for several yards around.

Some of it splashed on the men going to the villain's aid, and they leapt back lest they, too, combusted.

It also splashed, I must report, over Victor Marchmont Gray.

His screams were piteous, for he could not move because of the ropes that bound him. We stood around his flaming wagon, like worshipers round some pagan altar, and watched him burn to death. There was a terrible smell of burning hair, and crisped flesh that made me sick to my belly.

In the last moments before he was consumed, his voice, normally so quiet, rose to a piercing shriek.

"I curse you all," he cried, with a vehemence that curdled my very blood. "All that you have suffered, will be suffered again! Curse you! *Curse you!*"

The words turned into a long, drawn-out wail, that would have wrenched the heart of the foulest blackguard.

Then there was silence, save for the crackle of the flames and the sobbing of the women.

Lana was studying page 5, twin columns headed:

IT HAPPENED THEN	IT'S HAPPENING NOW!
Dead dog	5 dead dogs
Storm	Storm
Wheel off wagon	Wheel off Rev. Grindlay's car
Jack O'Brien suffocated	Cyrus Deen suffocated
Family feud	?
Romantic trouble	?
Sick horse	?
Theft	?
Fire	?
Murder	?????

What a checklist, she thought. *Tick off your own personal tragedy—and it's just a replay of the past.*

By lunchtime, every pupil and teacher in school had read the *Torch* from start to finish—and many had gone back to read it again.

Principal Reynolds had read it three times, trying to put together in his head just how he was going to tackle Chloe. Trouble was, everything she reported was factual. At no point did she come out and say *she* thought there was a curse on Smallville.

Then again, she never said there wasn't, either.

By late afternoon, the school newspaper was the talk of the town.

Families had discussed it over lunch.

Businessmen brought it up at meetings, and their original agendas were quickly abandoned.

Colleagues at work tossed the subject back and forth, laughing at their fears, but scaring themselves as well.

"That's right," a man said in a coffee bar. "It's got to be more than coincidence. Stands to reason, right?"

The owner wasn't convinced, but other diners nodded sagely.

"I knew a guy was cursed, once," a shoeshine told his captive client. "Vietnam, 1976. Guy was a native, see. Stopped eating, stopped sleeping. He was dead in a week."

"Makes you wonder, doesn't it?"

*   *   *

Deputy Sheriff Martin sat alone in his patrol car, parked outside the mall. He was sure his wife was having an affair with one of the desk clerks.

She'd hotly denied his accusations. They'd reconciled.

Now he found himself wondering all over again.

"Burned him alive?" said an old lady to the news vendor on Main Street. "How awful. No wonder he cursed them."

"Cursed us, too, if you ask me, Grandma."

"The Curse of Tutankhamen, right? You only had to look at the mummified remains, and you were dead within a year."

"But Tutankhamen's treasure went on tour. Internationally. Millions of people saw it. They didn't get cursed."

"How do you know?"

Sid Bickle hadn't spoken to his brother Ike in four years.

Curse or no curse, he wasn't starting again now.

Jean Brodick had tried a dozen times to end her affair with Ronnie.

He was married to her sister, for Pete's sake.

But every time, that sweet smile won her around. She was putty in his hands.

Her magazine's astrology column said she was going to face romantic turmoil in the near future. And now this. A curse.

Oh God! I just hope it doesn't end in murder!

*   *   *

"This is the twenty-first century. We've sent space-ships to Mars. We can nuke the Moon, for cripe's sake. How can a guy who's been dead 150 years put a curse on Smallville today?"

"Science don't know everything, pal. You know what they say: Once is happenstance. Twice is coincidence. Thrice is conspiracy."

"And four times is a curse? Einstein's Law, right?"

"Dad," little Holly Brown said slowly, "did Rebel die 'cause a bad man cussed him? Is that why, Dad? Is it?"

By early evening, the story was getting its first mention on the town radio station's *Smallville Today* show.

They trailed it as an item on the news bulletin and achieved their largest audience since a heavy metal tour got lost and ended up in Smallville.

By the time they finished dinner, almost everybody in Smallville knew about "the curse"—and, unknown even to themselves, were forming into two distinct camps.

Believers and scoffers.

And the former significantly outnumbered the latter.

CHAPTER 14

"I've been thinking, Clark. That whole curse thing . . . well, maybe it explains what happened last weekend out at the old bunker," Shirley said reflectively. "We could have died of suffocation, just like the man in the quicksand. And poor Mr. Deen, of course."

"I doubt it, Shirley. We didn't even know about the so-called curse then."

"You don't need to know about one to be affected by it," Shirley said scornfully. "Didn't you read the *Torch*? It explains everything."

They were walking down Peart Street, Shirley's arm linked lightly through his. It was a warm evening, with just the right amount of breeze.

"Maybe it was Mr. Deen digging up the journal that activated the curse," Shirley persisted. "I heard the witch's body was found buried under a huge slab carved with occult symbols and Satanic marks."

"First time I've heard that version," Clark admitted. "If I was you, Shirley, I'd take the whole thing with a grain of salt."

They walked on in silence for a little while. Then Shirley pointed out something Clark had just noticed himself.

"The town's really quiet," she said, her gaze sweeping

the near-deserted street. "Hardly any people around. Or traffic."

"Probably everybody's spooked by the curse," Clark said mockingly.

But the bowling alley was quiet, too. Its neon lights still shone, but none of the lanes were in play until Clark and Shirley arrived.

"It's the curse," the balding guy behind the ticket booth told them. "Everybody's staying home."

"And you?"

"I own the place. I have to risk it."

Shirley shot Clark a look that said, "I told you so," and flounced off to change into her bowling shoes.

Their game went well, although both found it slightly eerie playing alone, with the other lanes in darkness.

"No point wasting electricity," the balding guy said.

But instead of sounding quieter, the rumble of bowling balls on waxed wood seemed to overwhelm all else.

"Like a locomotive in a morgue," Clark joked.

Shirley was a good bowler, better than Clark, and she regularly picked up strikes.

At least, she's better than me if I don't use my powers.

She told him Phil used to get mad when she beat him, and go off in a huff for hours. But Clark had no problem with anyone, male or female, being better than he at anything. He was enjoying himself just watching her body move under her skimpy tank top and tight, cropped denims.

Perhaps breaking his attachment to Lana wouldn't be such a bad move.

And then Phil and Ed arrived.

Clark groaned under his breath. Couldn't these guys get a life? What kind of creep did you have to be, to make a hobby of following and harassing other people?

Phil glanced at the scoreboard. "You got him on the run, Shirl," he said loudly.

"Hey, a puppy could get Kent on the run, right, my man?"

Clark controlled his anger and concentrated on his shot. But he knew as the ball left his hand that it was a bad one. It slid into the gutter halfway down the lane, and Clark blushed as he turned away.

"Did nobody tell you, Kent?" Phil crowed. "You're supposed to knock the pins down. The gutter's for losers. Guess that's where you're headed, right?"

"Amen to that, bro." Ed laughed, and the two high-fived.

Clark was sick of sucking it in. He hated bullies in general, and with the powers he had, he had no intention of letting them get the better of him.

"We challenge you," he said boldly, surprising even himself. "Shirley and I versus you two. If we win, you leave. If you win—"

"Phil punches your snoot," Ed broke in nastily. "You're beat already, sucker."

And that's how it looked for the first three frames. Shirley hardly ever made her strike, and Clark . . . well, he wasn't all that good, anyway. It looked like Phil and Ed would be cleaning up. And Clark would have to deal with the threats when—and if—they turned violent.

But there was a steely look on Shirley's face as she did her best to shut out their rivals' taunts and concentrate on her game. She was rewarded with her first strike . . . and it opened the floodgates for more.

More or less single-handedly, she brought the scores level, Clark's major contribution being to act as cheerleader.

Phil lined up to take his final shot. Perspiration beaded his forehead as he focused on the ball, lining it up for the strike. He strode forward, his delivery arm sweeping through, sending the ball speeding down the lane.

"Looking good, my man!" Ed yelled.

Clark resisted the urge to employ his superbreath. One quick, judicious blast would be enough to spin the heavy ball aside. But as well as advising him how best to use his powers, Martha and Jonathan had taught him never to cheat.

It was hard, sometimes.

The ball hit high in the pocket, and nine pins exploded into the backnet. The tenth was caught a glancing blow and teetered on its base.

"Yes!" Phil yelled victoriously.

And prematurely. The pin slowly settled. It was still upright.

"I hate to say this," Clark told Shirley, "but we need a strike to win."

She winked at him. "I'm your girl," she said ambiguously.

Without hesitating, she stepped smoothly forward. The ball powered from her fingers, and hit solidly in the one-three pocket.

The pins tumbled.

"Stee-rike!" Clark couldn't contain himself. "You did it!"

He threw his arms around her and hugged her tight. Shirley made no move to pull away.

Over her shoulder, Clark saw a look of venom on Phil's face.

But he and Ed left with no further comment.

Clark realized that his arms were still around Shirley, and she still made no effort to release herself. He moved his head back a little so he could see her. She looked up into his eyes, and her lips moved imperceptibly toward his.

They kissed.

Clark liked it. And he could tell Shirley did, too.

Only the balding guy was a party pooper.

"Break it up, you two. I'm closing up for the night. This place is dead," he grunted. "Curse this damned curse!"

They walked slowly back to Shirley's house hand in hand, in no hurry to part from each other.

A new moon was shining in the sky. A new beginning?

At her gate, Shirley turned to face him. "That was fun, Clark. I really enjoyed myself. Thanks."

"No. Thank you. I'd like to do it again."

Their lips met, and he drew her close.

Suddenly, incongruously, he thought of Chloe's checklist in the *Torch*.

Romantic problems.

If his lips hadn't been pressed against Shirley's, he'd have smiled.

This kind of problem he could live with.

CHAPTER 15

"Peter Ross! Do my eyes deceive me—or are you doing schoolwork?"

"Full marks for observation, Dad." Pete was sitting at the table in the dining room, skimming through the pile of books and dictionaries heaped in front of him.

"Glad to see it, boy. You've been neglecting your studies of late."

Mr. Ross was inordinately proud of all his high-achieving children. Pete was the youngest of eight, and he had a lot to live up to.

So far, I haven't even come close.

"I won't interrupt you," his dad said, making to leave the room again. "I'm just glad you're back on track."

Pete bit his lip. He didn't like lying to his parents, but how could he confess what he was really doing? Searching the encyclopedias for any mention of a fruit or berry that matched with the ones Ed was supplying.

And, of course, reading up on curses.

He drew a blank with the weird berries. Most of the ones he found were toxic: foxglove, mandrake, deadly nightshade. And their fruits were nothing like Ed's berries.

In contrast, there were dozens of pages on curses—all backing up what Chloe had said in her feature.

If that's what's going on—if we really are cursed—it

would explain everything, Pete thought. *The near tragedy at the old bunker, for a start. Maybe it would even explain my use of drugs, too.*

As far as he knew, none of the others had taken Ed's fruit since last weekend. They'd all had too much of a scare to rush into doing it again. After four days without, Pete was feeling better than he had for weeks. The berries might fill you with energy, increase your power dramatically—but you paid for it later, in aches and pains and depression.

I don't really like Ed and his crowd anyway, he thought. *Maybe I won't be joining them again.*

"I'm sorry, Moira. I didn't mean to speak so sharply."

Michael Grindlay and his wife were preparing for bed. She'd hardly spoken a word to him since dinner.

"Perhaps this curse has affected your temper," she said tartly.

The minister sighed. "No. I was just a little over-wrought."

"Good." Moira plumped up her pillow and slipped between the sheets. "I don't think you should spare another thought for silly curses. It's all a lot of nonsense."

"Yes, dear. Of course."

No sense in provoking an argument, especially over such a controversial subject.

Moira closed her eyes and was asleep in seconds—an ability Michael had always envied. He was one of those people who lay awake at nights, fretting and worrying, even when there was little to fret or worry about.

While Moira dropped off to sleep like a rock.

Of course, Moira was right. It was all simply coincidence. He bet he couldn't find a single wagon train, ever, where horses and dogs didn't die.

They all ran into storms, too.

And probably hundreds—if not thousands—of the trekkers died.

But Cyrus Deen's death—suffocated in the same way as the prospector who died in the quicksand—wasn't so easily explained away.

For at least two thousand years, religious leaders had accepted the existence of demons as real. They were mentioned many times in the Bible, and the Koran even had a special section detailing the rights of the Djinn, the order of demons that lay between the angels and Mankind.

He could understand it happening 150 years ago.

But today? In Smallville?

The Reverend Grindlay shuddered and snuggled closer to his sleeping wife.

Jonathan Kent was one of the scoffers.

"A man makes his own luck," he told Martha—and not for the first time. "Creating a scapegoat is no solution to a run of misfortune."

Martha wasn't quite as convinced. "You have to admit—all of those coincidences are just a little bit unsettling. If you believed in that sort of thing. Not that I do," she added quickly.

"Really?" Jonathan teased.

She smiled. "Let's just say I like to hedge my bets. I did knock down that dog, though, didn't I?"

"Martha," he said wearily, "I've seen hundreds of

dead dogs. In the scheme of things, one dead dog is not a very significant event."

"There were five dead dogs, Jonathan."

"That just proves my point."

Jonathan rolled over, and his steady breathing soon told her he was fast asleep. But Martha lay there in the darkness, remembering the way the dog's leg had twitched. Remembering how its eyes seemed to be begging her for help . . .

Bill van Drey put down his beer glass, belched loudly, and headed for the bar's door.

"You're weaving, buddy," his friend Andy accused, staggering a little himself as he followed Bill out of the bar and onto the street.

They got together every Wednesday night for a drink and a game of pool, a habit they'd fallen into years ago, when they both worked in the creamed corn factory. The factory was little more than a shell, but old habits die hard.

Customers had been pretty sparse that night. To compensate for the lack of atmosphere in the bar, Bill and Andy had a drink or two more than usual.

Arms wrapped around each other's shoulders, they unsteadily made their way down the street.

As they approached a discarded cola can lying in the gutter, Bill drew back a foot to kick it. He lunged wildly, and his foot failed to connect with its target. Bill tottered, then lost his balance. He fell over, dragging Andy down with him.

There was a sickening crack as Andy's head slammed against the side of the curb.

"Andy? Andy!"

He wasn't breathing. Blood was running from his head.

By morning, "the curse" would have claimed another victim.

Lex reclined on his suite's chaise longue, staring out the window, eyes fixed on the bright moon that hung over Smallville.

He'd heard the story of the curse earlier, on the radio. Urban paranoia. He wondered how fast it would spread. Smallville was the perfect breeding ground for something like this: large enough for everybody not to know each other, but small enough for news to travel fast. It was isolated, too, with a large rural population.

A satellite gleamed as it tumbled in its orbit. Twenty-two thousand miles high, where superstition means nothing and hard scientific fact is all.

Curses are a manifestation of the primitive mind, Lex thought. *At least, until we acquire some scientific evidence to support their existence.*

In other towns, it had been UFOs, or Moth-Men. For some it was Alien Big Cats, or Black Dogs, or abducting Grays.

In Smallville, it was an ancient curse.

Lex began to chuckle softly.

It was a long time before he stopped.

Dr. Kincaid was returning from a late-night house call when he ran a red light and hit Art Dekker's flatbed truck.

The paramedics carted them both off to hospital. The

police measured skid marks and blood samples. The insurance companies would pick up the tab.

The curse had struck again.

Of course.

Daniel Arnally filched a bottle of vodka and a carton of cigarettes from the convenience store on Madison Street.

He couldn't believe it when the security guard stopped him and phoned for the cops.

"It's the curse, Danny," they told him. "You bad guys don't stand a chance."

A gang of homeys from one of the new developments on the fringes of town overturned their VW Beetle on a blind bend.

Nobody was hurt. Nobody was drunk.

A medic suggested that maybe the fact they had a lucky St. Christopher dangling from the rearview mirror had been enough to deflect the curse.

He didn't mention the nodding dog on the parcel shelf.

The veterinary doctor called Lana at midnight, causing Chloe's father to complain loudly as he banged on her bedroom door.

Lana pulled on a dressing gown and came out to the phone, trying to collect her dream-scattered thoughts.

"Sorry it's so late," the doctor told her, "but I thought you'd want to know at once. Czar . . . has taken a turn for the worse. It's not looking good."

Silence.

"I'm sorry, Lana. We'll try everything we can."

A tear slid down her cheek and dropped noiselessly to the floor.

"Sssh, Hercules!"

Amy Finelin put down her electric screwdriver and swept the long-haired Persian cat off the floor. She cradled it in her arms, stroking its long, silky fur.

"It's not what you're used to," she told the cat, as if it were another person, "but you'll just have to get used to it."

Proudly, she surveyed her handiwork. All on her own, she'd fitted two strong safety chains to the front door. And, just to be sure, she'd screwed a couple of planks to the doorframe. Even Hercules' cat flap had a padlock and chain.

"No curse is getting through that!"

Hercules purred loudly, as if to say, "What if the house burns up tonight? Didn't the radio mention death by fire?"

Sitting in the darkness of his loft, back propped against the wall, staring out into space, curses didn't figure much in Clark Kent's thinking.

Shirley Grainger did, though.

Dawn. The sun rose so quickly, it hardly gave Smallville time to adjust to the passing of night.

The sky was blue. The sun was hot.

And fear blanketed Smallville like a shroud. A fog of dark anxieties rolled slowly through the streets. Paranoia spread of its own accord, feeding on its own rumors. Invisible clouds sucked out the warmth of the day and chilled the morning air.

People shivered.

As if there was worse to come.

CHAPTER 16

The luxury touring coach swung off the highway exit just as the sun rose. All twelve passengers aboard were asleep. Only the driver saw the splendor of the Kansas dawn over the flat, near-featureless plains.

For an hour, he guided the coach along roads that became gradually smaller and narrower. Only when he saw the road sign did he switch on his microphone and use the intercom to waken his charges.

"Good morning, people," he announced. "Time to rise and shine. Journey's end in thirty minutes."

The eight members of the Mountain Man Touring Wrestling Show, and their four roadies, reluctantly abandoned their fitful sleep. Sprawled in their seats, one by one they opened their eyes and came to terms with another day. Another town. Another fight.

Brian Etienne knuckled the sleep from his eyes and ran his fingers through his short, blond spiky hair. He couldn't remember what he'd been dreaming about, but it must have been good, judging by his mind's reluctance to snap into waking mode.

His muscles ached in a dozen places, the result of the dozen bouts he'd fought over the previous five days. There was a dull throb from his ribs, where he hadn't moved quickly enough and his opponent's knee had connected way too hard.

I'm getting too old for life on the road already. And I'm only twenty-three. I never liked it, anyway.

"Everybody fit and happy?" Don Breed's rich, deep voice boomed.

The team leader's words were greeted by a chorus of groans and curses.

"We just did five straight shows in Metropolis," Merlyn the Mauler complained, in a nasal Brooklyn accent. He looked too slim and graceful to be a wrestler, but his sheer speed made up for what he lacked in bulk. "We'd be a lot happier and fitter if we had a night off!"

"Yeah. And healthier, too!"

"It's coming, my friends," Don replied. He tossed back his head to clear his long hair from his eyes. "Smallville tonight, Otisville on Saturday . . . then Sunday is all yours to do as you please."

"Smallville, Otisville, Hicksville," somebody else said, from the back of the bus. "They're all starting to blur into one."

You're way behind on that, Brian thought. *For the past twelve months, I haven't known whether I'm coming or going.* He glanced out of the coach's tinted window, and saw the sign announcing Smallville in just five miles. *But I know now . . .*

"Hey, that's the joy of life on tour." Don was laughing. "We get to meet the fans up close and personal. Besides, we're playing Dodge City all next week. You'll get entertainment and social life till it comes out your wazoo."

Not me, Brian said to himself. *Smallville is the end of the line. When I leave there, it'll be good-bye forever to pro wrestling and the never-ending tour.*

He settled back in his seat, half closed his eyes, and smiled.

"Your ball, Phil!"

The basketball struck the ground and spun up at a crazy angle. Phil lunged to reach it but missed and over-balanced, nearly falling.

Phil sucked in a deep breath. "Let's take five, guys," he suggested. "I'm whipped."

He and Ed and some of the others were playing an impromptu game of lunchtime basketball on Smallville High School's outside court. But after ten minutes, they were all blowing so hard they were glad to take the rest.

"We must be getting old," Ed joked. "We can't even do ten minutes' exercise without running ourselves into the ground."

"It must be the curse," Rob put in. "It's going to get us all!"

Phil joined in with the others' laughter, but he couldn't shake off his feeling of uneasiness. Once—and not long ago—he'd been a fair-to-middling basketball player. Now, he doubted if he'd last for even the first quarter in any kind of serious game.

Ed's berries, he thought. *Ever since I started taking them, I've been feeling rough. Not sleeping properly— waking up with a hangover—losing my temper way too often.*

His parents had been arguing again this morning, their raised voices spiking through his muddled thoughts. He hadn't stuck around for breakfast; instead, he'd walked to the end of his street and waited for Ed to come by in his pickup.

"Everybody going to the show tonight?" Ed asked, and there was a babble of muttered agreement.

"Are we flying?" someone wanted to know. Flying was their code word for tripping out on Ed's berries.

But Ed shook his head. "No way. Too many parents there, for a start. And then there's the security guards. We'll save the good times for Saturday, *muchachos*."

Phil would never have admitted it, but he was relieved. He seemed to feel permanently weak recently. Every time he got high, he paid for it by feeling low for days afterward.

Don't want the others to know that, though. Don't want them thinking I'm some kind of wuss.

"Hey, Shirley!"

Ed's voice jolted him out of his thoughts. He saw Shirley Grainger walking by with one of her friends, stopping to see what Ed wanted.

"You made a bad mistake, dumping Phil," Ed accused. "You've swapped a man for a mouse."

Phil felt himself flushing. He looked away, avoiding Shirley's eyes as she replied angrily to her tormentor.

"You're entitled to your opinion, Ed. So am I. And the way I see it, Clark Kent is twice the man you and your little gang will ever be."

The corners of her mouth turned down in a sneer, and she and her girlfriend walked away.

"No great loss, man," Ed said, clapping Phil on the back. "If she prefers to run around with losers, you're better off without her."

Phil stared sullenly after the departing girls. He'd felt rotten when Shirley dumped him, and even worse when she went out with the Kent nerd. He watched now as

Shirley and her friend parted ways, Shirley heading straight over to intercept Kent as he walked past the basketball court.

Phil's eyes narrowed dangerously. It was time he came up with some sort of plan to take care of that geek.

"Hey, Clark."

"Hi, Shirley."

"You doing anything tonight?"

"Um . . . as it happens, yes. Chloe and Lana—" Clark noticed how he put Chloe's name first. Sometimes it seemed that the whole school had known of his crush on Lana, and he didn't want Shirley to think she was some sort of second best. "Chloe and Lana got me a ticket for the wrestling show. I said I'd go along with them. Sorry."

He saw the look of disappointment on Shirley's face. It was obvious that she liked him as much as he liked her and wasn't just using him as a substitute for Phil.

"Maybe I'll see you there," Clark suggested.

Shirley shook her head. "I'm not much of a sports fan," she admitted. "Watching grown men throw each other around isn't really my idea of a fun night out."

"Tell you what," Clark ventured, "we could go out tomorrow night, if you're free. That is," he added, laughing, "if the Smallville Curse doesn't get us first."

Shirley smiled, and her eyes twinkled. "I don't believe in curses. Well, not much. Mister, you've got yourself a date."

The Reverend Grindlay finished reading the journal and flipped the book closed. He felt terrible.

He'd spent the entire morning reading and rereading

the entries, especially the final one: Victor Marchmont Gray's agonizing death in a burning wagon and the curse that he had cast on his traveling companions.

A shudder ran through him, and almost automatically he reached into his pocket to clasp the tiny green crucifix in his hand. Strange, how it seemed to comfort and soothe him. As if it were a real bridge between him and his faith.

Moira had interrupted only once, to bring him a welcome cup of coffee. When she saw that he was poring over the ancient journal with its copperplate writing, he witnessed an increasingly common sight: Moira in a temper.

"I don't know why you're wasting your time with that rubbish," she snapped. "There are a dozen things you could be getting on with a lot more profitably. The wiring . . . ?"

"Moira, you don't understand," he said soothingly. "You may not think curses are effective, but believe me there are plenty of heavyweight commentators who do."

He waved his hand vaguely in the direction of a pile of reference books on the edge of the desk. "And that includes the writers of the Bible," he added, trying to off-set her scathing look. "The Old Testament records how God cursed various people and lands—and it leaves no doubt that those curses actually *worked*."

"This is the twenty-first century," Moira said slowly and patiently, as if she were talking to a child. "Things like that just don't happen. Not in Smallville. Not any-where in the civilized world."

Michael took a deep, calming breath. He knew from experience that Moira's temper was on the point of exploding. It didn't happen often, but when it did . . . well, he sometimes wondered if he had married the right woman.

And the guilt he felt at that unworthy thought always made him apologize, even when he was in the right.

"Try to see it from my point of view," he told her, his voice almost pleading. "Cyrus Deen found the book, and days later he was dead. If this curse was activated when he dug up the old grave, then I have no choice. Cyrus may have unleashed the evil upon us—but somehow, I must find a way to *deactivate* it."

"You're a fool, Michael Grindlay!" his wife fumed. "A stubborn, obstinate fool."

She whirled on her heel and stormed out of the study, slamming the door so hard behind her that the pile of books, balanced precariously on the edge of the desk, toppled off onto the floor.

The minister's grip tightened around the green cross in his hand, as he struggled to control himself. He hated arguments of any kind. When Moira was in this kind of mood, there was no saying how long it might last. He could be made to suffer for days. Weeks, even.

He groaned inwardly. He and Moira needed to sit down and have a long chat. When folks had been married as long as they had, it wasn't unusual for them to start taking their relationship for granted. They needed to get to know each other all over again, to remind themselves of the love that had brought them together in the first place.

Right after this is sorted out, he promised himself. *Once I have a little more time . . .*

But he never seemed to have that "little more time." There was *always* something demanding his attention.

Sighing, he got up to retrieve the fallen books. He'd found a dozen or more rituals listed in their pages, incantations and ceremonies designed to abolish demons. They were rarely if ever used nowadays, but perhaps one of them might be what he needed.

Moira would go crazy if she knew what he planned.

Michael shuddered again. But he couldn't tell if it was fear of the curse or the thought of his wife's wrath.

The wrestling show was to take place in the school gymnasium. To minimize disruption while the tour's road crew set up the ring and all the accoutrements of modern wrestling, the entire school was given Friday afternoon off.

"Suck it in, everybody," Ed commanded, as he pushed open the Talon door. "Today we drink coffee with the geeks."

Phil, Rob, and Pete followed him inside. Usually, Ed's crowd preferred to hang out in one of the town's less salubrious cafes. But it was closed for redecoration, and the Talon was the only alternative.

Half the kids in school seemed to have had the same idea. The place was crowded. Yvonne the waitress had given up serving tables and was standing behind the counter, taking orders and money, letting the milling crowd of teenagers do their own legwork.

Phil glanced around, and a stab of anger shot through him.

Clark Kent was at the counter, picking up a tray with

three coffees on it. Lana Lang and Chloe Sullivan were seated at a table, waiting for him.

The door opened behind him, and Phil felt a nudge in his back.

"Hey, wait your turn," he snarled impatiently.

But his words tailed away as he turned to glance at the newcomer. He was tall, at least six-three, with short, spiky blond hair. Impossible muscles rippled under his thin shirt. His face was handsome, but spoiled by an arrogant sneer that seemed to be a permanent fixture at the side of his mouth.

Phil recognized him at once. His anger dissipated, and he stepped aside. "Sorry," he mumbled. "I thought it was someone else."

The stranger moved around him, and Phil saw Clark about to cross his path. Like a good nerd, Kent paused to let the newcomer go by.

Phil acted on a sudden impulse, surprising even himself.

Affecting an innocent look, he deliberately barged sideways into Kent. Clark staggered, was unable to retain his balance. The tray dipped in his hands, and three cups of coffee splashed over the stranger.

"I'm sorry, really," Kent apologized, looking flustered, and it was all Phil could do to suppress a smile. "Of course, I'll pay to have your shirt cleaned—"

The stranger glared down at Kent, and the sneer on his face deepened. Phil saw his fists clench. For a moment, Phil thought he was going to let loose a punch that would surely knock Kent into the middle of next week.

But he controlled himself well. Ignoring Kent, ignoring the stains on his shirt, he turned around and stalked back to the exit without saying a word.

"What was all that about?" Ed asked Phil, puzzled.

"Didn't you recognize him?" Phil nodded toward the newcomer's departing back as he exited from the cafe.

"He seemed familiar," Ed admitted. "Rock star?"

"Wrestler. That was Brian Etienne. Alias Kid Psycho."

"And you almost had him whipping Kent's butt?" Ed grinned widely, and clapped Phil on the back. "Phil, you are one bad dude!"

Suddenly, Phil had an idea. The king of all ideas.

It took all of his willpower not to laugh aloud.

CHAPTER 17

"Nice job, boys." Don Breed congratulated his road crew. "Let's just hope it makes 'em spend."

The school gym was almost unrecognizable. Huge banners bearing images of the wrestlers adorned the walls. A large flexiscreen had been erected, on which the bouts would be shown, allowing for giant close-ups of the action. A full-sized ring had also been set up, its corners festooned with American flags.

A booth outside the entry door would sell souvenir programs, posters, magazines, Don's book, *Tough Guys in Spandex*, and the tour's single biggest money-spinner: T-shirts.

"Okay, you guys won't be needed again till around seven o'clock." Don fished a large-denomination bill from his wallet and handed it to Tom Verden, the road crew manager. "Get yourselves something to eat—catch a movie—whatever. But don't be late getting back."

Don leapt lithely up onto the ringside, moving easily for a man of his bulk. He was a big guy, but he'd always been light on his feet. He vaulted over the top rope.

"Practice, guys," he yelled across the auditorium. "Let's get warmed up here."

The other wrestlers shuffled out of the changing room area. They wore T-shirts and shorts, unwilling to risk their expensive Spandex costumes in practice bouts.

"Pair off, and let's get started."

Stanley Markss swung himself up into the ring, ready to grapple with his boss. Don faced him, spread the fingers of each hand wide, and began to circle his opponent.

Tom Verden folded the banknote Don had given him and strolled toward the exit. His three crewmen followed.

"Wait up, Tom." Verden flinched at the whining note in Sam Fozter's voice. "I'll just take my share now, if that's okay."

"Our company not good enough for you, Foz?" Tom asked, as they filed out into the warm afternoon.

Foz shrugged. "You know me. I like to look around. Visit the museums and stuff. All you guys ever want is burgers and beer."

Tom gave him a ten-spot. "I owe you two-fifty."

"I won't let you forget."

"I know."

Tom watched through hooded eyes as Fozter pocketed the money and veered away from the others.

"Are we looking for a bar, Tom?" Rudy Sillars wanted to know. "I got a friend passed through here once, told me there's only one halfway-decent bar in town. With the emphasis on *halfway*."

Tom grinned. Rudy had a rep for knowing the best bar in every town and city in the nation. If he hadn't been there personally, he knew someone who had.

But Tom wasn't thinking about beer. His thoughts were on Sam Fozter. He watched Foz round a corner and disappear from sight, then came to a sudden decision. He handed Don's fifty-dollar bill to Rudy.

"You guys go on without me. I'll catch up with you."

Without waiting for a reply, he hurried off in the same direction Foz had taken.

Rudy looked at the note, then at the fourth roadie, Aaron Z. "How the devil's he going to join us when he doesn't know where we've gone?"

"Clark! Aren't you finished with your shower yet?"

"I'll be right out, Dad."

Clark studied his reflection with your mirror for the umpteenth time. He ran his fingers through his thick, black hair and let it spring back into shape. He splashed on an extra dab of aftershave. Sure, it was only a wrestling show, but he was going with Lana—and Chloe, of course—and wanted to look his best.

Funny, he found himself thinking, *I'm going out with Shirley now, but I'm still making the effort for Lana. Guess old habits die hard.*

But in his heart, he knew it was more than habit. A lot more. He'd worshiped Lana from afar for more than half his life. Shirley might have made a strong impression on him, but she hadn't made his feelings for Lana go away.

Satisfied, he ran his fingers through his hair one more time.

"Clark! Are you finished yet?"

Sam Fozter strolled lazily along a broad, tree-lined street, to all intents and purposes a tourist enjoying the late-afternoon sun.

Nobody seeing him would give him a second glance.

He'd already taken a quick look at Main Street. A few nice shops, all with closed-circuit television coverage.

Sam never took chances. Big cities like Metropolis were always best for shops; there, he was just one face among millions.

Here, in Smallville, he could be identified easily.

He examined the glass-encased tourist map in the town square, then sauntered off in the direction of the church. Often, these hick town churches and chapels had silver candlesticks and plate, even money lying around. For the taking.

The church's old oak door stood open, a blatant invitation to a man like Sam.

He entered, trying to look respectful. But there was nobody there to impress. Nice stained glass. Pity it wasn't transportable. The folks on Nob Hill would pay plenty for it.

Still, anything silver would be nice.

The altar was festooned with fresh-cut flowers, but the candlesticks were all electroplated nickel silver. Cheapskates. There was nothing worth taking the risk of stealing.

Foz was reluctant to leave without something to justify his time and effort. The wages Don paid, he'd be in debt all his life. He wouldn't be on the tour at all, if it weren't for his profitable sideline. And Barney in Frisco had some great contacts.

Disappointed, he was on the point of leaving when he saw a doorway he hadn't previously noticed. No harm trying.

Unlocked.

Foz darted a glance at the church entrance. Still nobody around. Slipping through the door, he closed it behind him with the gentlest of clicks.

He found himself in a short, windowless hallway. There was only one door in the wall, standing half-open, before it turned the corner that led, presumably, to the rest of the house.

Foz could hear a very faint murmur of voices. Somebody was home.

He peered in through the open doorway. A study, its walls lined with old books. Might be worth something, but they were too bulky to carry. Too hard to conceal.

College and family photographs adorned the walls. Nice Oriental carpet—but what could he do?

"If it don't fit in a padded bag," Barney had told him, "leave it."

He picked up several of the books and glanced at their covers. Old, but not old enough. Then he saw the journal, lying flat on the desktop. It looked really old. Foz picked it up and flicked through a few pages, impressed by the dates of the entries.

This was more like it.

Just as he slid it into his coat pocket, the telephone rang.

Foz almost had a heart attack. He moved faster than he ever had in his life before, shooting out of the study and back through the door into the church before the phone rang three times.

That was close. He had to be more careful. He had a sweet little racket, and there was no point taking stupid chances.

He crossed himself as he passed the altar and was whistling happily as he walked down the aisle to the exit.

*   *   *

Clark didn't know when his mood changed, but it must have been on the drive to town.

"Thanks for this, Dad."

"No problem, Clark." At the wheel, Jonathan threw his son a sideways smile. "I'm always happy to chauffeur my son around on his romantic jaunts."

Jonathan slowed the truck as he approached the end of the farm drive, then accelerated out into the road, tires scattering gravel.

"You could always have run," he added. "That would impress Lana a lot more than my pickup truck."

"And Chloe," Clark said quickly, reddening with embarrassment. "She's coming, too."

He was silent as they drove into town, and the cornfields began to give way to buildings. Lana tonight, Shirley tomorrow. He ought to feel great. But thoughts of Pete haunted him. His best friend should have been with them. Instead, he would be with his new friends, a bunch of troublemakers and losers.

Clark felt a strange sense of foreboding, as if some malevolent force were nearby, definable only by its evil emanations.

"Why so glum all of a sudden?" his father asked. He hesitated before going on. "You're not taking this curse business seriously, I hope?"

"Of course not."

This was it, of course. The perfect opportunity to tell his father about Pete and what he was up to. Clark tried—as he'd tried before—but he just couldn't find the words. He'd always enjoyed a great relationship with his father, and respected the older man's judgment on everything.

But it would be betraying Pete. It might destroy his future. Friends are supposed to look out for each other. He'd tried to get help from the Reverend Grindlay, but to little avail. Clark had to solve this problem himself.

He made a determined effort to shake off the unsettling mood. Pursing his lips, he began to whistle, tapping out the beat with his fingers on the car seat.

"That's more like it." His father laughed, as the truck turned into the Sullivans' road.

It seemed like the whole town had turned out for the show.

Curse or no curse, the promise of an evening's entertainment was too much to resist. Or, maybe, a night out was something they all needed: a chance to relax, to forget their fears and niggling worries in the company of friends.

A chance to watch big men in colorful costumes bashing each other's brains out.

Clark, Lana, and Chloe walked into the schoolyard together, arguing good-naturedly.

"But surely you went over the top," Clark accused Chloe. "I mean, a *checklist* of tragedies? That's supermarket tabloid material."

"That's exactly what I told her," Lana agreed.

"Hey, it struck a chord with Smallville," Chloe protested. "I'm proud of that piece. And how many of our stories get picked up by radio and the newspapers?" She didn't wait for a reply. "None, that's how many. Except my curse story. I'm proud of it," she repeated.

"And so you should be," Clark complimented her.

"It's just . . . well, you've got half the town worried sick."

"Huh!" Chloe snorted, and indicated the mass of people heading toward the gym. "I guess it must be the *other* half of the town that's worried, right?"

Before Clark could reply, he saw Pete, fooling around with his new friends. Clark hoped he would come over, but—as usual—Pete's eyes slid guiltily away from his.

"Oh man, am I looking forward to this!" said Phil, beaming.

Phil looked so smug, Pete couldn't help wondering what he meant.

"I didn't know you were a big grapple fan," Pete told him.

"I'm not," Phil confessed. "But somehow, I think we're in for a very pleasant surprise tonight."

"What are you talking about?" Ed demanded.

But Phil wasn't sharing his secret just yet. "You'll see," he told the others tantalizingly. "Oh yeah, we'll all see!"

Principal Reynolds felt strangely exposed as he filed into the gym.

Despite his fears about Chloe's newspaper feature, it didn't seem to have made people stay home. The place was thronged.

But usually, he was in charge.

Tonight, it wasn't *his* school at all.

Lex Luthor was conspicuous by his absence.

"Everything okay?" Don Breed asked.

Manning the sales booth, Tom Verden nodded. "Not much action yet," he conceded, "but it'll perk up later, once the show gets their adrenaline buzzing." Tom hesitated. "I need to have a word with you, Don."

"Fire away."

"Not now. After the show."

"Good man." Don began to saunter away. "The show always comes first."

Michael and Moira Grindlay were among the last to arrive.

As minister, Michael felt it was his duty to support Smallville's social life. He'd attended rock concerts, operatic recitals and avant garde theater plays, all in the line of civic duty. Besides, what little he'd seen of pro wrestling on television was vastly entertaining.

Moira had been frosty ever since their spat that morning. She'd hardly spoken to him at all—until he'd made the mistake of joking while they got ready to go out.

"Young hunks in spandex," he'd said. "I'm sure you'll enjoy yourself."

It was said innocently enough, but it unleashed such a torrent of high-pitched abuse from Moira that he wished he'd never spoken.

Since then, her frostiness had turned to ice.

CHAPTER 18

"Ladeez and gentlemen," Don announced from the center of the ring, the PA system amplifying his deep bass voice and drowning out the background chatter. "Welcome to the Mountain Man Touring Wrestling Show's evening of unerudite and positively antieducational entertainment!"

He was dressed in a spangled red, white, and blue costume, complete with matching top hat. He was well aware that the paying customer liked a little showmanship with his entertainment and did his best to deliver it. Look at where it had gotten Don King and Steve MacMahon.

Don raised one hand, the signal for the roadie handling the lighting to douse the main lights. The spectators were plunged into darkness, only the ring left illuminated by powerful lights. The audience fell silent.

Towering over him on one wall, Don's image addressed the throng from the giant screen.

"We come to the first bout in our extraspectacular extravaganza," Don went on, in the type of language that had become second nature to him. "Iron Man Vasquez—scourge of the square ring—will fight three, three-minute rounds with the British All-Star ex-champion, Merlyn the Mauler."

Each name was greeted by a muted roar from the crowd.

At least some of them are hip to us, Don thought. *The schoolkids, no doubt.*

He just hoped none of them spoke to Merlyn afterward, though. The wrestler's thick Brooklyn accent was a sure giveaway he'd never been within a thousand miles of Britain in his life.

The two fighters emerged into the gym and vaulted over the ropes into the ring. Iron Man Vasquez stuck out a foot as his opponent landed, and Merlyn went sprawling to the canvas.

The audience roared. They liked their heroes and villains to be defined from the get-go.

"Your referee for tonight's contests is Mr. Rudy Sillars of California, flown in at great expense to officiate in this chiller-diller-thriller."

Rudy stood in the spotlight and took a bow.

It always gave him a kick when Don introduced him like that. As far as anybody knew, it was the truth. Unless, of course, they'd seen him arrive on the coach with the others that morning.

He strode to the center of the ring and beckoned to the wrestlers.

"I want a good, clean fight. Best of three falls or submissions wins. No biting. No gouging. Apart from that, anything goes."

He stepped back as acting timekeeper Aaron Z. sounded the bell to begin Round One.

"Wow! Look at that!"

Pete whistled as, straight from the bell, Iron Man

soared across the ring in a double-footed dropkick. His feet slammed into Merlyn's chest and sent him staggering back against the ropes.

"It's all fixed," Ed said derisively. "They know how to roll with the moves. They spend weeks practicing. It's not really fighting—more like dancing. Girl stuff."

Pete shrugged. "If you say so," he murmured, his eyes never leaving the men in the ring. He'd felt guilty snubbing Clark earlier, but his regrets were soon forgotten as he immersed himself in the spectacle.

Merlyn rebounded from the top rope, using its elasticity to give himself momentum. He shot at Iron Man, who recognized the danger and dropped to the canvas on all fours.

Merlyn leapt over his opponent's body, hit the ropes on the far side and bounced back—just as Iron Man was springing to his feet. A blow from Merlyn's elbow took him in the head, sending him crashing heavily back to the canvas.

Pete was impressed. Even if Ed was right, and the fighters had choreographed every second of this, it was still brilliant entertainment.

He wondered idly how the wrestlers would fare if they'd eaten Ed's berries. Now that would *really* be some wrestling match! They'd be stronger, faster, even more athletic. Of course, the comedowns would soon take the edge off their athletic performance.

He was more determined than ever to say no.

The bout ended in a win by knockout for Iron Man.

The unfortunate Merlyn was helped out of the ring by Foz, who supported him till they were back in the changing area, out of the audience's sight. Only then did Merlyn make a remarkable and immediate recovery.

"That's seven straight losses, Tony," he said to Iron Man. "What am I doing wrong?"

While the wrestlers' set pieces were indeed highly choreographed, the results of the bouts still depended on the fighters themselves. Contrary to uninformed gossip, the outcome was never fixed.

"Maybe it's the name," Tony suggested. "I mean, *Merlyn*? Great, if you're a Harry Potter fan. How about changing it to Gandalf the Goofy?" He grinned disarmingly. "Or maybe I'm just the better wrestler. Ever think of that?"

He ducked to avoid the towel that flew at him from Merlyn's hand.

Like Pete, Chloe was more than impressed with the show.

"They're, like, two hundred pounds of solid muscle . . . and yet they're lighter on their feet than ballet dancers."

"Don't you mean battering rams?" Lana queried. "This is *so* aggressive!"

"That's half the fun, Lana," Chloe explained. "Didn't you know? All that testosterone . . . hunks in tight costumes . . . Good versus Evil." She sighed and rolled her eyes, pretending she was going to swoon.

She was seated between Lana and Clark, a little arrangement she'd mischievously decided on. That way, they couldn't get wrapped up in each other's company and leave Chloe out in the cold. Of course, the number of times she'd sensed them glance at each other was enough to make her paranoid, anyway.

The second bout began, the aptly named Big Lizard facing up to the Fist. Big Lizard was at least 280 pounds, his skin tinted green like lizards' scales, a tattooed dragon emblazoned on his broad, rippling back.

The Fist was a minimum fifty pounds lighter, wearing an all-black outfit with a target on its chest.

Really starting to get into the swing of things, Chloe gasped as the bigger man lunged. The Fist ducked under the clutching hands, but Big Lizard managed to grab his arm. Whipping down on it, he sent the hapless Fist spinning through the air.

There was a collective intake of breath from the crowd.

At the last moment, before he seemed destined to slam into the padded cornerpost with frightening force, the Fist somersaulted in the air. His feet landed on the bottom rope.

Chloe clapped in delight as he barely paused before kicking off again, soaring over Big Lizard's head, to land directly behind him. His foot shot out, to sweep away the bigger man's ankles.

Five seconds later, the Fist had won the first fall.

The applause was deafening. As Chloe stamped and yelled her approval, she was aware that, on either side, Clark and Lana were still casting each other sly glances.

After the second bout ended—in a knockout for Big Lizard—Don Breed sprang back into the ring, microphone in hand.

"Ladeez and gentlemen, show your appreciation please for two gallant grapplers!"

He waited for the applause to die away before making his next announcement.

"It is the Mountain Man crew's proud boast that we will pay one thousand dollars to any male able to endure three minutes in the ring with our up-and-coming star, Kid Psycho. Do we have any takers tonight?"

No reply.

"Come on, gentlemen of Smallville. You can't all be overage and overweight. Are you telling me this tintabulating town can't raise one single soul bold enough to face the Kid?"

Theatrically, Don shook his head and tutted noisily. "Oh man, wait till I tell them this over in Otisville tomorrow!"

He reached into the waistband of his tights and pulled out a sheet of paper. He made a great play of unfolding it, peering at it as if he couldn't read it, piquing the crowd's curiosity.

"Well, well, well," he said at last, feigning surprise. "Smallville *does* have a saving grace. It seems one man *is* willing to put his head above the parapet. One man *is* willing to impress the ladies, and put his all on the line for a considerable cash reward."

He looked up into the rows of seats, shielding his eyes from the spotlights, as if seeking out a particular face in the darkness.

"Mr. Clark Kent! Please—come on down!"

CHAPTER 19

As the echoes of Don Breed's voice died away, Phil laughed out loud. He clutched his belly with both hands and rocked rhythmically back and forward in his seat.

Ed, Rob, and Pete stared at him, wondering what the heck was wrong with him.

Then they got it.

There was respect in Ed's voice as he whispered: "Oh, dude. You are the Main Man. You are the *King!*"

Lana looked at Clark in surprise. "I didn't know you were a closet wrestler."

"I'm not," Clark all but sputtered. "I don't know anything about this!"

Same way I didn't know I was "volunteering" for the charity calendar, Clark thought.

He knew immediately who had put his name forward. Phil Meara.

The spotlight hovered close to them, moving in slow, lazy circles over the heads of the crowd.

"I read about this Kid Psycho on the Internet," Chloe hissed. "He's tough as nails. If you need a thousand bucks that badly, Clark, Smallville Savings and Loan is doing great deals for students."

"Ha-ha."

"And don't forget," Chloe added mysteriously, "the curse."

"But I didn't volunteer," Clark protested hotly. "Somebody put my name down—but it wasn't me."

"Then ignore it," Lana advised, settling back in her seat. "This whole thing is getting very silly, anyway."

The spotlight danced over the people seated around them. Several teenagers got to their feet, yelling and pointing in Clark's direction.

A second later, he was illuminated in the powerful beam of light. Center stage. Caught like a butterfly pinned to a board.

"Clark Kent," the master of ceremonies' voice boomed. "Come on down, o ye of stout heart and muscular physique."

Laughter rippled through the auditorium. Several voices called out, echoing Don Breed: "Go for it, Kent!" "Have you *seen* Kid Psycho? You *deserve* a thousand bucks!" "Do it for Smallville!"

Clark froze, not knowing what to do. Humiliate himself in front of Lana and the whole town by backing down from the bout? Or humiliate himself by going into the ring and making a complete fool of himself?

Some choice!

It was Phil who made his mind up for him.

"Nah," he catcalled, his voice cutting above the general noise. "Kent's a coward. Five bucks says he won't fight!"

Stung to anger, Clark shot to his feet and raised a hand in the air.

"I'm here," he yelled.

Once more applause erupted through the gymnasium.

"Clark?" Lana was incredulous. "Are you insane? What do you think you're *doing*?"

Clark shrugged, wondering precisely that himself. "It looks like I don't have much choice, Lana. Wish me luck."

"Brother, you'll need it," Chloe said, shaking her head sadly. "Want me to write your obituary for the *Torch*?"

"Thanks, Chloe. You have a real knack for making me feel good."

"I'll say you were an unwilling volunteer," she shot back. "You'll be a hero!"

Lana was shaking her head slowly, as if still unable to come to terms with this.

"Luck, Lana?" Clark prompted, moving past her toward the aisle.

Lana looked startled. She thought for a moment—then blew him a kiss off the tips of her fingers.

This is how champions must feel, Clark told himself, as he made his way down to the ring amidst tumultuous applause. *Except for the embarrassment, of course. And maybe the fear of making a total idiot of myself!*

Flashes strobed him as spectators sought to capture the moment on camera.

"Yeah, take his picture." Phil's voice rose above the din. "It'll be something to remember him by!"

Five minutes later, Clark stood in the center of the ring fitted out in purple tights and matching spangled tank top.

He'd been taken back to the changing rooms and offered a choice of cheesy costumes.

"I'll pass on the hornet," he said, indicating a black-

and-yellow-striped Spandex monstrosity. He also gave the thumbs down to a red and blue all-over outfit, with an oversize 'S' highlighted in a diamond.

"It used to belong to SavageMan," the roadie told him. "Remember him?"

Clark shook his head. "He got a new job?"

"Sort of. Kid Psycho broke his arm. In three places."

Clark pointed to the purple outfit in silence. The anger that had welled up in him at Phil's gibe had dissipated.

Now he was wondering what on Earth he'd let himself in for.

"Introducing, in the blue corner, the bravest sophomore student at Smallville High. Ladeez and gentlemen, give it up for Cla-aaaaaaaark Kent!"

Self-consciously, Clark raised his hand in acknowledgment as the crowd cheered his name, drowning out the catcalls from Phil and Ed.

"And in the red corner, Clark's opponent tonight. Weighing in at two hundred pounds, the man who has won all of his past twenty-three contests—show your appreciation, please, for Ki-iiiiiid Psycho!"

Brian Etienne—aka Kid Psycho—flexed his impressive biceps and swelled his chest as he stalked the ring, snarling at the crowd. Everybody knew he was the villain of the piece. He sneered and shook a fist at them, encouraging the chorus of boos and hisses to grow louder.

He walked up to Clark, looming over the teenager, bending slightly to thrust his face closer. "Remember me, clumsy?" he asked quietly.

Clark gulped and nodded reluctantly. It was the guy he'd spilled coffee on in the Talon.

"Good. I guess I don't need to tell you—expect no favors."

Clark sighed inaudibly. Before he could think of some witty comeback, the referee stepped between them. He ran through his usual preliminary spiel, then sent them back to their corners.

If I could use my powers, Clark thought, *I'm sure I could take him down with no problems. Superspeed . . . superstrength . . . I could probably do it with one hand tied behind my back.*

The bell rang, and Clark walked forward, extending his hand in a goodwill gesture.

Next thing he knew, he was flipping through the air, to land with a sickening thump on the canvas.

Half-winded, he struggled to his feet.

I wasn't expecting that. He's fast. I'll have to watch out for—

Before he'd even finished the thought, Kid Psycho gripped his wrist, twisted, and sent him crashing back down.

Kid Psycho's living up to his name. He's taking no prisoners. It's about time I got my act together!

Each time Clark hit the canvas, Phil and Ed and Rob cheered and whooped at the top of their voices.

Only Pete remained silent, hunched over in his seat, feeling lousy and ashamed.

"Give it a rest," he hissed at the trio, aware someplace inside that he was blaming them for the shame he felt at seeing Clark humiliated.

"Relax, Petey. I know you and Kent used to be buddies—but I told you, it's all a fix," Ed assured him. "Kid

Psycho knows how to make it look good without *really* hurting him."

Of course, Clark *couldn't* be hurt—Pete knew that. His alien body conferred powers on him that mere humans couldn't begin to emulate. But Clark couldn't use those powers in plain view. And with no training or skills in wrestling, he was the perfect patsy for Kid Psycho's fluent moves.

Pete winced in sympathy as, in the ring, Clark's tumbling body once more shook the canvas.

"Ouch!" Chloe flinched, seeing her friend slammed down on his back for what seemed the tenth time. "Even if it's choreographed, that's *gotta* hurt!"

Lana had her hands over her eyes, unable to watch any more of the punishment being inflicted in the ring. "Poor Clark! That brute will kill him," she muttered. "You've got to stop this, Chloe!"

"Me?" Chloe's eyes stayed glued to the ring in horrible fascination. "Like, my ringcraft is strictly limited to Hunk Admiration. And you have to admit, Clark is looking pretty hot. Apart from losing, that is."

Lana risked a peek through the gaps between her fingers. Kid Psycho was delivering a forearm smash to Clark's chest, a ferocious blow that sent him staggering back against the ropes.

"Please, Chloe." Lana's voice cracked, surprising even herself at how close she was to tears. "I can't bear to see Clark being hurt any more."

"What the heck can we do?" Chloe said impatiently. "Nobody made Clark go into the ring." Her voice softened. "Calm down, Lana. Kid Psycho's a professional.

It's his job to make it look like he's delivering a beating."

She thought for a moment. "Look, if Clark was really hurt; he wouldn't keep getting up, would he?" she asked, as if that clinched it.

Lana looked far from convinced.

"Having fun, clumsy?" Kid Psycho muttered.

He gripped both Clark's forearms in his powerful hands. Even as he felt the boy brace himself to resist, the wrestler was falling backward, pulling Clark with him. His feet came up to take Clark in the chest, sending the boy soaring over his head.

The ring shook as he landed.

The crowd groaned, and Kid Psycho turned to roar at the ringside seats. He threw several mock-punches, gesturing with his other hand for the groaners to get up into the ring with him.

Brian grinned to himself. *That'll teach him to splatter me with coffee. Now, a few more throws to show him not to be such a lippy brat. Then it's time for the coup de grace.*

Clark soared high over Kid Psycho's shoulder and crashed headfirst to the canvas.

He rolled over once and pushed himself into a sitting position, clutching the bottom rope. He'd seen enough combat sport on television to know that when you were hurt, you should stay down until you recover.

Not that he was hurt, exactly. More that his head was spinning, his senses reeling, totally befuddled and disoriented by the series of vicious throws and falls Kid Psycho had used against him.

His body wasn't completely invulnerable—at least, not as far as he knew—but it was plenty strong enough to resist anything the wrestler could do to him.

He shook his head, trying to clear it, desperate to stop the multiple images that swarmed and spun in his field of vision.

Dimly, he heard the referee's voice. "Six—"

Maybe I should just stay down. Let him count me out. Get it over with.

"Seven—"

Humiliated in front of the whole school. "A brave defeat," they'll say.

Things were starting to come back into focus.

"Eight—"

Made to look like a clown in front of Phil . . .

"Nine—"

A chump in front of Lana.

He was on his feet before the referee could finish the count.

Kid Psycho looked displeased—not that he often seemed to look any other way. Obviously that last forearm smash and Irish Whip were meant to be the final move. He brushed aside the referee and lunged at Clark.

Clark let the angry wrestler grab his wrist. But this time, when he tried to snap it downward, Clark resisted and held firm. Not with all his strength, but enough.

He saw the surprise in Kid Psycho's eyes.

Clark didn't give him time to figure out what was happening. He jerked his own wrist backward, breaking the wrestler's grip. Then he grabbed Kid Psycho's arm and hand, applying pressure under the elbow just as the Kid had done to him a dozen times.

Kid Psycho yelped with pain. With a mighty effort, he kicked up and back, his whole body sweeping off the floor in a backward somersault. Halfway through the turn, Clark released him.

Not expecting it, without Clark's arm as pivot, Kid Psycho's own weight brought him crashing down face-first on the canvas with bone-jarring force. He twitched and lay still.

The cheer that went up from the crowd could have lifted the roof. Even Lana was on her feet, stamping and clapping and chanting his name.

The referee counted Kid Psycho out.

CHAPTER 20

The prize-giving passed in a cacophony of cheering and a blizzard of flashbulbs, as Smallville recorded the moment for posterity.

Don Breed raised Clark's arm in triumph, proclaiming him: "The Toughest Teen In Town! Ladeez and gentlemen, do not—I repeat DO NOT—tangle with this man!"

Beaming broadly, Clark accepted the thousand dollars in crisp, new notes. But he drew a blank when he tried to find a pocket in his costume to put the money in.

"Where do you guys carry your wallets?" he asked jokingly.

"We don't usually need 'em," Don told him. "This is the first time ever we've had to pay out."

A couple of photographers from the local paper climbed into the ring, seeking some close shots of Clark. As they posed together, Don went on: "So tell me, son— how *did* you beat the Kid?"

Clark considered. He couldn't confess it was a tiny, judicious use of his superstrength that had won the contest for him.

"I paid attention to what Kid Psycho was doing to me," he said at last. "When I got the chance, I tried to do the same thing to him."

"In spades, son. In spades."

Don parted the ringside ropes, and Clark clambered out between them.

"If you're looking for work, kid," the wrestling boss told him, "you could do worse than the grapple game."

"Thanks, but no thanks," Clark replied. He looked down at his purple-sequined outfit. "Despite appearances, I'm not really the showman type."

Don announced a fifteen-minute interval before the main bouts, and the houselights came up.

He walked over to where Rudy Sillars was squeezing a dripping sponge over the groggy Kid Psycho's head and shoulders.

"What happened, Kid?"

Brian started to shake his head, but the motion hurt too much. "I dunno," he confessed. "I couldn't throw him. I just sort of . . . lost my strength. Either that, or the kid was King Kong in disguise."

"Look to your laurels," Don told him. "Guys who cost me a thousand bucks don't stay employed for very long."

Chicken feed, compared to what's coming my way, Etienne thought. But, wisely, he said nothing. He'd collect what was coming to him and split, leave them a man short halfway through a major tour. He'd laugh in Don Breed's face if the Mountain Man dared to complain.

"Better clear your head," Don commented as he turned to walk away again. "You still have to fight HammerHead in the second half."

Half a hundred hands reached out to clap Clark on the back as, once again in his regular clothes, he went to reclaim his seat.

Lana rose to her feet to greet him, a look of intense relief on her face. To his astonishment, she threw her arms around him and hugged him.

"Oh, Clark! I'm so glad you're all right. I was so worried about you!"

Clark made the most of the moment, holding her warm body against him, breathing in the faint smell of her perfume.

If this is the kind of reception I get, maybe I should listen to Don Breed and take up wrestling!

Lana gently disengaged herself and stepped back. She raised an admonishing finger. "You should never have gotten into that ring," she scolded. "You could have been seriously hurt."

"No, he couldn't," Chloe put in, sounding slightly exasperated. "I told you—Kid Psycho knows exactly what he's doing. Am I right, Clark? These throws didn't hurt you, did they?"

"We-ell . . ." Clark debated telling them just how close Kid Psycho came to living up to his name. If it hadn't been for his superpowers, he'd be a hospital case. But in the end he merely said, "No. I guess not."

He sat back down, basking in the glow of victory. The thousand dollars in his pants pocket wasn't exactly unwelcome, either. And he was over the moon at how Lana had reacted to his predicament.

It doesn't get much better than this.

If Chloe hadn't been sitting between them, he was sure he and Lana would be holding hands.

He twisted a little in his seat, his eyes sweeping the spectators in search of Pete. There he was, talking with Ed and Phil. Clark wondered how Phil felt about his triumph, especially as it was obviously Phil who'd signed him up for the fight.

Clark didn't normally eavesdrop on his friends, but he figured that, on this occasion, it was justified. He focused all his thoughts on his hearing, screening out the hubbub of the arena, trying to zero in on Pete's crowd.

"It's a stinkin' fix," Phil fumed. "It's gotta be. That dweeb Kent isn't capable of beating a guy like Kid Psycho."

"Chill out, man," Ed told him.

"But he won the thousand bucks! He got Shirley, too!"

"We'll enjoy ourselves more tomorrow," Ed promised.

"Where we meeting?" Rob wanted to know.

"The old Jakobs place. Noon." Ed laughed. "Nice and private. Be there, dudes, or be square."

The third bout was athletic and dramatic enough, but still an anticlimax after Clark's valiant victory.

Kid Psycho wasn't in the best of moods after his unscheduled defeat. He beat HammerHead by two submissions to one fall. HammerHead's arm would hurt for days.

But the triumph did little to cheer up Kid Psycho. He just couldn't figure what that schoolkid had done to him.

"Clark? There's something you ought to know."

Chloe spoke reluctantly. She didn't want to be the good fairy who brought Lana and Clark together—she'd rather have him all for herself. But, by the same token, she knew she couldn't stand in her friend's way.

Lana had slipped out to buy some drinks in the break

between bouts, and Chloe waited till her friend was out of earshot before turning to Clark.

"You want to borrow a thousand dollars?" he asked mischievously.

"No, you clown. It's about Lana."

Ha! That piqued his interest!

"She told me she's jealous of Shirley Grainger," Chloe went on. "She was quite . . . emotional about it."

"Like . . . ?" Clark prompted.

"Like, crying. Like, saying she didn't realize how much you meant to her. Like . . . what more do you need me to say, Clark?"

"Just keep talking, Chloe. It's music to my ears."

"She wouldn't even *look* when Kid Psycho was tossing you all around the ring. She kept saying he would kill you, so we had to stop the fight."

A faraway look came into Clark's eyes.

"Are you all right?" There was suspicion in Chloe's voice. "You look like you're in some sort of trance."

Clark smiled. "I guess I am."

Some of the sparkle had gone out of the night.

Don Breed—the Mountain Man himself—did his best to resurrect the magic, by fighting an exemplary bout with his longtime sparring partner Stan Marks, alias Monstroso.

Both men tested each other to the extreme, putting everything they had into the display. When the referee finally announced a draw, nobody felt cheated.

Least of all, the crowd.

*   *   *

The evening over, the spectators filed out into the balmy night.

Don joined Tom at the sales booth. There were still a few stragglers picking up their souvenirs. One saw Don, and had him sign a copy of his book.

"So how'd we do, Tom?"

"Fantastic, boss." Tom gestured to a shoe box stuffed with money, out of sight under the counter. "I'd say you made your thousand dollars back, with interest. Just a pity we didn't have a Clark Kent T-shirt for sale, too. We'd have cleaned up."

"You said earlier you wanted to speak to me?"

Tom frowned. "It could be something, or nothing, boss. You know how Sam Fozter always splits off on his own when we hit town? Well, I've been getting kind of suspicious about it. So I followed him this afternoon."

"And . . . ?"

"He went to the church." Now that Tom was voicing his suspicions, Don could see he was beginning to doubt them himself. "He was inside for a long time," he added lamely.

"You think he was . . . ?" Don Breed purposefully let his words hang.

"Stealing."

"Any proof?"

"No. Just a hunch. There's something . . . underhanded about Foz. He doesn't hang with the other guys." He started boxing up the remainders, as the last of the spectators filed out.

Don stroked his chin thoughtfully. "Leave it to me, Tom."

*   *   *

It was getting late by the time the roadies and wrestlers had dismantled and packed all of their gear. Amazing how much space it took up in the back of the coach.

"Beer and poker, gentlemen?" Don pulled a pack of playing cards from his pocket. "We got a few hours before we need to leave. It's 150 miles to Otisville, and we're putting on a Saturday matinee as well as the main show."

"Oh, man." Tony Vasquez groaned, massaging his arm muscles. "I *ache*."

"Where you going, Kid?" Don asked, as Brian Etienne started down the steps at the front of the coach.

"Guess that's my business, boss. Right?"

"Make sure you're back before we leave."

"I will."

The coach door closed behind him with a sharp hiss of compressed air.

Later, Clark lay awake in his bed for a long time, going over the events of the night.

When he fell asleep, it was to dream of Lana.

And Shirley.

They were having a tug of war, using him as the rope.

Then they both let go.

Even later that night, Lex Luthor stood in his suite with his back to the window, confronting a part of his life he thought he'd left behind long ago.

"It's been a long time, Lex."

"Six years, Brian? You're looking well."

"I look like what I am, Lex."

"A debt collector?"

Despite himself, a smile played round the corners of Etienne's mouth. "A pro wrestler, Lex. A good one, too. Guess the receptionist recognized me because she said you didn't want callers, but let me in anyway."

Lex gestured to the chairs set round the coffee table, still stacked with untidy piles of books. "Excuse my rudeness. Sit. I'm surprised to see you after all this time."

The duo sat down opposite each other, still fencing with each other, sounding each other out. A lot of things can change in six years.

"Drink?" Lex offered.

Brian shook his head. "I'll get straight to the point, Lex. I'm here to collect what you owe me."

Lex raised a quizzical eyebrow. "I owe you?" he repeated. "But surely that was paid last time we saw each other . . . ?"

"The price went up, Lex."

"Retrospectively? Every retailer in the country would like to learn that trick, Brian."

"Listen." Etienne's voice dropped an octave, and he did little to disguise his hostility. "You got caught with cocaine. I took the rap."

"We were young and stupid."

"I was young and in jail."

"You got the twenty thousand I promised you." Lex shrugged. "Case closed, Brian."

"No, Lex. I did four years in prison. Five thousand bucks per year. A hundred a week for living in a concrete box with lunatics and losers."

Etienne's eyes flashed as he remembered the hardships and indignities he'd suffered. The indignities that had spurred him to start bodybuilding and working out. That had eventually resulted in him becoming a professional wrestler.

"Fourteen bucks a day, Lex, for living in Hell. Retrospective-ly," he added mockingly, drawing the word out, "that was not a good deal."

"You took it."

Etienne leaned forward in his seat. "I want the same again, Lex. And even that's cheap for the time that was stolen out of my life."

Lex steepled his fingers together and gazed levelly at his former acquaintance, completely unintimidated. "And if I refuse, Brian . . . ?"

Etienne's clenched fist slammed into the open palm of his other hand with a crack that echoed sharply in the room. "Sorry, Lex," he said, and there was sincerity in his voice despite his threatening action. "I liked you. I still do. We had some good times together. But I have to get out of the situation I'm in . . . and you're my ticket."

The sneer returned to Etienne's mouth. "Besides, what's twenty grand to you? Chump change. Your dad's a billionaire."

My dad's a monster, Lex thought. *And maybe the biggest tightwad you ever met.*

Aloud, he said, "I'll need an hour or so to raise it."

Brian got to his feet. "I'll be back."

"No. Don't come to the hotel again. I'll meet you someplace."

"The schoolyard. One hour."

He opened the room door and stepped out into the hallway before turning for one last comment. "Be there," he said affably, but there was a cold, hard glint in his eyes.

Lex Luthor knew a threat, even when it was uttered with a smile.

CHAPTER 21

"What the hell do you think you're doing?" Sam Fozter blustered. "Those are my things."

They'd been playing their usual game of post-fight poker when Don had excused himself and disappeared to the far end of the coach. Five minutes later, he still hadn't returned.

With a knot of apprehension growing in his stomach, Foz had followed his boss. He found Don back in the personal quarters, rifling through his open suitcase.

"Maybe they are your things, maybe they aren't," Don said cryptically. He pulled several large, padded envelopes out of Foz's battered case. They were all stuffed and sealed, all addressed to the same place: Barney Fozter in San Francisco. "Looks like you've been running a sweet little racket, Foz."

"I dunno what you mean."

Don ripped the parcel tape off the first envelope and slit it open. Curiously, he examined its contents. An old leather-bound journal—the one Foz had lifted from the church that afternoon.

"I'm not stupid, Foz. You've been using the tour as cover, to go robbing. Then you parcel up whatever you've stolen and send it to your brother back in 'Frisco."

As he spoke, Don slit open more of the envelopes and

lifted out their contents. A silver chain and emerald pendant that Foz had stolen from a jeweler in Metropolis. A small Japanese stone carving and a gold cigarette case that had come from a city antique store. A Rolex watch.

Sam felt suddenly afraid. Yes, that's exactly what he'd been doing. But now he was faced with the price of his crimes, he didn't feel nearly so confident.

"Y-you're not going to hand me over to the cops, are you?" he stuttered.

Don shook his head. "That's not the kind of publicity this tour needs. No. You'll tell us where you got this stuff, and we'll send it back to them. As for you, Foz—"

The Mountain Man stretched to his full height, and loomed threateningly over Foz. A look of terror crossed the latter's face, and he cringed away from the bigger man.

"You are off the bus."

Foz was frozen to the spot with fear. Don was a fearsome sight; a man like that could crush a skull with one blow.

"Write down where you stole those things, then go."

Sam hurried to obey, scrawling the names of the shops and museums where he'd stolen his haul of treasures on a piece of paper.

When he finished, he looked up at Don. "My belongings—" he began.

Don snatched up the suitcase, and hurled it at him.

"You have ten seconds. Go."

"But—we're in the middle of nowhere," Foz whined. "I got no money. I don't know anybody around here. What the hell am I supposed to do?"

"That's your problem. Five seconds."

Don clenched his massive fists, and Foz took the hint. Muttering under his breath, he got down off the coach and strode away cursing, into an alien night.

Alone again in his suite, Lex Luthor pondered his problem.

And how to get out of it.

Lex was no coward. He had a little training in basic martial arts, and what he lacked in skill he made up for in courage. Even so, he knew he'd take a fearsome beating if this quarrel with Brian deteriorated into actual physical violence.

Come on, Lex urged himself. *I've being trying to convince myself I'm a genius. So how about a little master-play?*

What he needed was something to extricate him from the situation. Something, preferably, that showed him a profit, too. But there was nothing in his business books that covered a situation like this. As *Cassandra's Secret* had revealed, the nitty-gritty, bottom line of all reality was: You're on your own. Figure it out for yourself.

Lex felt a thrill course through him. The human mind *wants* to solve problems. That's what it had evolved for.

And then he had it, like a lightbulb going on over his head.

He went down to the lobby, in search of a phone to call his lawyer.

Michael Grindlay waited until he was sure Moira was fast asleep, and slid soundlessly out of bed. Leaving his slippers by the bedside, he padded across the carpet in his bare feet.

Twenty seconds later, he was standing in his study. He had things to get ready for tomorrow, and Moira must know nothing about it.

He pulled three or four old volumes from his bookshelf and stacked them on the desk. He'd brought a half-dozen small candles in from the church earlier, and he arranged them on the desk, too. From a drawer he took a tiny phial of holy water he'd siphoned from the baptismal font.

And the journal. He needed the journal.

Strange, it wasn't where he'd left it. Maybe Moira had come in, and—no. Moira had been at the arena with him all evening. When they got home, she'd made them both a cup of hot chocolate they'd drunk in awkward silence, then gone to bed.

Perhaps he'd dropped it on the floor. He got down on his hands and knees and searched underneath the desk. Nothing.

It wasn't in any of the drawers, or on the bookshelves. Then he noticed that his stack of books had been moved. They weren't in the same order in which he'd left them.

With a growing sense of horror, he began to realize he'd been robbed.

Brian Etienne stood ramrod-straight outside the schoolyard.

He had no doubt Lex would come. He'd always been a man of his word, even when they were running wild. He'd bring the money, too, and maybe Brian would be able to start on that new life he'd always dreamed of.

I didn't like threatening him like that, but I didn't have a lot of choice.

He nodded with satisfaction as he saw a figure approaching, light from a streetlamp reflecting off his bald head.

"Good to see you. Did you do as I said?"

"I did." Lex pulled a bulging envelope from inside his loose-fitting designer jacket. "Twenty thousand dollars."

Casually, Lex threw the package down on the sidewalk, about six feet away from where they stood. It landed with a slap.

Etienne was puzzled, but Lex didn't give him time to ask questions.

"If you want it," Lex said steadily, "you'll have to fight me for it."

"What?" Etienne was astonished. "In case it escaped your notice, Lex, I'm bigger than you. Heavier. And I wasn't kidding about being a pro wrestler. I'll chew you up."

"Maybe so," Lex admitted, with a slight shrug. "But I worked for that money. It's mine. I can't allow you to steal it from me without putting up a fight. That's not my style."

"Don't be stupid. I'd kill you, Lex."

Lex's eyes bored into his, neither of them willing to look away first.

"If you want the money that badly, Brian, maybe that's what you'll have to do."

Brian scratched his head through his spiky hair. What did he do now? This hadn't figured in any of the scenarios he'd imagined.

"Of course," Lex went on smoothly, "there's always an alternative."

He reached into the other side of his jacket and pulled

out another, bulkier envelope. He tossed it down carelessly, to land beside the first on the curbside.

Brian's eyes narrowed. What was going on here? What kind of trick was this?

"There's forty thousand in that envelope, Brian. It could be yours, too—and without the fight, I should add."

"If . . . ?"

"If you allow me to invest it in you."

"Invest? In me?" Etienne snorted. "You must be crazy."

"Maybe I am. But look at it from where I'm standing," Lex said. "It took me a long time to realize it, but I should never have let you take the rap for me. I should have had the guts to do my own prison time. I haven't touched drugs since then—and I bet you haven't, either. But you're right—a hundred dollars a week for going to jail was an insult. I owe you a lot more than that."

Lex's eyes never wavered from his. "But I can't let you take money from me by force, Brian. Or coercion. That would be making criminals out of both of us. So let's say I invest the whole sixty thou in you. You start a business—wrestling tours, martial arts school, whatever you fancy. You call the shots."

Brian couldn't quite believe what he was hearing. "What's in it for you?" he asked, feeling it was somehow inadequate.

"Silent partner. No interference. Fifty percent of the profit. Deal?"

Lex held out his hand, but Brian didn't move.

"Or would you rather fight to the death for it?" Lex added.

Brian laughed, and stretched out his own hand to shake Lex's. "Deal," he said, bewildered at the speed at which events had moved. "Just one thing. Tell me I'm not dreaming."

In answer, Lex pulled a sheet of paper from his pocket. "Legal contract," he explained. "Read it, and sign when you're ready."

A slow grin spread over Brian's face. "You got a lawyer out of bed at *this* time of night? Man, you *must* be rich!"

In the schoolyard, the coach engine was ticking over.

Otisville was waiting. They all needed a good night's sleep. Two full shows the next day.

Sam was long gone, and Don was glancing impatiently at his watch when Kid Psycho returned.

"Five more minutes, and you'd have been left stranded," Don told him.

"Don't matter, boss. I'm off the tour."

"You're off your head, is what you are," Don snapped. "Come on. We don't have time for jokes."

"No joke, boss. I'm staying here. I got an offer I couldn't refuse."

Don stared at him in disbelief. "In Smallville?" he said doubtfully. "But—you can't just ditch the tour."

"Sorry, boss. I can. And I have."

Somehow, Brian's anger with his boss had gone. It wasn't Don's fault Brian had always hated working for other folk. Lex's offer was the best chance he'd ever had in his life.

He had no intention of throwing it away.

CHAPTER 22

By half past sunrise, Clark had his whole day's chores done.

Logs were cut and stacked. The animals were cleaned, fed and watered. The slow leak in the water tank was fixed. And the truck was loaded with the dozens of crates they'd be taking to market.

When Martha and Jonathan came downstairs, they found waffles and honey waiting, with a pot of coffee warming on the kitchen stove.

"Why, Clark," his mother said, "how thoughtful of you."

"That's okay, Mom. The chores are all done, too."

"Great," his father said. "You certainly haven't allowed winning a thousand dollars to go to your head." There was a long pause, then, "What's the favor?"

Clark did his best to sound aggrieved. "I knew Mom was upset by those telephone calls last night—"

Their phone had rung off the hook the night before. Reporters and photographers, on the trail of a story. His parents had been irritated at first, and finally angry, when the callers refused to take "no" for an answer. The Smallville Curse was big news, and they wanted to talk with anybody even remotely involved—even a farmer's wife who'd run down a dog.

"So," Clark went on, "I thought I'd give you a little treat, start the day well, you know, like that."

"Sure." Jonathan raised one eyebrow. "Now—what's the favor?"

All three burst out laughing.

"You can see right through me," Clark admitted. "I want to skip market today."

"Must be something important," his mother said pensively. "A girl, maybe. Lana? Am I right?"

"No. Shirley. And that's tonight."

Clark took a deep breath. Lying was anathema to him, yet ever since this whole drugs business began with Pete, he seemed to be doing little else. "I'm hoping to meet up with Pete."

Of course, it wasn't exactly a lie. But it was unlikely he'd be "meeting up" with Pete in any way his parents could imagine.

"Haven't seen a lot of Pete lately," Jonathan observed. He poured coffee into the cups Clark had set out and passed them around. "Is everything all right between you two?"

"Mmm," Clark said noncommittally. "There's just something I need to sort out with him."

"Then you go ahead, son," his father told him. He sipped appreciatively at his coffee. "Friends are the best investment you can make in life."

"Are you sure you don't want me to call the doctor?"

Moira Grindlay's tone was softer than it had been since their quarrel. She put down a wicker tray of orange juice and thinly buttered toast on the bedside table.

Her husband squirmed under the bedclothes. "No,

dear. I'm just feeling out of sorts. Too much stress, I shouldn't wonder. This has been a week we won't forget in a hurry."

"If you're really sure, Michael . . . ?"

"Yes, dear. A few hours' sleep and I'll be fine. You run along to the market. I'm only sorry I can't go with you."

"I'll manage."

She threw him a last, concerned glance, and left the room.

The Reverend Grindlay lay still for a long time, the warmth of the duvet taking the edge off the chill of fear that prickled his skin. He'd never felt dread before, but that was the only word that came anywhere close to describing his feelings.

Dread.

The knowledge that he was going to confront evil terrified him.

He summoned all his strength, and murmured a brief prayer. He rolled out of bed, dressed himself, and quickly made his way to his study.

He'd checked everywhere the previous night, but there was no doubt the journal was missing. He'd wracked his mind, trying to work out what might have happened to it, but in vain. He'd just have to proceed without it.

Originally, he had intended to hold the ritual inside the church. But something had changed his mind. It seemed wrong, somehow, to introduce an evil to that hallowed space—even if his purpose was to negate that very evil.

Instead, his study would suffice.

Doing his best to still the tremble in his arm, he

reached for the stack of books on the desk. He knew exactly which pages he needed to consult, and he laid them open where he could see.

He stroked the little green cross in his pocket, and its warm glow gave him fresh heart. He said another prayer, of protection this time, then began to chant the words his predecessors in the Church had used to fight against demonic incursion.

Unfamiliar, old-fashioned phrases tripped awkwardly off his tongue.

Images of devils and demons swirled in his mind. Their faces leered at him, snarling and baring their teeth, as if defying him to move against them. Their eyes flashed red sparks.

Michael could almost taste his own fear.

His voice faltered, his lips suddenly too dry to speak. He licked them with the tip of his tongue.

He steeled himself against the visions, praying fervently that his faith would protect him, and read on.

An exorcism—in Smallville! He didn't know whether to laugh, or cry.

The sun was high in the sky.

Clark sped through the cornfields, his legs moving like pistons as he cleared sixty miles an hour. The cornstalks blurred together, forming a long, green tunnel as he sprinted between the rows. He loved the feeling of exhilaration being able to really open up gave him.

But there was little joy in him.

His sensitive hearing had picked up Ed Wall's words at the gym the night before. The gang was getting together at the old Jakobs' cornmeal factory off the highway. Its owners had gone bankrupt a decade earlier, crushed by the deep pockets of the big operators. The factory was the only testament to the fact they'd ever been there.

A concrete box on a concrete platform, weeds and briars growing through the cracks. Like a neglected tomb.

Clark saw the building ahead, and slowed instantly to a walk.

"No big party this week," Ed told his acolytes, gathered round him in the cool of the old factory. "Strictly the Main Men chilling out."

Sunlight streamed in through broken windows, casting pools of golden light on the debris-strewn floor, reflecting off the oily water in a rusting drum. Parts for machines with forgotten names and purposes lay in jumbled heaps in the semidarkness. Here and there, a ceiling beam had collapsed.

Ed pulled out a polyethylene bag, and carefully tipped out its contents. Five of the luscious green berries.

"One each," he told them. "One for backup."

Ed. Phil. Rob. And me, Pete thought unhappily. He remembered his resolution not to take any more. He'd even considered telling Ed that to his face.

Easier thought than done.

"Come on, Petey," Ed challenged him when he hesitated. "What's wrong? Not afraid, are you?"

"Why would I be afraid?" Pete demanded hotly.

He took the small green fruit between thumb and forefinger, careful not to damage it. Feeling Ed's eyes on him, he popped it in his mouth with a flourish, and turned away.

The road to Hell is paved with good intentions, he thought.

And then, out of nowhere, Lex Luthor's words came back to him. What he'd said at the end of his lecture. Something like:

"When you stand alone in the cold, impersonal cosmos, there's nobody to help you. No gods. No gurus. No teachers. No friends. There's only one person you can rely on: yourself."

The words had made an impression on Pete at the time. But only now could he see what they really meant. Nobody else could do anything to save him. He held the future in his own hands. Only by his own actions could he ever change anything.

There was another point Lex had made, about essences. Pete tried it now, asking himself: What is the essence of taking drugs?

Pleasure. Being part of a group. Rebellion. No. These were all superficial answers.

The real essence of taking drugs was escaping from reality. Hiding the truth behind an intoxicating smoke screen.

Lex was right. If he wanted things to change in his life, only he could change them.

Surreptitiously, so the others wouldn't see, Pete spat the berry out into his palm and dropped it into his shirt pocket.

The Reverend Grindlay spoke the last words of the incantation and waited until his voice died away.

He crossed himself, said a prayer of cleansing, and left

the study. He had to be back in bed before Moira returned.

It had gone well, though. Throughout the ritual, he'd felt increasingly confident that it would work. Even without the journal on which to focus, he was sure it had been effective. The Smallville Curse would trouble nobody again. The evil was gone.

His footsteps were a lot lighter on the way upstairs than they had been coming down.

Ten yards from the factory wall, Clark flexed his leg muscles—and soared upward like a jump jet. He landed lithely on the roof, picking his way across broken struts and loose tiles to reach a skylight.

He'd tried peering in through a ground-floor window, realizing instantaneously that he'd be backlit by the sun. If any of them looked his way, it would be impossible to miss him.

Hence the surveillance from above.

The skylight's glass panes had long since disappeared, victim of the weather, or vandals. Clark crouched by it, holding on to a decaying strut for support as he craned to look into the factory below.

It was an eerie scene, with dust swirling in shafts of sunlight and rusting metal everywhere. Like the building was still there, but its heart had long since disappeared.

He saw Phil and Rob take their drugs, heard Ed taunting Pete, and saw Pete put something in his mouth.

Pain stabbed his heart. His best friend, reduced to this—and all Clark could do was spy on him. Well, this was the last time. One way or another, he was going to have things out with Pete that day. He'd *force* him to listen, if need be.

There was a screech of metal as the strut he was holding sheared away from its support bracket. Thrown off balance, Clark tried to stop himself from sliding down the roof. His thrashing hand gripped another stanchion—and it, too, promptly ripped away.

The whole section of roof collapsed with a teeth-grinding shriek.

Unable to halt his fall, Clark plunged down through the air and landed with a bone jarring thud on the factory floor.

CHAPTER 23

Half-winded by the fall, Clark lay on his back on the factory floor and looked up.

Ed was standing over him. The pupils of the football player's eyes were enormous, and there was a leer on his face.

"Seems we have a spy," he said menacingly. "Right, 007? What gives? Some kind of *Revenge of the Nerds* scenario?"

Clark gasped for breath. His body might be nearly invulnerable to harm, but the thirty-foot fall hadn't done him any good. A shaft of sunlight shone in his face, making it hard for him to see.

"What'll we do with him, Ed?" Rob's face came into view. "We don't want him telling anybody."

"Let's show him what life really is all about." In the strange, ethereal light, Ed's face was near-feral. "Let's turn him on."

Phil giggled, and gave a whoop. "Okay! Let's show him Smallville is only the beginning. It's time for him to *fly.*"

Clark's reeling senses were starting to clear. But before he realized what they were talking about, they were on him.

Phil and Rob each pinned a shoulder to the ground. In Clark's dazed state—and with their own strength enhanced by drugs—they were able to hold him fast, despite his struggles.

Ed was laughing as he pulled out a plastic bag.

Pete stared, aghast, at the nightmare unfolding before him. He watched in total disbelief as Ed took the final berry from his bag, and held it up so Clark could see.

"You're about to join the Main Men, Kent."

"Stop!" The word burst from Pete's mouth. "You can't do this. You can't force him to take drugs!"

Ed made a loud clucking noise. "Going chicken on us, Petey?" he taunted. "Well, you just stand back and watch. The fun starts here."

Ed moved his hand closer to Clark, and Pete didn't stop to think.

"Leave him alone!"

He charged forward at Ed, fists balled and arms flailing.

But Ed stepped aside. As Pete stumbled past him, Ed lashed out with a fist that caught Pete on the side of the head. Enhanced by the strange fruit's powers, the blow packed the wallop of a jackhammer.

"That's for being a loser," Ed snarled.

Pete felt pain crackle like lightning. He staggered into the brick wall, then everything went black.

Ed's hand grew larger in Clark's vision.

What's that he's holding. Surely it can't be—

Suddenly realizing the danger he was in, Clark fought to break free. But it was too late. His arms were pinned, and Ed was pressing down with one knee on his chest. Ed's other hand reached out to grab Clark around the jaw, forcing it open.

Clark felt his lips tingle as the berry brushed against them. Then the inside of his mouth flared with pain.

Desperately, he tried to spit the berry out. But Ed's hands were clamped around his mouth, trying to make him swallow. The fruit burst in his mouth, and the thick, viscous juice ran down his throat.

"Aaaaaaaaagh!"

Clark screamed, as the pain of only moments ago was completely obliterated by the white-hot fire that surged through his veins. Agony coursed through his body like a barbed-wire serpent.

In blind panic, he tore his arms free, sending Phil and Rob staggering back, away from him. He tried to get to his feet, but failed. He fell forward onto his face, burying it in his hands, whimpering and groaning as his body was wracked by convulsions.

The inside of his skull felt as if it were being eaten away by fire ants. He'd never imagined such agony could exist.

A low, moaning sound filled his ears, and he realized it was the sound of his own voice.

Rob looked down at Clark's twitching body, and shivered.

"Th-that's not natural, man," he said shakily. "That's not a good reaction, right?"

But it was hard to tell what was really happening and what he was hallucinating. Sometimes Clark seemed to be laughing, fit to burst at some personal cosmic joke. Then things would switch, and Clark was crying as if every demon in Hell were burning him up.

From the inside.

"Maybe we should take him home. Or to a doctor, or something."

"Chill," Ed said coolly. "He'll never enjoy it if he fights against it. His choice, guys. Right?"

Rob peered at Clark again. Laughs . . . or sobs? He wondered if Ed or Phil could see the little insects crawling around just out of view? Or was that just his imagination?

"This is boring," Ed said at last.

Clark had grown quieter. His face was turned away from them, his body drawn up in a fetal position, wracked by the occasional shudder.

Rob reached out his hand into a beam of sunlight, experimenting. He withdrew it swiftly, as if he'd been burned by a laser.

"Yeah. Let's go."

Phil was staring at Clark, mesmerized. "You sure he's okay, Ed? I mean, I wouldn't want him to get hurt . . ."

Ed clapped his buddy on the shoulder. "How many times have we taken this stuff, Phil? Dozens. Has anybody ever come to any harm? No. Will Kent be the first? I seriously doubt it."

He scooped up a half brick from the ground and sent it arcing through the air. It ricocheted off a rusting conveyor and slammed into a wall. The echoes seemed to take forever to die away.

"Let's go flying, dudes."

They left at a run.

By the time they emerged outside, blinking in the afternoon light, they'd forgotten all about Clark Kent and Pete Ross.

*   *   *

"Tell me something, honestly—" Lana began.

"Are you implying something?" Chloe butted in. "I'm always honest."

"No. Don't be silly."

They were in the Talon. Lana was working her shift, but the cafe was almost empty. Not only was Pete absent, but Clark hadn't shown up either.

"Okay, Lana. Let's hear it."

Sometimes, Chloe felt a little exasperated with Lana's naïveté. She was too good to be true. Yes, Lana Lang had it all: straight As, good looks, dancing eyes, and the love of a good man.

And no parents, Chloe reminded herself, feeling instantly guilty. Lana had known tragedy like few people ever experienced: the death of her parents just when she needed them most. That she hadn't turned out a traumatized wreck was testament to her aunt Nell.

"This curse," Lana said slowly. "I know that journalists don't always believe what they write. But I'd like to know if you do."

Chloe didn't hesitate. "Yes. I've done more than enough research to be convinced that curses do exist. They have a long and inglorious history, from the earliest written records, right up to the present day."

Lana's brows wrinkled. "But how can something that happened so long ago—to a completely different set of people—come back to haunt Smallville?"

"That, Lana, is the sixty-four-thousand-dollar question. That checklist I did might have been more at home in a supermarket tabloid, but it served a purpose. It allowed me—and the readers—to make a comparison. Dead dogs. Suffocation."

Chloe began to enumerate the points of similarity on her fingers, but Lana interrupted. "There's probably a lot we don't know about. Family fights. Petty theft." She bit her lip. "Romantic problems."

Chloe was surprised. "Are you saying *you* have romantic problems? Good grief, Clark would do anything for you."

Lana was stung. "That's not fair. I never try to encourage Clark." Suddenly, she deflated. Her shoulders slumped. She picked up her cold coffee and took a sip before going on, "I don't even know if I want to encourage him. Since Whitney died, everything's turned into a mess."

Chloe could see she was close to tears. "And you think that's because of the curse?" she prompted.

"Yes. No. I don't know." Lana shook her head sadly. "All I know is nothing feels right anymore. The only time I'm happy is when I'm with you, or with Clark."

She glanced around the cafe.

"And now even Clark's deserted me."

Every fiber in Clark's body pulsed with pain.

Even his mind felt like it was on fire, assaulted by wave after wave of piercing green torture.

Memories danced in his head like ghosts. A toddler walking unscathed from a downed spacecraft. (Flare of green pain.) The night his parents told him he was an alien. (Shower of burning emerald sparks.) The day he realized what he felt for Lana Lang was love. (Curtain of shimmering agony.) The painful reaction he'd suffered from Lana's meteor necklace. (Column of toxic green fire.)

The same green pain.

(The same green pain.)

He seemed to be looking down on his body, watching it through a prism of green crystal, its thousand hues enveloping him. Shutting out the world. Sucking his vitality like a vampire.

Somewhere, far away in his mind, he knew he was dying.

Death was green.

And it hurt like hell.

"Clark! Clark! Oh God! Clark!"

Pete bent in concern over the trembling body of his friend. He grabbed Clark's arm and shook him, but there was no response except a terrible moan.

Pete's head was throbbing from Ed's blow, but he had no thought for his own condition. He'd come to and found Clark convulsing in a pool of sunlight, green bile dribbling from the corners of his mouth. His eyes were rolled back in his head, blinking rapidly every few seconds.

"Clark?" Pete's blood ran cold at the thought of what would happen if he couldn't revive him. "Please, Clark," he tried again. "It's Pete. I need you to hear me!"

Clark Kent was an awareness—an intelligence—drifting through interstellar space. A green, roiling cloud, a billion miles across, that swirled between the stars.

A comet flashed through him, twisting and turning as it tumbled in its aeons-old orbit. A red star flared to giant size, then disappeared. A black hole swirled as he passed it, sucking in matter, only to spew it out into a brand new Universe.

He was returning to the place of his birth, somewhere out here in the eternal cosmos, a planet orbiting any one of those trillions of suns.

Spaceboy was coming home.

But why was home so cold and dark and unwelcoming?

"Spaceboy!"

Who called him that?

"Spaceboy!"

A word or a thought? He felt so weak, he wanted nothing more than to drift off into oblivion. A place where the pain would go away, and he would be at peace.

Suddenly, a vision of Lex Luthor's face flashed through the green mists in his mind. Lex was mouthing words silently . . . but somehow Clark knew what he was saying.

"When you stand alone in the cold light of the cosmos, there will be no one to help you."

Immediate understanding fired through his reeling brain. He could live . . . or he could die. The choice was his.

Nobody else could make it for him.

"Snap out of it. Do you hear me?"

The voice spoke again, louder. Clark tried to open his eyes, but it felt like they'd been nailed shut. A maelstrom of flaring green sparks burned his sockets.

"Spaceboy!"

He tried again. His eyelids lifted, sending a wave of nausea through him. Golden light. Heaven.

Then a face swam into view.

"Spaceboy!"

"P-Pete." The words were barely a croak. "D-don't you ever call me that again."

"Will you be all right if I go call a doctor?"

Clark's grip tightened so weakly on his wrist, Pete barely felt it.

"No. No . . . doctor," Clark gasped. "No hospital."

Pete sighed in dismay. He knew exactly why Clark couldn't be subjected to any kind of medical attention, for even the most cursory examination would reveal his superpowers.

"But this is serious, Clark. I don't know what to do."

"Dr-dri—" Clark's voice broke off, as he was consumed by another convulsion.

"What?" Pete shook him gently. "What are you saying? You have to tell me, Clark."

"D-drink. Make sick."

Of course! Pete shot to his feet, and glanced around. No liquid in here, except—

Sunlight glinted off the multihued surface of the barrel. Water. Filthy water, that might have been there for years.

The oil drum was only a few feet away. The bung was rusted solid, but part of the upper rim closest to Clark had largely rotted away. There was nothing else for it.

Jamming his shoulder against the back of the drum, Pete exerted as much force as he could muster. He felt the decayed metal give.

"Open your mouth, Clark. Now!"

Dirty water sloshed over the top, splashing on Clark's

chest. Suddenly, the whole drum gave, and Clark was immersed in a deluge of fetid, oily water.

The effect was almost immediate. His body began to convulse again—but this time he was retching, too. A thin stream of gleaming green liquid spread across the factory floor. Where the sunlight caught it, it writhed and twisted like a living thing.

Clark retched so much, he thought he'd die of that rather than meteor poisoning. But with every bout of sickness, his body's remarkable healing powers recovered more.

Pete sat beside him on the floor as the shafts of sunlight rose higher up the walls and finally disappeared. The sun was setting.

It was almost dark before Clark felt well enough to move.

Pete set out for Smallville, supporting the weight of his best friend.

CHAPTER 24

It was a three mile hike on the back roads from the corn-meal factory to the Kent farm. It took Pete and Clark more than three hours, the latter leaning on the former each step of the way.

Every hundred yards or so they had to stop, either to allow Pete to rest or let Clark have another retching fit.

Pete's heart was pounding, and not just from effort. He knew without a shadow of a doubt that this tragedy was all his fault. He was the one who felt so intimidated by Clark that he'd deliberately snubbed him and sought out new friends. He was the one who'd let himself be talked into taking drugs.

He was the one who'd behaved like a jerk.

His parents would be furious. He'd be grounded for life. And how would he be able to face Jonathan and Martha Kent and tell them what happened to Clark?

All along, Clark had done nothing but play the part of a true friend.

And this is where it had gotten him.

Stars filled the sky, and they still had a mile to go.

Pete was so preoccupied with his own gloomy thoughts, he failed to notice that Clark's strength was slowly returning. Though pain still wracked his body, more and more, he was able to support himself.

Several times, car headlights blazed out of the night. Clark let Pete hustle him off the road, into cover on the fringes of the cornfields. The sudden movement made him nauseous, and he was sick again and again.

Then it was back on the road. One foot after another. Don't look up, it makes you giddy. Green starbursts obscured his vision. His thoughts were chaotic: memories from his childhood mingling with scenes from an alien green hell.

Several times, he tried to tame his mind, to focus on a single rational thought.

Like: Ed's berry did this. Must be contaminated in the same way as Lana's necklace. The meteor swarm that fragmented over Smallville. The meteors that carried my spacecraft to Earth.

Did the meteors awaken the curse?

Problem was, language seemed to take on a life of its own. Any one of the words involved was enough to send his thoughts jetting off at the most obscure tangent.

And all the time, it hurt so bad he wanted to cry.

The night was still and calm, a late-rising moon casting an ethereal glow on the flat countryside. Cornstalks swayed in the breeze like exotic dancers.

They were halfway down the drive to the Kents' farm when Pete drew to a halt. Clark sat down on the grass verge, resting his head between his knees. Pete knew this was neither the time nor the place for what he was going to say. But it had to be said, anyway.

"I want to apologize, Clark. For all the trouble I've caused. For all you've had to suffer because of me."

"Okay," Clark croaked. He looked up, moving his head slowly. "We're . . . friends. Yes?"

Pete felt deeply ashamed as he nodded. "Yes. Friends. Though I haven't behaved like one." He pointed to the lights of the farmhouse, just a few hundred yards ahead. "All hell is going to break loose when I take you in there," he said ruefully. "Your parents will go ape. *My* parents will go ape. I'll be expelled from school. Ed might go to jail."

He paused, looking deep into Clark's upturned eyes. "Are you taking this in? You look like you're on another planet."

Clark nodded, and almost smiled. "Spaceboy," he mouthed. "Don't tell parents. Not . . . necessary."

"But look at you! They'd have to be blind not to notice something is wrong. Very wrong. Besides, where else can I take you?"

"Barn." Clark raised his hand and pointed vaguely. The shape of the massive barn was silhouetted by the lights from the house behind. "My den. Get . . . getting better. All time."

"I'm not buying that," Pete said skeptically.

"Honest."

The effort must have been too much. Pete winced as Clark fell forward, coughing and spluttering and spitting into the weeds. He could only stand and watch, tortured at the extent of his friend's torment.

At last, Clark's spasms died away. He straightened up, his voice louder and more confident.

"Honest, Pete. The barn. I'll sit there for a while. Recover."

* * *

It was another fifteen minutes before Pete managed to maneuver Clark up the wooden steps and through the trapdoor into Clark's den. He half-carried Clark across to the wall and sat him on a floor cushion.

Pete had been there before, at Clark's invitation. He knew there was always fruit juice in the tiny freezer chest. He pulled out a couple of bottles, and together they sat and drank in silence.

"Oh no!"

Pete started as Clark shot upright from his slouch. "What is it? You're not getting sick again?"

"Worse. I had a date with Shirley."

Pete was reluctant to leave, but Clark insisted. Pete's parents would be getting worried—and besides, Clark argued, he needed Pete to call Shirley and explain to her.

"Are you sure?"

"Look, I'm getting better by the minute." He spread his hands theatrically. "I'll sit here for a half hour or so, then go into the house."

"Promise?"

"On my honor."

Pete turned to leave, but Clark spoke again. "Thanks, Pete," he said earnestly. "You saved my life."

"And you might just have saved mine. Thank *you*."

Both smiled, and Pete shinned down the ladder to the ground.

"Shirley?"

"Yes," she said curtly.

"This is Pete Ross."

Shirley was silent. She was sitting on her bed, staring

at the television, aimlessly channel-surfing. Her date outfit was back in the wardrobe. Her tears had long since dried, and her anger had given way to a cool detachment.

The voice at the other end of the line got fed up waiting, and went on: "I'm calling on behalf of Clark Kent. He says to tell you he's sorry he couldn't make it tonight."

"I've been waiting for *hours*," Shirley said icily. "Couldn't you have called earlier?"

"Not really. Clark got sick."

Despite her resolution, Shirley felt concern. "What happened? Is Clark all right? Did he—?"

"Look, I'm in a real hurry. I have to go. Clark will call you after. He'll explain. Bye."

There was a click, and Shirley glared at her cell phone, her mind in turmoil. *Was* Clark okay?

Or had he just used his friend to dump her?

More than anything, Clark wanted to sleep.

His back was propped against the barn wall, and his head kept lolling onto his chest. But every time his eyes closed, a blast of pain jolted him back to wakefulness.

He should have asked Pete to switch off the light before he left. He would do it himself, but felt dizzy every time he moved.

Seemed all he could do was think.

Shirley. How could I have forgotten about our date?

Easy. I forgot about her almost the moment I heard from Chloe that Lana was jealous.

I like Shirley, sure. Maybe with time it could be more. But I love Lana.

As if merely thinking about Lana gave him strength,

he lurched to his feet and reached an optimistic hand for the light switch. The world spun around in green waves. Groaning, he staggered against the makeshift wooden shelves that held his astronomy books.

Shelves and books went crashing to the floor.

An instant later, Clark's unconscious body landed atop them.

"One o'clock." Jonathan's voice was grim. "And not a word."

He was pacing the floor in the farmhouse kitchen, while Martha sat on the easy chair by the stove. The telephone was by her side, and she stared at it every now and again, as if willing it to ring.

"I really am beginning to worry that something's happened to him," she confessed. "Perhaps we should call the hospital."

"That's the last place Clark would go if he was hurt, Martha."

They'd gone over this a thousand times over the years, drumming into Clark that he was so different, he could never take the chance of being discovered. So, no hospitals. No police. No official contact of any kind.

If the authorities ever discovered the truth about their son, he'd end up as little more than a rat in a lab. People *always* feared what they didn't know; and scientists assuaged their fears by taking things to pieces.

That wouldn't happen to their son.

"But he's always called before if he's out as late as this."

Jonathan stopped his pacing and swung himself into a

chair. "He said he had something to sort out with Pete. We've called the Rosses, and Pete isn't home, either."

"And he had a date with this Shirley girl. Perhaps we should call her."

"Maybe you're right." Jonathan shrugged, and broke off abruptly. He was a strong, independent man, used to thinking and acting for himself, but this was turning him into a nervous wreck. "My only worry is—if everything is okay, he's going to end up not trusting us."

"I feel so helpless . . ."

Jonathan went over to stand by her side, laying a comforting arm on her shoulder. He and Martha couldn't have children of their own. When Clark—almost literally—dropped into their laps, they thought it was a miracle. No blood relation could ever love their son more.

The phone rang with a piercing shrillness that half-scared them out of their wits. The first ring had barely died away before Martha had the receiver pressed tightly to her ear.

"Yes?" she gasped.

Jonathan stared at her in alarm, as she made a series of monosyllabic answers. When she put the phone back in its cradle, her face was ashen.

"That was Pete's father." She got to her feet, and Jonathan's arm tightened around her. "Pete came home a little while ago."

"And Clark—?"

"Mr. Ross put Pete on the line. He claims Clark wasn't feeling well." She went across to the back door, and Jonathan followed. "He said Clark was going to sit up in his den for a while."

"And he didn't tell us?"

Jonathan snatched up his flashlight and moved past Martha into the yard. He heard her footsteps behind him as he ran toward the barn door.

"Clark?"

His voice echoed through the cavernous interior of the barn. But there was no reply.

Jonathan climbed the steps to the floor he'd turned into a den for Clark.

A light was on.

"Are you there?" Jonathan eased himself up through the trapdoor.

He stared in sudden fear at the figure sprawled among the fallen bookshelves.

Whirling the flashlight to light up the trapdoor, he called out, "Martha! You'd better get up here."

Sam Fozter downed the last of his rum and Coke and slammed the glass down on the bar. He nodded toward the empty bar seats.

"You always as quiet as this?"

"They're staying home," the barman told him. "Because of the curse. Have you heard about it?"

"No. And I don't want to."

"More of the same?" the barkeep asked, hand already reaching for the rum bottle.

Foz shook his head. "I'd like to," he admitted. "But I got thirty bucks to my name. Which happens to be coffee, eggs and toast in the morning, followed by the first bus to Metropolis."

"Staying at the hotel?"

"With a friend."

A friend called Jesus, Foz thought.

He walked out of the bar and along the near-deserted Main Street, his old suitcase getting heavier by the minute.

Curse? Curse Don Breed, more like.

He'd been intending to sleep rough, not too shabby a prospect on a warm night like this. Then he remembered the church. The door was open when he went yesterday. In a place like Smallville, he'd be willing to bet it stayed open twenty-four/seven. If not, the lock would be a cinch to force.

Who knows? Maybe even be some wafers and wine lying around. Or is that some other religion?

He was right on the first score—the door was open—but wrong on the second. No food or drink.

And the door that led through to the minister's house—the one that had been unlocked when he called Friday—was tonight firmly bolted.

The empty church spooked him a little, pale moonlight bathing the stained-glass windows, making them glow like ghostlights.

Foz rested a hand on the back of a wooden pew. He wouldn't be sleeping on that. The aisle was carpeted, but with concrete flooring beneath.

It was then he noticed the ladder leading upwards, into darkness. The bell tower, obviously. Might be worth taking a look.

He clambered up the wooden rungs, dragging his case behind him. Trepidatiously, he stuck his head through into the loft room above. There were large slatted windows in two of the four sides, but the moonlight that penetrated was wan and weak.

Foz put down his case and waited for his sight to adjust. He was in the electronic control room for the church bells.

A small, computerized timer was attached to a larger console. Part of its front panel had been removed, and a couple of electric wires spiraled out. They snaked down onto the floor and disappeared into the deep shadows.

Screwing up his eyes in the dim light, Foz was able to make out a pile of heavy-duty dustsheets lying in the corner. Just what the doctor ordered.

Or maybe that should be bishop?

He took a step toward the untidy heap and felt a tug at his ankle.

Instinctively, he yelped and jerked his foot away.

He felt something snap. There was a slight blue fizz of electricity.

Idiot. It was only the wire.

Minutes later, he was curled up under half a dozen dustsheets, drifting off into a dream about pounding Don Breed's face to pulp.

CHAPTER 25

He's drunk! was the first, furious thought that flashed through Jonathan's head.

He felt instantly ashamed. He should know better than to judge Clark like that. The boy had never shown any liking for alcohol. If he *had* been going to drink, Jonathan was willing to bet he'd have talked it over with Martha and him first.

Using his thumb and forefinger, he felt for Clark's pulse, while Martha checked his breathing.

"Pulse is weak," he reported. "His breathing's shallow and irregular."

They maneuvered Clark so that his head was supported by a cushion and made his body as comfortable as they could. Then they debated what to do about this extraordinary situation.

Jonathan wanted to carry Clark back to the house and nurse him there. Martha protested it would be too hard to manipulate him through the trapdoor. Jonathan pointed out the old winch and rope still secured to the barn wall outside the den window. Martha said no son of hers would be lowered on a hook.

In the end, they decided to leave him where he was.

Martha returned to the house for an eiderdown and pillows, as well as a flask of coffee.

By the time she got back, Jonathan had straightened

up most of the mess. The bookshelf had cracked in half, so he stacked the books against the wall. Underneath them he found a sheaf of old newspaper pages and cuttings that had been damaged when Clark fell.

Barely glancing at them, he collected them as best he could and set them down on top of the books.

They settled down with a cup of strong coffee each, to keep vigil through the night.

Clark dreamed of nothing at all, as if his hallucinations had used up all of his imagination.

As the sun rose, turning the sky into a paint box, he stirred. In a matter of seconds, sunlight was filtering in through the chinks in the century-old wooden walls.

Memory returned instantly. And with it, anxiety. His parents . . . !

He jerked himself upright, and groaned.

They were sitting on the floor on either side of him. But there was no accusation, no threat of retribution on their faces. They shone with love.

And relief.

Clark felt almost well again.

The deep sleep was what he'd needed, giving his recuperative powers time to do their work without any interference from his conscious mind.

Martha cooked him the largest breakfast ever seen in Kansas and carried it from the house to the barn. He ate every last bite before consenting to face his parents' barrage of questions. But he had already decided what his line was going to be.

"I understand how worried you've been," he began.

"And you deserve an explanation of what's been going on. But if I tell you what this is all about, it's not just my life and future which will be jeopardized. It's my friend's. And my enemies', too."

"Clark, whatever happened to you last night was serious," Jonathan said quietly. "We can't help you unless we know what's wrong."

"I know, Dad. But this is something I have to do on my own. After it's all over . . . I'll tell you then."

Jonathan pondered long and hard before replying. "I figure you do owe us that explanation, son," he said at last. "But you're a teenager, not far off being a man. So I also figure we have to trust you."

Martha nodded her agreement. "Just know that, if you need us, we're here for you. Always."

"Thanks, Mom," Clark told her sincerely. "Fortunately, I don't anticipate any more trouble like last night. I'm confident I can take care of things from here on in."

"We're confident, too," Jonathan told him. "Good luck."

They left him alone then, and Clark lay for a long time watching the bands of sunlight knifing between the wallboards. Occasionally, flashes of green intruded on his vision.

He'd read someplace that the mind can't remember pain, that memory of trauma would be sufficient in itself to prolong—if not cause—even more trauma. But though it was true, he couldn't relive the bone-searing agony he'd suffered last night, he had learned a valuable lesson.

Clark didn't think he had ever experienced pain like

that before. And he had no wish ever to feel such intense agony ever again.

Dust danced in the sunbeams, and he sighed as he surveyed the damage his fall had caused. Nothing that couldn't be fixed.

Then he noticed the newspapers, lying on a pile of astronomy books. His gaze would have passed on by, but for the top clipping. It was one he didn't remember seeing before.

He stood up, moving slowly and carefully, testing his balance before he committed himself. Okay. He picked up the top page, obviously one of those that had been so dry and brittle he hadn't tried to separate it from the others.

A little giddiness, but otherwise all right.

The clipping was from a London newspaper dated 1849, and was another paean of praise to Victor Marchmont Gray's amazing psychic abilities. It featured an interview with a lord and lady of the manor, who attested to Gray contacting the spirit of their ancestor.

Evidently his conversation with the "spirit" had led directly to the discovery of an ancient treasure that restored the impoverished family to their former aristocratic glory.

The old newspaper crackled in his hand, and Clark realized there was another sheet underneath. He pried them gently apart and laid out the new page flat on the floor. The whole of the bottom portion of the page was missing, but the headline and story were still more or less intact.

What he read there was like being kicked in the head.

*   *   *

The Reverend Grindlay slept late and wakened in a cold sweat.

He'd been dreaming he'd overslept and missed his service, and that some demon from Hell stood in the pulpit in his place. Its fierce eyes gleamed malevolently, as it mouthed profanities and screamed abuse at his flock.

Grimly, he shook away the memory.

"Moira," he yelled, starting to hurriedly pull on his clothes, "you should have called me."

Moira bustled into the room. "There's no pleasing some people," she snapped. "You were so ill yesterday, I thought I was doing you a favor by not wakening you."

Michael was immediately contrite. He'd jumped down her throat, yet she only had his own best interests at heart.

"I'm sorry, dear," he muttered, stooping to lace up his shoes. *How many times have I said that before?* "But I'd hoped to get that wiring finished before I sound the bells."

"You should have done it last week, when I told you," Moira pointed out. "But no. You were more interested in your stupid curse."

Michael flushed. That was true, too. But the curse was lifted now. He'd let the town know that during his sermon this morning—and Moira would find out with the others.

"I'm sorry," he said again.

"Easy said, and soon forgotten," Moira sniffed, and flounced huffily from the room.

Dispiritedly, Michael followed her through to the

kitchen, knowing there would be boiled eggs and toast for breakfast.

And there were.

"You have to go to *church*?"

Jonathan tilted his head to one side and considered his son. He blinked as a sudden thought struck him. "You're not arranging a wedding, are you?"

Clark laughed. "No, sir. I have to see the minister," Clark told him. "I have something important to tell him."

"And how do you propose to get there?"

Clark shrugged. "Run? I could be there in minutes."

"And risk someone seeing you?"

"Cycle, then."

"Clark, you've been sick—something that doesn't happen very often," Martha put in. "I think you should take it easy for a while. Just till we're sure you're back to normal."

"I'm getting there, Mom," Clark assured her. "But there's something the Reverend Grindlay really should know."

"Drink your coffee," Jonathan said, "and I'll take you in the truck."

"So what is this piece of news that just won't wait?" Jonathan asked, as he steered the pickup out of the farm-yard.

"Sorry, Dad. No can tell." Clark turned to wink at his father. "I think you'll get a kick out of it, though. Only thing is, the Reverend Grindlay has the right to know first."

Clark felt suddenly worried. "Is that all right? I mean, I'm not holding out on you, or anything."

"I told you, son. I trust you."

He hit the gas, and they sped out onto the road.

Sam Fozter enjoyed the best night's sleep he'd known in a year—since he'd joined Don Breed's show.

The coach had probably been a luxury vehicle when it was built, but that was a long time ago. The suspension was so shot, passengers hit the roof every time the bus encountered a pothole.

Even a pile of dustcovers was better.

Downstairs in the church, the Reverend Grindlay stood for a moment in the diffused sunlight, drinking in the atmosphere.

He hadn't had time to cut and arrange new flowers for the altar, but Moira had. A beautiful display, too. He must remember to thank her later.

He hit a switch, and electric light flooded the interior. Instantly, the church somehow seemed a less holy place.

Crossing his fingers, he hit the button for the prerecorded electronic bells. If they didn't work, he'd get another tongue-lashing from Moira.

But to his great relief, the bells began to ring out, calling the faithful of Smallville to their Sunday morning worship.

DONG DONG DONG!

Sam sat bolt upright, blasted awake by the noise, hands to his ears in a futile attempt to block it out.

It took him a moment to figure what was going on.

The church bells. Of course!

Time he was out of there.

He slid back the trapdoor and peered cautiously down into the church. Damn! The minister was there, fiddling around with the flowers on the altar. The end of the ladder was in plain view. If Foz tried to get down that way, he'd be spotted at once.

The bells were blaring in his ears, knocking his senses haywire, making it difficult to even think. He quested around for another exit.

But the only way was up, a thin-slatted ladder leading up into the confines of the clock tower. Once, in the days of hand-ringing, the tower had housed the bells, too, but now that they were prerecorded, the speakers were in the chamber where he'd slept.

Leaving his suitcase where it lay, Sam grasped the rungs. Cursing his luck, railing against the unholy din, he began to clamber upward.

Below, on the floor, he didn't notice the telltale sparks fizzing around the end of the cable he'd blundered into Saturday night.

And the first, faint smells of burning totally eluded him.

Sam climbed high into the narrowing clock tower, as far away from those damned bells as he could get.

At last, the noise began to die away. Comparatively, at least.

Peering out through the slats set into the tower wall, he could see people streaming toward the church.

Like ants, he thought, *drawn to honey.*

There was a faint smell of smoke in the air. Some old

geek burning off his garden trash, no doubt. That's what old folks did on Sundays in Hicksville.

Wedging himself into the angle between two cross-beams, Sam settled down to wait.

An hour, tops, and the service would be over.

And he'd be on the first bus to anywhere.

CHAPTER 26

There were at least 50 percent more people in the congregation than usual.

Standing in the sculpted wooden box of his pulpit, the Reverend Grindlay observed the fact with some satisfaction. The increase was largely due to the curse and the prominent place it had occupied all week in the local media.

He recognized a reporter for the local morning paper, and a couple from the radio, too. The press had been pestering him all week, but he'd flatly refused to talk to them. As a result, he'd seen Chloe's feature reprinted and regurgitated in a variety of guises.

Soon, he'd be able to set all of their minds at rest.

Moira was in her usual place in the front pew. In all their years of marriage, she'd never missed a single one of his sermons. He smiled at her, but was disappointed that she affected not to notice.

It would take more than a smile to work his way back into her good graces. And it would be harder still, he knew, once she heard what he had to say that morning.

He raised both arms in the air, and the murmur of idle chatter died away. A chorus of self-conscious coughs broke the silence, and he waited for them to subside before saying his opening prayer.

*   *   *

High above in the clock tower, Sam clung to his wooden cradle, and cursed again. First the bells, now *this* racket.

He tried to jam his fingers in his ears to block out the bad singing, but nearly overbalanced as he relaxed his grip on the beams. Nothing else to do. He'd just have to tolerate it until the service was done.

The burning smell was getting stronger, making his nostrils twitch and his eyes sting.

Foz wondered what he'd ever done to deserve this.

Ed left his home at eleven o'clock, telling his parents he was going to hang out with the gang. Like they cared.

He was out of berries. It was time to replenish the stock.

The strange, green fruits had been responsible for major changes in Ed's life. When Whitney had been around, Ed was only number two in the pecking order. With Whitney gone, the spotlight fell on Ed.

But Ed was sufficiently self-aware to know he wasn't a natural leader. The little gang of friends he headed was starting to drift apart.

And then he'd discovered the berries.

He'd been in Riverside Park, practicing mountain bike runs on the dirt track with Phil and Rob. Waiting for the other two to finish their run, he'd picked a few wild raspberries from a clump of bushes by the riverbank.

They tasted so good, he absentmindedly pulled some more, one eye on his buddies' cycling maneuvers.

As soon as he bit down on it, he knew it wasn't a raspberry. A warm sticky flavor flooded his taste buds, at the same time somehow cool and refreshing. There was a tingle in his cheekbones.

He became aware of Phil calling him. "Slay us, maestro!"

With a sense of amazement, Ed felt an odd energy surge through him. He hauled his bike upright and swung himself into the saddle. His leg muscles were throbbing with power.

Tentatively, he stood up on the pedals and pulled back on the handlebars. The front wheel rose eighteen inches in the air.

Ed kept his balance effortlessly, as he raced along the track on only his rear wheel, his legs pumping. He must have hit forty miles an hour as he streaked down the long slope, dust flying up from the spinning rear wheel.

Phil and Rob were astonished.

Ed was astonished.

But he was still sufficiently in control of himself not to mention a word about the weird fruit he'd found.

Later, after the others had gone, he lingered in the park and combed through the cluster of undergrowth. There they were, slender brown canes growing in with the wild raspberries. Each one bore a small cluster of shiny green berries at its tip.

Next morning, he discovered that the comedown wasn't pleasant. Blurred vision, slight nausea, aching muscles. But it was far outweighed by the sheer elation and strength that the berry had given him—if only temporarily.

He'd had worse hangovers from beer.

He experimented a few more times on his own before introducing Phil and Rob to his discovery.

The group was connected again. It even started to enlarge.

And Ed was the lynchpin, the hub around which everything revolved.

He made his way along the gravel path that wound down to the Smallville River and crossed the footbridge into the park. Much of the area had been landscaped, but large patches had been left to grow wild, to host whatever Kansas wildlife it could.

He felt an anticipatory tingle in his mouth. Almost as if the strange fruits were crying out to him.

And he was responding.

Two hundred yards behind him, Pete followed doggedly.

He'd been waiting near Ed's house for two hours, knowing that Ed would have to restock his supply after forcing the last berry down Clark's throat.

Pete was lucky his parents hadn't grounded him. His father had ranted on at length about trust and responsibility, but he'd finally accepted that Pete had only been trying to help a sick friend. The berries were never mentioned. All the same, his dad had insisted on calling the Kents first thing, just to be sure Clark's story was the same as Pete's.

He hung back in the shadows, constantly alert for Ed turning around and spotting him.

But it was obvious Ed's thoughts were elsewhere. He kept his head down until he reached the path on the far side of the river. Even then, he gave only a cursory glance around before heading off across the grass.

Hidden behind a flowering bush, Pete remained unobserved. Crouching low to minimize the possibility of detection, he inched his way forward to get a better view of what Ed was doing.

"My friends," the Reverend Grindlay solemnly addressed his congregation, "it has been said that the Lord works in mysterious ways. During the past week, many among us must have wondered what dread purpose lay behind the fear and paranoia that has enveloped our town.

"What had we, the people of Smallville, done wrong, that we should apparently fall victim to a curse?"

He paused, glancing around the pews as he let his words sink in. Moira's brow was knitted in disapproval, just as he'd expected. But the serious looks on many of the other faces told him that he was right: they *were* worried about this supernatural intrusion into their lives.

"Were we being tested, perhaps? Or were we the target of something far more sinister? For make no mistake, my friends—"

His voice rose, echoing around the church. "Evil exists."

He gave an incongruous little laugh. "Of course, this is the twenty-first century. People only believe in evil when they see it at the movies. They read about evil in horror stories, never dreaming for a moment that it might worm its pernicious way into their own lives. Our society has trivialized evil—" His voice rose again. "—and perhaps that is why it has come to haunt us."

Again that little laugh. "But I speak of evil, and curses. What proof do we have? An entry in an ancient journal. Rabble-rousing shows on the radio. Features in our newspapers. And a checklist, to see if Smallville suffers in the same way as a pioneer wagon train. Can these trivial details truly be evidence of evil?"

The Reverend Grindlay leveled his gaze and kept his voice steady. "I personally believe that they can. For centuries, our faith has allowed that the demonic can interact with us here on Earth. And, by the same token, we on Earth have the power—through faith—to banish demons. Yesterday, I took it upon myself to do precisely that." He paused, casting a defiant look at Moira before continuing:

"Yesterday, I exorcised the curse."

Moira bristled at her husband's words and glared at him.

She knew instantly what he was talking about. He'd lied to her, pretended that he was ill, and all the time he was planning some sort of absurd exorcism.

Wait till she got him alone!

Up in the clock tower, the smoke was thickening, stinging Sam's eyes and making him cough. He didn't know how much more of this he could bear.

This can't be a garden fire!

Grimacing, he turned his face away from the slatted openings in the wall. It was then he glanced down—and saw the flames in the control room twenty feet below, already licking at the bottom of the ladder.

Ed didn't hear the footsteps on the grass behind him until it was too late. He whirled—to find Pete Ross facing him.

"Latest harvest?" Pete asked, indicating the slender canes with their ripe green fruits.

"You followed me!" Ed exploded. "Well, you can forget about muscling in. This is my patch. I found it. I'm keeping it!"

"I don't think so, Ed." Pete kept his voice level, though his adrenaline was racing. "I'm taking over."

"Oh yeah?" Ed sneered, unconsciously puffing out his chest to emphasize the difference in their physical stature. "You and what army, Petey?"

Pete pulled himself up to his full height. He felt afraid, sure. Ed was taller and heavier. But Pete's mind was made up. He was going through with this, no matter what.

"If this is the way you want it, Ed."

Before Pete finished speaking, Ed brought up his fist in a roundhouse swing that would have knocked Pete senseless if it had connected. But Pete saw it coming and ducked easily aside.

He swung his own fist, and it sank satisfyingly deep into Ed's belly. Ed gasped and cursed, but flung his arms around Pete's neck and tried to wrestle him to the grass.

Pete writhed and squirmed, resisting as best he could. At close quarters, Ed's greater bulk would soon wear him down. He managed to get in several punches to Ed's ribs, causing Ed to release his grip and stagger back.

"You're going to be sorry, Petey—" he blustered.

But Pete didn't wait to hear out the threat. He waded into Ed with his fists flailing, feeling pain shoot through his knuckles every time he was lucky enough to land a blow.

Ed retreated under the pressure of the attack, but Pete

didn't stop. He lowered his head, pushing against Ed's chest, his fists still crashing in on the bigger man from all directions.

Whatever else he may have been—arrogant, contemptuous, a bully—Ed wasn't a fighter. Unable to defend himself against Pete's ongoing attack, he made a last effort to push Pete away.

But his foot slipped on the grass, and he lurched sideways—just as Pete threw his hardest punch yet. It caught Ed flush on the point of the chin. His eyes closed, and he sagged to the ground.

"And that's another thing." Pete struggled to control his breathing. "Don't ever call me Petey again."

He gave himself a moment to recover. Then, turning his back on the prone Ed, he grasped the nearest cane and tugged.

Its roots resisted only momentarily before it came out of the ground in his hand. He held it up, peering closely at the single green fruit.

Such a little thing . . . yet it's caused so much trouble.

"The service isn't finished yet."

Clark pointed to the collection of cars parked outside the church, as Jonathan found a space and eased the pickup in.

"I guess I'll wait by the graveyard."

Clark picked up the manila envelope he'd brought with him, and slid out of the pickup. His feet crunched on the gravel driveway, as he strode toward a row of marble tombstones, glinting in the sunshine.

Funny. There was an acrid smell in the air. Something was burning.

Clark swiveled his head and looked all around. Nothing that could be the source of the smell. Then he glanced up—and saw flames and thick, black smoke starting to pour out through the slats in the clock tower.

"Fire!"

Fire—it's the only way, Pete thought.

He'd heaped the berry canes on a gravel beach by a bend in the river. Half a dozen sheets of newspaper, retrieved from a park trash can, were crumpled underneath for kindling.

Pete pulled a box of safety matches from his pocket. Nobody in his family was a smoker, so he'd had to buy the matches before he settled down to wait outside Ed's house. This had been his intention all along.

He struck a match, and it sparked into life. He held it low, watched the flames licking at the edges of the newspaper. Then the whole heap flared, crackling as the fire took hold of the woody canes.

Ethereal tendrils of green smoke twisted in the orange flames.

Pete reached into his pocket again and pulled out the single green fruit that he had secreted yesterday. He held it up to the sun and marveled for one last time at how it seemed to pulse with its own strange energy.

Maybe he should keep it. Just in case. You never knew when something was going to be needed. Or come in handy. Or . . .

Pete smiled wryly to himself. *We're good at rationalizing our own behavior,* he thought.

Without even a twinge of regret, he dropped the berry

onto the fire. There was a brief, green explosion, and it vanished in the flames.

He turned back toward where Ed was picking himself off the ground, rubbing his bruised jaw.

It wouldn't be easy to convince Ed that what he'd done was for the best. But Pete knew it was.

And that was enough.

CHAPTER 27

Discovery no longer mattered to Sam Fozter.

Survival was all that counted now.

The fire in the bell chamber below was spreading fast, sending up columns of heat that scorched his exposed skin. No point trying to climb higher inside the tower—he'd only be putting himself in greater danger.

The only way out was down.

He gripped a cross-strut in both hands, intending to swing himself back onto the ladder. But he couldn't—his left foot was solidly wedged in the angle between the beams. Desperately, he tugged at it, attempting to turn his foot this way and that, trying to work it loose.

No use. He was caught fast.

He looked down and felt panic welling in him. The flames were roaring, and the heat was quickly becoming unbearable. There was only one thing left for him to do.

"Help! *Help!*"

"For centuries, certain men have taken it upon themselves to combat evil for the common good."

The Reverend Grindlay felt every eye on him and basked in being the focus of attention. It might only be because they were afraid, but he would settle for that.

"History does not record these men. Their names are unknown to the world. They worked quietly, privately, under the aegis of the Church. And they were effective. Their rituals—based on their unflappable faith— worked."

He had become aware of a distant roaring sound, but was unable to figure out what it was. All his thoughts were on his sermon.

The minister had no way of knowing that, above, the fire had been following the path of least resistance. It spread into the ducts housing the electrical wiring and shot along them, following the contours of the roof.

Everywhere it touched, new flames licked.

Tentacles of thick, black smoke began to rise, roiling above the growing inferno.

"I searched the old books. I pored over the message they contain. And I did what I had to do." The Reverend Grindlay's nose twitched. Surely that was smoke . . . ?

Suddenly, there was a miniature explosion, and the trapdoor to the tower blew open, belching sparks and flame.

"Fire!" someone screamed, and a dozen others took up the call.

With the demise of the trapdoor, fresh air could reach the flames. It rushed in, giving them new, magnified life.

Michael looked around in horror. Thin tendrils of flame webbed the church ceiling, radiating out from the bell chamber. The church interior was rapidly filling with dense, clinging smoke.

A beam came crashing down on the pews. Burning embers scattered everywhere, igniting a wave of new fires.

"Open the door!" someone shouted, galvanizing the minister into action. Feeling his way, he began to scramble down from the pulpit.

"No!" he shrieked, hardly able to hear over the crackle of burning and the cries of terrified people. "Leave the door! If the air gets in—!"

A reporter from the local radio station reached the door first, coughing and spluttering, his face blackened with smoke. He didn't even hear the minister's desperate warning. His hands scrabbled at the door handle, and he breathed in cool air as the door clattered open.

Sucked in by the partial vacuum created by the flames, air rushed into the porch and down the aisle. Fires had broken out in a dozen places, and their flames responded greedily to this fresh fuel.

The inferno surged in its intensity.

The long stained-glass window closest to the tower cracked, and suddenly shattered in the intense heat. A group of terrified ladies, crouching under the side pews, were sprayed with shards of hundred-year-old glass.

"Moira!"

Michael yelled his wife's name, but he could discern no answering call over the raucous din. Black, oily smoke was rapidly filling the building, making it almost impossible to see more than a few yards.

He tripped and barked his shin as he cleared the pulpit steps.

"Moira!" he shouted again, and was rewarded by a lungful of smoke. He began to cough uncontrollably, gasping for breath, his eyes streaming and his ears filled with the roar of the fire.

I've failed. I've failed everybody. The curse isn't lifted at all. The only thing I've done is make it worse!

The fresh air turned the tower into the equivalent of a chimney.

Flames grew to three times their previous size. Another ceiling beam came plunging down, trailing smoke and sparks. It fell on the altar, smashing it, scattering Moira's flowers. Blazing embers flew everywhere, setting alight everything that was flammable.

His foot still trapped in the crevice, his skin crackling in the intense heat, Sam Fozter screamed.

Jonathan had leapt out of his truck as soon as he heard his son's urgent shout.

Flames and smoke had started to pour from the tower, threatening to engulf the whole structure. There was a terrified scream from someplace high up its side.

"Check out the main doors, Dad," Clark called, his voice urgent. "I'll take care of whoever's in the tower."

Wondering at how naturally authority seemed to come to his son, Jonathan ran along the path to the front of the building.

A couple of dozen people had managed to get out. They lay collapsed on the grass, spitting and coughing. One man was unconscious, a deep gash on his forehead dripping blood onto his face.

Shielding his eyes against the fierce heat inside, Jonathan ducked in through the open door. It was a long time since he'd set foot in the church, but if he remembered correctly there was a small washroom just inside the porch.

He shouldered the washroom door open. The fire hadn't spread this far yet, though the choking smoke was already seeping in. He turned on both taps at the wash basin, and used wadded-up toilet paper to block the drain. Ripping the cotton towels off their wall hooks, he plunged them into the water spilling over the edge of the sink.

Wrapping one towel around his nose and mouth, he left the washroom and ran into the inferno.

Satisfied there was nobody around who might see him, Clark leapt into the air and soared up to the tower. He had no idea *how* he was able to do this; he only knew that he could.

The screams were coming from near the top, by the clock face.

Clark took a deep breath. He plunged through the thick, choking smoke. His fingers drove into the sides of the clock, digging into the wooden surround as if it was putty.

He wrenched hard with both hands, and the heavy clock face came away from the wood. Using his supervision to pierce the smoke, he saw there was nobody around below. He dropped the clock face, and heard it clatter to the gravel thirty feet below, trailing cogs and gears behind it.

Clark gulped in more air before the escaping smoke enveloped him. It was impossible to see anything with normal vision. He blinked, and his super-vision came into play again. He could see the interior of the tower as plain as if the smoke were transparent.

A man was thrashing around in terror, his foot caught where the beams converged. But his movements were weakening; he didn't have much time left.

Clark forced his way inside, past the remnants of the clock mechanism. The heat wouldn't harm him, but he could already feel it charring his shirt and jeans.

He smashed a beam with a blow from the edge of his hand, and the victim's foot came free. Clark grabbed him, shielding him as best he could from the blizzard of sparks and flame. He kicked off against the wall, scraping back out of the opening as a six foot length of timberboard crashed down inside.

Clark was a blur as he leapt back down to ground level and laid the injured man out on the grass, in shade. The man's breathing had stopped almost completely. Clark stooped down to pinch his nostrils, applying his lips to the unmoving victim's mouth. Taking care not to breathe too hard, he sucked the smoke out of the man's lungs.

The man's body shuddered as his breathing restarted.

The church fire alarm was screeching by then.

Windows shattered in a series of mini-explosions. Each time one broke, more air rushed in to feed the conflagration.

Clark rushed around to the main entrance, just as his father led out a group of three worshipers. One man's jacket and hair were smoldering, and Clark snatched his father's wet towel to douse the flames.

Water was spilling out of the washroom, splashing around their ankles.

Clark saw his father doubled over, retching from the effects of the smoke. He needed time to recover.

Running into the washroom, Clark grabbed the ends of its heavy drapes and yanked them off their rod. Soaking them in the water from the sink, he flew back out into the flaming church.

A family was huddled in the space between the end of the pews and the wall, lost in the smoke, waiting for death with streaming eyes and smokefilled lungs. The father had positioned his body to shield his children, a final human gesture in the face of impending tragedy.

Clark wrapped the soaking-wet drape around them, then guided them quickly to the door, and safety.

As far as he could tell, almost everyone had managed to get out now. Blaring sirens announced the imminent arrival of the fire department.

"Moira . . ."

His enhanced hearing picked up the strangled voice before he saw the minister. He was crawling along the floor, using the line of the pews to guide him through the smoke.

Clark snatched him up and ran back to the entrance. He swerved to avoid a shower of blazing wood that dropped from the ceiling. He reached the doorway and thrust the minister's body into the hands of his waiting father.

"His wife's still inside!" Clark turned to reenter the burning church.

"Be careful, son," his father hissed.

Clark didn't answer, merely dived back inside the

church. The entire edifice was ablaze, flames filling the interior and leaping thirty feet or more from the roof.

Scanning with his super-vision, he saw Moira Grindlay's unconscious body. She was lying near the remains of the altar, her legs trapped under a fallen beam. One arm lay next to a blazing pew, her skin charring from the heat. Her hair was starting to sizzle.

Clark flung the beam aside as if it was made of papier-mâché.

Moments later, Moira was lying in the sunshine on the cemetery grass, with paramedics administering oxygen to her scorched lungs. Still coughing and retching, her husband crouched at her side.

An ambulance was already racing away, ferrying the worst-affected to the nearest hospital.

A fire team was hosing down the outside walls, sending jets of water gushing into the church. Another team was working on the minister's house, trying futilely to contain the spread of the blaze. Rescue workers in protective clothing and breathing apparatus moved into the church.

"I think everyone's out now," Clark told the lead fireman, making sure by giving the church a final surreptitious scan with his super-vision.

The fireman took in Clark's disheveled state and charred clothing. "You did well, son. Better let the medics take a look at you."

"Thanks. I will."

But, of course, he didn't.

CHAPTER 28

SMALLVILLE CURSE STRIKES AGAIN!
Exorcism Fails: 1 Dead, 27 Injured in Church Blaze!

The Monday morning newspapers had a field day.

Sam Fozter died on the operating table in Smallville Hospital, his lungs too badly damaged by smoke inhalation for the respirator to cope. His wallet and ID had been melted beyond recognition, but the metal GI-style dog tags around his neck survived.

And every reporter drew the salient parallel: a man had died in a blazing wagon 150 years before another died in a burned-out church.

If Smallville had been afraid before, now it was terrified.

"Mr. Hennessy? This is Virna Frame. Todd's wife. I'm afraid Todd won't be coming to work today. No. He's not sick. It's just . . . with this fire and everything, he thinks it best not to take chances."

Dear Mrs. Williamson,

Please excuse my son, Eric, and daughter, June, from class today. Although my husband and I do not believe in curses, we feel that safety lies in not tempting fate.

Yours sincerely,
Margaret Fodor

"Hello? I'm trying to get through to the day-shift supervisor."

"The line's busy, ma'am."

"I know that. I've been trying for an hour."

"Can I help you?"

"You can pass on a message. Tell the supervisor Renee Wilson won't be at work today."

"You and half the shift, ma'am."

"Yes, this is the Transport Department. Yes, we know the 10.00 A.M. bus didn't show this morning. Or the 11 A.M. I'm afraid that's because the drivers didn't show, either. Thank you for calling Smallville Transport. We're always at your service."

"Hi. I can't answer the phone right now, as I've taken the family to Metropolis. Please leave your message after the beep."

Clark had been waiting for ten minutes at the road's end before the school bus arrived. It was going to be a special day, and he had no intention of getting off on the wrong foot.

"Yo, Clark," Pete greeted him, as he sprang up the steps. "Kept your seat warm."

"Hold that thought, Pete."

They'd spoken together on the phone Sunday night for over an hour. Clark told him all about the fire at the church, playing down his own part in the rescue.

In return, Pete described how he'd thrashed Ed and burned the drugged fruits that had caused so much heartbreak.

It was only when Pete had asked why Clark was at

church in the first place that Clark remembered the clippings in his manila envelope. He'd stashed it behind a tombstone before going up to the clock tower.

Afterward, he'd forgotten all about it. The urgency of his message had been eclipsed by the reality of the fire.

"What's the problem?" Pete asked now, with mock-concern, as Clark moved past him down the aisle. "My company not good enough?"

"Your company is of the highest quality," Clark teased. "But you're just not as attractive as a certain lady I know."

His eyes locked on Lana's as he made his way to the back of the bus, where she sat with Chloe.

"Hi, Lana. I'm really glad Czar's is going to be okay. I know how much the horse means to you." He greeted her with his most dazzling smile. "Chloe."

Lana smiled back at him, her pretty face glowing. But her eyes were moist, as if she'd been crying. Chloe threw him an enigmatic glance, and Clark wondered what that boded.

It wasn't long before he found out.

"Look," Lana said. She held up a letter, a few hand-written pages.

Clark stared at it, bemused. "I'm looking."

"It's from Whitney," Lana went on. "His commanding officer found it among his possessions." Fresh tears glistened the corners of her eyes. "It's the last letter he ever wrote me, before . . . before . . ."

Her voice trailed away, and she hugged the letter to her, as if it were the most important thing in the world.

Clark sat down beside them in a daze, an icy chill coursing through his veins. Even from beyond the grave,

Whitney had come back to haunt him. He stared out of the window, seeing nothing, as his world crumbled around him.

Shirley Grainger was standing in the schoolyard with a group of friends when the bus pulled in.

Clark was last to shuffle off, his footsteps as leaden as his heart. Lana and Pete were walking ahead, chattering away, but he hung back. He had nothing to say to anyone.

He caught Shirley's eye, and did his best to lighten up and smile. She stared through him as if he weren't there, then turned back to her friends, ignoring him completely.

"Taking flak from all sides, Clark?" Chloe said.

He hadn't realized she was beside him. "Women can be very cruel," he said miserably.

"Can be," Chloe agreed. "And often are. Maybe it's the curse . . ."

Michael Grindlay sat by his wife's bedside in an accident ward at Smallville Hospital.

Moira was unconscious, a result of the strong medication they'd given her to combat the pain of a broken ankle and badly burned arm. A nurse came in every half hour, to change her dressings and check the drip.

I had to almost lose her before I realized how much she means to me.

He murmured a prayer for her recovery, then reached down to clasp her hand.

"I'm sorry, Moira," he said quietly, more to himself than her. "I've been wrapped up in myself for too long. And now we've lost everything—the house, the church, our belongings." He gave a rueful little smile. "All they saved was the car. It took us years to build our life together—and only an hour to smash it apart. But I promise you this, Moira—things are going to be different once you're well again."

He felt tears prickle at the back of his eyes. "I'll make it all up to you somehow—if you'll just give me the chance."

He felt her squeeze his hand weakly.

Her eyes opened, and she looked up at him with no trace of accusation. "Of course I will, Michael," she said feebly, and he rejoiced to hear her voice. "I love you, don't I?"

Her eyes closed, and she drifted back into her medicated dreams.

Michael kept his vigil at her side, with tears trickling unashamedly down his cheeks.

Midnight.

The scarred skeleton of the church was silhouetted by the moon, looking more like the ribs of some giant animal than a building. The air was still heavy with the smell of stale, wet smoke.

The fire department had spent hours dousing the flames, making safe what little of the church remained.

POLICE LINE—DO NOT CROSS tapes surrounded the entire perimeter, putting even the graveyard out of bounds. But they were no barrier to Clark. He picked his way among the tombstones, feeling a strange sense of sadness at being here at all.

This church had seen a lot of Smallville's life. It was here that children were christened—the young married—

and the old were buried. For more than a hundred years, this church had been the community's servant. It was one of the last places of refuge for those in trouble.

And now it was no more than a burned, empty shell.

The envelope was where he'd left it, slightly damp from the spray from the firemen's hoses. Clark picked it up, tucked it inside his windbreaker, and was back home less than three minutes later.

CHAPTER 29

The Reverend Grindlay was staying at the Smallville Hotel. As soon as the management heard about the fire, they'd offered him free accommodation until his affairs were back in order.

Smallville folks looked after their own.

A package containing the journal of Andrew Seddon had been delivered to him that morning, redirected from the church. Whoever had stolen the diary, they'd clearly had second thoughts. A brief note on a sheet of paper said, "Taken in error. Sorry."

The postmark was Otisville.

Michael put the journal aside without opening it.

Used to the light, airy atmosphere of the church, he felt confined in the hotel room. It might be luxurious, it might be free—but it was still a prison for him.

Punishment for my crimes, he thought.

The telephone rang.

Michael was tempted to ignore it. He'd fended off a dozen calls from newspapers, magazines and broadcasters, all eager to interview him. All eager to translate Smallville's misfortunes into an increase in audience share. It made him sick.

"Yes?"

"There's a young man here to see you, Reverend," the receptionist told him. "A Mr. Clark Kent."

The teenager who'd come to see him about his friend's drug problem. What could he possibly want?

"Send him up, please."

Clark had almost taken Chloe into his confidence.

It had been her piece on the curse that had started the whole furore. She could be instrumental in bringing it to an end, by publishing an extra edition of the *Torch*. But he'd finally decided to go with his original decision.

The minister was the one who had to hear the truth first.

"I was sorry to hear about your wife, sir," Clark said, as Michael ushered him into the spacious room. "How is she?"

"Recovering. At least she's alive—unlike that poor wretch who was hiding in the bell tower."

"According to the radio, he was one of the wrestling tour's road crew. It seems they'd fired him on Saturday. On suspicion of theft."

"No man deserves to die like that." He gestured for Clark to sit. "Now, how can I help you? I trust your friend hasn't made things worse . . . ?"

"No, sir. In fact, one of my reasons for coming is to thank you for your advice. He's come to his senses. I think everything is all right now."

Michael touched his fingertips together. "Thank Heaven."

"But I have another reason, too."

Clark took the envelope from his pocket and tipped its contents onto the coffee table. The minister stared at them, puzzled.

"These are clippings about Victor Marchmont Gray,"

Clark explained. "They were found in a cave outside town. All of them are glowing testimonials to his spiritual ability. All except this one."

He unfolded the cracked and torn page.

Michael frowned as he leaned forward for a better look. He started, his eyes widening as he peered closer. Then he sat back, with a look of shock on his face.

"This can't be true!"

"I think you should read it all, sir."

The old newspaper's headline read: CRYSTAL GAZER EXPOSED AS FRAUD! There was an artist's rendition of Victor Gray, looking considerably less affluent than in the previous clippings.

The story beneath related how Gray had colluded with two minor aristocrats to fabricate an imaginary treasure. Then, pretending to be guided by the spirit world, Gray had "found" the treasure. His popularity—and fees— soared.

But Gray had gotten greedy. He cheated his partners out of the payment he'd promised them. They had decided to pay him back by publicly exposing him and his contact with spirits as a hoax.

Suddenly friendless, hounded from his home by his creditors and sued in the courts by those he had duped, Victor Gray was reported as having left Great Britain in disgrace.

The Reverend Grindlay finished reading and sat back. He looked stunned.

"He came here," he said, disbelievingly. "He was burned alive in his wagon, and buried on the land that would become Smallville."

"That's not the important part, sir," Clark pointed out

gently. "What's important is—he was a *fraud.* A confidence trickster. He was never in league with demons, or anything else. He was a man who dreamed up a hoax. His curse *couldn't* have worked!"

"But it did!" the minister protested. "That girl from the school—Chloe. She pointed out all of the similarities between then and now. Good grief, my own church went up in flames, killing a man. Just like Gray was burned to death in his wagon."

"Coincidence," Clark said. "Tragic, but only coincidence."

"But there has to be something else!" The minister was adamant. "Everything tallies. The dead dog. Theft. Fire. Death. Everything Chloe mentioned in her feature." He shook his head, as if unwilling—or unable—to accept the truth. "I even carried out an exorcism. There *has* to be more, I tell you!"

"There is, sir." Clark sighed.

Now came the hard part.

Over the past year or so, Clark had helped Chloe with her investigations into a dozen or more weird happenings in town. A man who seemingly turned into a dragon, and went on a murder spree. A schoolgirl who could transform herself into other people. A classmate whose fascination with insects led him to kill—and devour—his own mother.

That's why Chloe had designated Smallville as "Weird Capital of America." So much that remained unexplained, in such a small place.

And all of the cases had one thing in common.

The strange, green substance from the meteors seemed to be involved. It had scattered over a dozen square miles, and there was no telling where dust or fragments might turn up.

It was the same material in Lana's pendant that caused Clark's skin to crawl, and his veins to writhe, if he came anyplace close to it. He didn't know how the meteors were implicated, only that they irrefutably were.

"Reverend Grindlay, as you know, several strange things have happened in town over the past twelve or thirteen years," Clark began, choosing his words with care. "It's been speculated that, somehow, the meteor swarm that fell on us is to blame. I was wondering . . . do *you* have any part of a meteor?"

He could tell from the way the minister looked at him that he'd hit the nail on the head.

"Well, yes I do," Michael admitted. "But I don't see what that has to do with anything." He reached into his pocket, and brought out the cross-shaped fragment of rock. "This."

Instinctively, Clark moved back in his seat, away from the substance that had so recently almost killed him.

"It's only a piece of rock." The minister shrugged. "It can't possibly have played any part in the business of the curse."

"I can't prove that it did," Clark confessed. "But I strongly suspect it. I know this is a strange request—but I think it would be for the best if you destroyed it."

"Best? For whom?"

"For Smallville." Clark hesitated before going on to state his suspicion. "If the meteor does have some strange power, then *you* might be the link between the curse and its manifestation."

"Me?" Grindlay echoed, outraged. "Young man, I think you have overstayed your welcome."

Long after Clark had left, Michael sat deep in thought.

He held the little green cross in his hand, feeling its warmth soothe and console him. How could this innocent artifact have played any part in the events of the past week? How could any inanimate object act as a catalyst for evil?

The short answer was, it couldn't. It was absurd to even think it.

Of course, that was the very argument Moira used against the curse.

The teenager's words had planted the seeds of doubt in his mind.

CHAPTER 30

On Friday morning, Lex Luthor received his first call from his new business partner.

"First contracts are signed, Lex," Brian Etienne told him. "I'm in LA. I have a meeting with the head of sports programming for a cable company later today. Things are looking good."

"I knew I could rely on you," Lex replied.

His gamble had paid off. He'd turned an assault against him into future profits. Aikido of the mind. That was *Cassandra's* real secret—the ability to create your own future, the way you wanted it, whatever external circumstance might throw at you.

There was a long silence at the other end of the line, before Brian said: "Thanks, Lex. You don't know what this means to me."

"Yes," Lex contradicted him, "I do. Too many creative minds turn to crime because there seems no other way." He changed the subject. "But this is only the start, Brian. My father always taught me to expect a good return on my money. I'm looking forward to the day I bank my profits."

"Join the club." Brian laughed. "I'll call you tonight with the details."

"I'll be back home," Lex told him. "Call me at the castle."

Lex hung up the phone.

Home, he thought. *I've never called anywhere "home" before.*

"Sam Fozter died alone. He had no family, except a brother, who sadly cannot be with us today."

Because he's in jail, Michael Grindlay thought unhappily. But he went on, "He has nobody to miss him. Nobody to mourn him. Except we few gathered here today."

He stood by the graveside, Bible in hand. Opposite him, only Clark Kent and his parents had shown up for the funeral. They sheltered under a large umbrella, for, contrary to the forecasters' predictions, the day was gray, with a warm drizzle falling.

How awful to die, and have only strangers at your burial.

Michael had expected to feel a terrible sadness at seeing what little remained of his church and home. The fire-blackened beams were ugly and out of place in the lush, green cemetery. Like intruders from some alien world. Or the aftermath of war.

But the sadness just wasn't there. Instead, he felt quiet optimism. The doctors were pleased with Moira's progress. She'd be released within the week. They were talking to each other in a way they hadn't done for years.

And, at the end of the day, a church was only a building. A place, like any other. It was the spirit that filled that place that was important. One day, he knew, another church would rise on this spot.

The Kent family turned to leave.

Michael watched them until they exited through the cemetery gates.

He reached into his pocket, and pulled out his little green cross. He held it up, marveling anew at how perfectly formed it was. Even in the light rain, its green surface seemed to weave and flow.

Surely nothing so beautiful could ever be the cause of evil?

But he was making a new start. He'd promised Moira. Everything tangible in their lives was gone.

Only their love remained.

And his faith.

What was it the apostle had said? "Though ye have faith, and have not charity, ye are become as a sounding brass . . ."

He could afford to be a little charitable to the Kent boy.

He tossed the tiny green cross into Sam Fozter's grave. It dislodged a lump of earth and disappeared under the soil.

Lex paced the battlements of his castle in bright moonlight. The light rain had cleared hours ago, leaving the world refreshed.

"Home." The word seemed strange to him. And yet, he couldn't deny that he belonged to Smallville, more than anywhere else he'd ever stayed. And that included a lot of places.

He was amazed at the difference in himself since he'd come across that book. His mind was sharper, one hundred percent focused on whatever he did. Like King Midas, all he touched could turn to gold.

I can make losers into winners. Turn hatred into gratitude.

But this phenomenon new power he'd discovered was amoral. Neither good nor evil, it just was. It was how men would use it that would define it.

He gazed away from the moon, out into the endless cosmos. A billion stars twinkled, as if calling him, beckoning him to greatness.

A man who used this power for good could transform the Universe.

A man who used it for evil could *rule* the Universe.

Lex Luthor had a decision to make.

Five miles away, Clark sat in his den and watched the same stars wheel in their long, slow cycles.

He found himself wondering about Andrew Seddon and the other pioneers on that ill-fated expedition. Did they ever make it to California? Or did they settle along the trail, perhaps even in the group of sodbusters' huts that would one day become Smallville?

Did they ever find their gold?

The ache in his heart had dulled a little. He should never have let himself get so carried away over Lana. Sometimes he wondered if their relationship was cursed . . .

He had to smile at that, despite himself.

Already, Chloe was working on her special edition, exposing the curse as a hoax. Good news is never picked up on with the same speed as bad news, but eventually it would filter down. People would feel sheepish, and wonder what they had ever worried about. They'd laugh at themselves, make jokes at their own expense, and boast how they alone were the only ones in the entire town who never believed.

Normal life would return. A lovers' quarrel would be no more than a lovers' quarrel. A fire might be tragic, but it would only be a fire. Accidents would happen, without any need for supernatural explanation.

The scapegoat had been driven out into the wilderness.

Until the next time.

ABOUT THE AUTHOR

ALAN GRANT was born in Bristol, England in 1949. After finishing school, he edited wildlife, romance, and fashion magazines before becoming a freelance writer. With longtime writing partner John Wagner, he scripted Judge Dredd and a dozen other science fiction series for the British comic book publisher 200 AD. Since 1987 he has written over 200 Batman stories for DC Comics. He is the author of *The Stone King,* a Justice League novel published by Pocket Books. Alan works in a Gothic mansion in the Scottish border country with his wife and guardian angel, Sue.

READ MORE
SMALLVILLE
NOVELS!

STRANGE VISITORS
(0-446-61213-8)
By Roger Stern

DRAGON
(0-446-61214-6)
By Alan Grant

HAUNTINGS
(0-446-61215-4)
By Nancy Holder

WHODUNNIT
(0-446-61216-2)
By Dean Wesley Smith

SHADOWS
(0-446-61360-6)
By Diana G. Gallagher

SILENCE
(0-446-61359-2)
By Nancy Holder

AVAILABLE AT BOOKSTORES EVERYWHERE FROM WARNER ASPECT

VISIT WARNER ASPECT ON-LINE!

THE WARNER ASPECT HOMEPAGE

You'll find us at: www.twbookmark.com then by clicking on Science Fiction and Fantasy.

NEW AND UPCOMING TITLES

Each month we feature our new titles and reader favorites.

AUTHOR INFO

Author bios, bibliographies and links to personal Web sites.

CONTESTS AND OTHER FUN STUFF

Advance galley giveaways, autographed copies, and more.

THE ASPECT BUZZ

What's new, hot and upcoming from Warner Aspect: awards news, bestsellers, movie tie-in information . . .